SUMMER KING
WINTER FOOL

Tor books by Lisa Goldstein

The Red Magician
Strange Devices of the Sun and Moon
Summer King, Winter Fool

SUMMER KING
WINTER FOOL

LISA GOLDSTEIN

TOR

A TOM DOHERTY ASSOCIATES BOOK
NEW YORK

SUMMER KING, WINTER FOOL

Copyright © 1994 by Lisa Goldstein

Map by Michaela Roessner and Ellisa Mitchell

This book is printed on acid-free paper.

A Tor Book
Published by Tom Doherty Associates, Inc.
175 Fifth Avenue
New York, N.Y. 10010

Tor ® is a registered trademark of Tom Doherty Associates, Inc.

Design by Lynn Newmark

Library of Congress Cataloging-in-Publication Data

Goldstein, Lisa.
    Summer king, winter fool / Lisa Goldstein.
        p.   cm.
    "A Tom Doherty Associates book."
    ISBN 0-312-85632-6 (hardcover)
    I. Title.
    PS3557.0397S86   1994
    813'.54—dc20   94-117
                                                                            CIP

First edition: May 1994

Printed in the United States of America

0 9 8 7 6 5 4 3 2 1

To Doug, once again

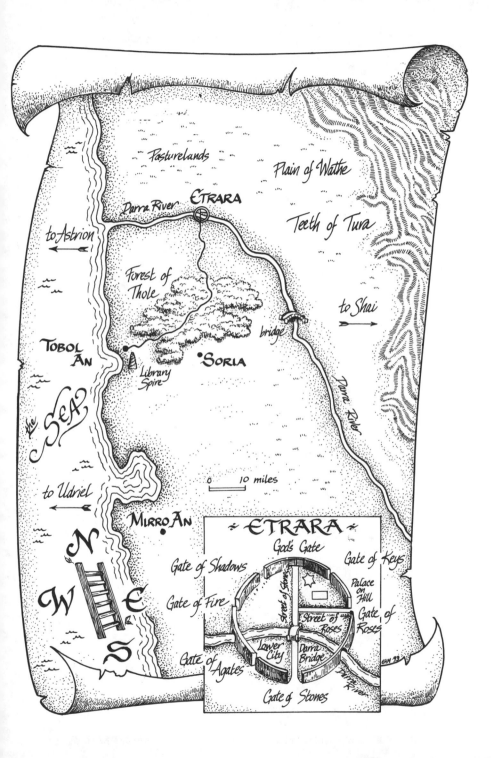

SUMMER KING

······················

WINTER FOOL

One

· · · · · · · ·

O
N A COLD WINTER NIGHT IN ETRARA,
two figures strode toward the palace. A loud wind
blew, and the torches of first one and then the other
flared into brightness, casting their faces into light and
shadow.

One of the men was tall, with brown hair and slate-gray
eyes. But the other was taller, his hair and eyes nearly black.
Their cloaks coursed behind them in the rough wind. The
lighted windows of the palace shone before them; they pulled
their cloaks closer and hurried on.

They passed Sbona's fountain, a statue of the goddess
creating the waters with her tears. Wind gusted through the
yard and sent an icy spray of water over them. The torches
guttered and nearly went out.

"Cold," Valemar said to his cousin. "They say this is the
coldest winter anyone can remember."

Narrion said nothing. The wind blew his long black hair
behind him, and he paused to fit his half-mask over his head.

Valemar did the same. His silver mask gleamed in the
dim light.

"Listen," Narrion said. His tone was low, conspiratorial,
though there was no one in the courtyard to overhear him. "I
have some business to attend to tonight. You can come with

me or not, as you choose. But don't ask questions, and don't hinder me."

"When have I ever hindered you? You've always done as you pleased."

But Narrion had hurried on ahead. What business? Val thought. He saw his cousin knock at the outer palace door and go inside.

The door closed as Val came up to it. He knocked, and the porter opened the small spy-hole. "Who is it?" the porter asked.

"I—" Val said, his mind still on Narrion. What business?

The porter began to close the spy-hole. "It's Valemar, of the house of the willow tree," Val said.

The outer palace door opened. A fire burned in the grate in the entrance room and candles lit the walls; compared to the chill outside the palace seemed almost hot.

Valemar handed his cloak and torch to the porter and went into the banquet room. A page came to escort him and his cousin to their places. Valemar sat and looked around at the other guests, searching for Tamra and not finding her anywhere. She had told him she would be at the banquet. Perhaps she had come in a clever disguise, but he felt certain he could recognize her from her mouth and figure alone.

The half-masks hid the eyes and foreheads of all the guests but, as always, Val could make fair guesses at who they were from their position in the room. The king's half-brothers and half-sisters sat on the raised dais, two each on either side of the carved chair reserved for Gobro IV. At one of the lower tables Val saw the King's Pen and at another the King's Axe; he looked around for the King's Coin and found him at the far end of the hall, nearly opposite the king. The treasurer had refused to grant more money to the private purse and was still suffering Gobro's displeasure.

The broad-shouldered man near the front of the hall had to be Andosto, said by some to be the grandson of the god Callabrion—said in whispers, because his grandparents were still alive. He sat next to Riel, talking to her in a low voice.

Appropriate, Val thought, because Riel, a former lover of the king, was herself rumored to be the daughter of the god Scathiel. Her beauty, at any rate, was legendary; even men who had never met her composed sonnets to it. On her other side sat her husband, newly ennobled by the king in gratitude for his wife's favors. He looked startled and confused and delighted; the gold ring of his knighthood reflected back to the candlelight.

Now Val could see three or four of the king's old lovers scattered throughout the room. And in the shadows at the far corners sat a few cripples and beggars; it was the king's custom to welcome the Wandering God in all weathers and not just at the changing of the seasons.

Trumpets sounded. Conversation stopped as the herald announced the king: "Gobro IV, King of Etrara and the Southern Marches, Ruler of Udriel and Astrion, Master of the Seas and the Son of Sbona." The king was a short plump man, addicted to sweets made of vanilla and ginger; folks whispered that his hands were always sticky. His clothes and mask were gold and black and white, the royal colors.

"Look where he comes, the Ascending God," Narrion said as the king climbed heavily to the dais. A few folks at the table laughed; Gobro was not popular with either the nobility or the people.

The trumpets sounded again and a train of knights came into the room, carrying several dishes. One of the knights tasted the meal and then set the dishes before the king. Gobro nodded, and at that signal pages began to pass through the room with trays of food.

A page set a dish of oysters covered with sauce in front of Val, then moved on to set another dish before Narrion. Val took a bite; it was too sweet, as were all the dishes served by the king. Near him he heard someone talking about King Tariel III and his legendary banquets. Tariel, Gobro's father, had died five years before; Val had been seventeen then and too young to be called to court.

The pages returned and poured the wine. Val sipped at

his and recognized with surprise a vintage from the inland country of Shai. Narrion nodded in approval and held out his glass for more.

The candles burned low, casting a golden light on the lords and ladies at the tables, on the rich tapestries of the Seven Virtues and Seven Vices lining the walls. Jewels winked and glittered in the darkness at the edges of the room. Silks changed color in the soft light.

The sound of a drum reverberated through the room, and trumpets answered. A troupe of actors danced into the banquet hall and climbed to the stage behind the dais. The guests applauded, and a few people at Val's table murmured in approval. "He's learned something, has old King Gobro," Narrion said. "This banquet might not be as tedious as I thought."

"Quiet," Val said. He was applauding too, but for a different reason: he had seen Tamra among the actors. She stood serenely on stage, her reddish gold hair framing her face; he thought he could almost see the blue eyes he had once compared to the sea in a poem.

He would like to have acted with her but of course that was impossible; twenty years ago King Tariel had passed an edict making it illegal for men to act in plays. Having to pretend to be someone else, Tariel had said, robbed men of their dignity.

The men and women on the dais turned their chairs to face the stage. The Prologue, a tall woman dressed in a man's breeches and tunic, came forward to set the scene: it would be a play of mistaken identities and a king forced into exile.

"Daring, aren't they?" Narrion whispered beside him. Val nodded. The actors were indeed taking a chance by presenting this particular play; the king did not like to be reminded of the dangers that beset his throne. One of the king's brothers—Arion?—applauded a little too loudly at the end of the Prologue's speech.

Tamra and another actor came forward. Tamra began to

speak, but at that moment six women in black rags stepped to the stage and began to dance.

At first they seemed to be part of the play. Then Val felt rather than saw Narrion grow alert beside him, heard gasps and exclamations from around the banqueting hall. The women turned as they danced, showing their hoods of badger skin to the audience. The Maegrim. Someone's fortune was about to change.

The women danced faster. Now Val saw seven people where before he had seen six. The king sank back in his chair, looking pale. He had reached the pinnacle of his fortune; if the Maegrim had come for him his fall from the ladder was assured. He glanced nervously at the four dukes and duchesses. Arion seemed eager, Mariel shocked, Callia apprehensive; Talenor had no expression at all on his face.

The Maegrim sank to the stage. One of them took out her bundle of flat conjuring sticks and threw one down. "Winter!" she called, meaning that the stick had shown a winter face.

Val wondered which face the stick had shown; he would have to ask Tamra about it later. Tamra stood just behind the Maegrim on the stage, frozen by their nearness. Had the conjurers come for her? She had high birth, beauty, wealth; if her fortune changed she, like the king, could only fall from the ladder.

"Summer!" the Maegra called.

The king groaned aloud.

"Summer!" the Maegra said again. She stood heavily. Had she finished? Two summer casts in a winter month was an ill omen indeed.

Another stick fell from her hand. She stood unmoving, still as a statue. Tamra walked forward tentatively and looked at the stick on the stage. She said something in a low voice, and then, realizing that no one had heard her, she repeated it: "Winter!"

The king sank back in his chair. Two summer casts and two winter ones. The Maegra gathered up her sticks and she and the other women left the stage. Val turned to Narrion. "Four casts," he said, whispering.

Narrion nodded. "I never heard of a cast that wasn't an odd number. Always three or five—sometimes seven, like the Maegrim themselves, but never four."

"Maybe that last one was an accident."

"Don't say that too loudly," Narrion said. He was whispering as well. "The king doesn't want to hear ill omens. If anyone asks you saw four casts, just like everyone else. I wonder what they were."

"We'll ask Tamra after the banquet," Val said.

But later, when everyone had gathered in the Duchess Sbarra's room, Val did not see Tamra anywhere. Sbarra was the wife of Duke Talenor, a beautiful and witty woman whose hospitality was legendary. King Gobro retired early and woke late, and after he had gone to bed the nobles and courtiers met in her apartments. No one knew if the king was aware of this arrangement or not, but the thought that he might not be, that the true business of the court was decided without him, added spice to the gatherings.

The people who met in Sbarra's room had another bond as well: most of them thought the reign of King Gobro would be a short one. King Tariel had fathered five illegitimate children on five different women, and when he had died suddenly, of a fall from a horse, he had not had time to designate an heir. After months of rancorous argument among the five siblings they had compromised on Gobro as the next king. His brothers and sisters thought him stupid and ineffectual, and no doubt one or two of them had agreed to him for precisely that reason; he would be easy to overthrow.

Gobro responded to his election as everyone thought he would. He behaved modestly for the first few months of his reign, deferring to his brothers and sisters in everything. Gradually, though, he realized he had real power. He bought fabulous suits of clothing and arranged lavish entertainments. He took women to his bed nearly every night, and when he grew tired of them he showered them and their husbands with land, money and titles, until the King's Pen complained that there was no land left to give, and the King's Coin told him most of the money was gone from the treasury, and the nobles complained that he was cheapening their titles.

"Really, Arion, you shouldn't have applauded so loudly at the Prologue," Duchess Mariel said. "Our brother has ways of showing his displeasure."

"What do I care?" Arion said. "After tonight his fall from the ladder is assured."

"Do you think so?" Sbarra asked. She sat in a high-backed chair under a tapestry depicting the battle of Arbono. Her poet sat in a smaller chair at her feet.

"Of course. You saw the Maegrim."

"The Maegrim could have come for any of us in the room," Sbarra said. "For you or me, or even for Narrion here."

Everyone laughed. Narrion had been singled out because he seemed proof against Sbarra's charm; his silence at her gatherings had become the stuff of gossip. Val was certain his cousin had his own plans, his own designs, that he used Sbarra's gatherings as a place to collect the information he needed to act.

Suddenly he remembered that Narrion had said he had business that night. Should he go with him?

"What were the casts?" Duchess Mariel asked. "Did anyone see them?"

"The actors did," Val said.

"And where are they?" Sbarra said. "Carousing across the river, no doubt. The king must have rewarded them handsomely—they did well to continue the play after the Maegrim left."

"What could Gobro have given them?" Callia asked. "The King's Coin has a tight hold on the purse strings."

"Did you see the poor man?—sent to the outer reaches of exile. It must have taken him hours just to get his first course."

"Ah, but no doubt he had a wonderful conversation with the Wandering God," Arion said, meaning the beggars King Gobro sat at the ends of the banqueting hall.

"The King's Coin isn't here either," Sbarra said. "I suppose my influence must be waning."

A chorus of voices protested. At that moment the door opened and Tamra and her companions entered. "You do know your cues," someone said. "Your names were mentioned just a minute ago."

"Favorably, I hope," Tamra said. She and the other actors were still in their costumes; she wore a green satin dress with the flowering skirts fashionable a generation ago.

"That depends," Mariel said. "We wanted to know what the casts were."

"Everyone's been asking me that," Tamra said. "And I always wanted to be famous for my beauty."

A dozen courteous flatteries rose to Val's mind in an instant. He opened his mouth to speak, remembered just in time that Sbarra, as their hostess, should be praised before anyone else. Tamra should not have been so tactless.

"Don't worry, my dear—your beauty is legendary," Sbarra said gently, and the awkward moment passed.

"The casts," Tamra said. "Let's see. The first one was winter, wasn't it?" She closed her eyes to better call up the conjuring sticks; she seemed to be enjoying the attention. "The Sun Obscured by Clouds. And the two summer casts were the Tree in Flower, and the Running Brook."

For the first time Val wondered if the casts had been intended for him, if the Maegrim had come to announce that his fortune was about to change. And what did it mean if they had? His family could trace their ancestors back twenty generations, to the reign of Ellara the Good, but at present they were not high in the king's favor. He could rise on the ladder, then. He touched the charm at his throat for luck.

The room around him had grown silent. "And the fourth cast?" Sbarra asked.

"You know, I don't remember," Tamra said. "I was terrified—I didn't even know if she'd meant to drop that stick, or if I should be announcing it. . . . It was a winter cast, I remember that."

A few people looked dissatisfied. "We should go, Tamra," the woman who had played the Prologue said. "They're waiting for us across the river."

Tamra stood and smoothed the skirts of her costume. "That's true, they are," she said. "Good fortune."

Several people called for her to stay. She walked to the door and turned to face the gathering, brushing back her red hair. Her hand touched the earring Val had given her. It was a gesture as old as the court itself; he rose from his seat and followed her.

As he went he saw Narrion frown. Val knew that Narrion paid court to Tamra as well, and he smiled to think that for this one evening, at least, she had favored him over his cousin. He went with the actors into the hall and closed the door behind them.

"I thank you for the sonnet," Tamra said.

"Ah," he said. "How did you know it was mine?"

"You asked everyone I know for the names of my favorite flowers. Hardly discreet, Val, especially when you included those flowers in your rhyme."

"Ah," he said again, pleased. He had wanted her to know the poem was his, and she knew he had wanted it; the court game had been played out to the end. "Did you like it?"

But Tamra seemed to be thinking of something else. "Listen," she said suddenly. "I have to tell you something. But you must swear never to repeat it to anyone, on the honor of your house."

"Of course."

"Do you remember that last cast, the one I said was winter? It was a summer cast, just like the two before it."

"Three summer and one winter, in a winter month?"

"Aye. A terrible omen. I doubt the king will last the year."

What did she expect him to do with this knowledge? He could give it to Narrion, of course, but Narrion would use it

for his own ends, and lately Val had come to suspect that those
ends included the overthrow of King Gobro. And what would
happen then? Val had come to adulthood during the long
and peaceful reign of Tariel III, and he feared the chaos of
civil war.

But she had sworn him to silence, he remembered. The
choice was not his to make, all the gods be thanked. "Good
fortune, Val!" she said. She kissed him and hurried down the
corridor with the other actors.

He watched her go, reluctant to return to Sbarra's rooms.
She seemed to have more life within her than all the rest of the
court combined; for a moment he felt tempted to go with her
across the river. Could she save him? Could she rescue him
from the tedium and hypocrisy of the court?

He shook his head. No, not her, and not any of the
women whose favors he had sought in the past few years: they
were, if anything, more frivolous than he was. Perhaps he
should leave the warmth of the court, see what the great world
around him had to offer.

He laughed at his fancies. Sign on for a voyage across the
great ocean to Astrion or Udriel, perhaps, or fight in a border
war against the Shai! No, it was best to stay with what he knew,
to remain at court and be himself.

Narrion looked up as he came into Sbarra's room. An old
man was speaking, someone Val didn't know. He wore a long
unadorned tunic in a style that had been popular among the
nobility five or six years ago, and his breeches were nearly
worn through at the knees.

If he hadn't seen him at Sbarra's gathering Val would
have taken the man for one of Gobro's beggars. But who was
he? King Gobro raised or lowered those around him almost at
his whim, but Val thought he knew all the players at court,
both those who stood high in the king's favor and those who
had fallen.

"Two summer casts and two winter ones could mean
balance," the old man said. "Stability."

"Or stagnation," Lord Varra, the King's Pen, said. "No one falls from the ladder, but no one rises either."

"Would that be such a bad thing?" Duke Talenor asked. The candle flames glinted on his newfangled spectacles as he looked up.

Everyone stared at him in surprise. Like Narrion he almost never spoke at Sbarra's gatherings, but unlike Narrion he was not resented for it. Everyone knew that he spent his days studying old strange books, musty volumes of philosophy, and that he barely seemed to notice anything that happened outside his library. It had taken a philosophical question to rouse him from his musings.

"Of course," Duchess Callia said. Her golden hair—unusual among the darker folk of Etrara—caught the light as she spoke. "The world exists only because of change. Without it summer would never succeed winter—the crops would die."

"But if stagnation meant that Gobro's reign was long and filled with peace?" the old man asked.

"And cold," Sbarra's poet said, shivering. "It does sometimes seem as if this winter will never end."

"Gobro's reign is peaceful only by accident," Callia said. "He has no idea what he's doing."

"But we need wars," Arion said suddenly, ignoring the last few speakers. "How else would we prove our bravery, our skill at arms? How else can we gain honor?"

"Is honor so important, then?"

The talk turned to the Virtues. The old man interrupted Arion's defense of honor and valor to champion love as the chief Virtue. Duchess Sbarra spoke up for loyalty. "Loyalty!" Mariel said, laughing.

Val yawned. It seemed to him that he had heard this discussion hundreds of times before. "Listen," Narrion whispered to him. "This is tedious. Let's go—you can help me with the business I spoke of."

Val nodded. What could Narrion's business be? He had heard rumors that his cousin belonged to the Society of Fools, a group of men and women who used the early winter months to spread misrule as a reminder of the cold about to come. But winter had nearly ended; in a month the summer god Callabrion would ascend to the heavens and wed the goddess Sbona, and the days would begin to lengthen. Val had heard nothing about the Society of Fools for months.

They murmured excuses and moved toward the door. Val heard laughter behind them; probably someone had speculated that they were going to look for Tamra. "Love!" the old man shouted as they stepped into the corridor. "Love is the only Virtue!"

Val felt his interest grow as he walked through the palace with his cousin. He had desired excitement, adventure; it was almost as if the gods had heard him and granted his wish. They stopped at the porter's room and retrieved their cloaks and torches, lit the torches from the fire in the entrance room and went outside.

The wind had died down during their stay in the palace. The air was cold and sharp as crystal. Val stretched his arms and felt its clearness suffuse him; he knew at once that he belonged here, hurrying down Palace Hill toward the city, and not in the stuffy rooms of the palace, discussing Virtues long dead.

The full moon was up and gazing benevolently over the glittering gold and white city, its light picking out arches and turrets, towers and gateways. From the hill Val could see past the city to Darra River, its changing surface reflecting back the unchanging light from the moon. Beyond the river the lower city lay shrouded in darkness.

Bells pealed out from the tall clock tower at the university. He and Narrion made their way down the hill, passing the great manors of the nobility. Three or four ladders leaned against each of the houses, their rungs plaited with ribbons and bells and ivy. Narrion turned at the theater and again at the university, and finally came out on the Street of Stones.

"Dotards!" Narrion said. "When will they do something useful?"

"As well expect fish to fly," Val said. "They're ornaments,

jewels on the fingers of the king. Does Gobro ask his rings for advice?"

"He might do better if he did. We're headed for ruin as long as that man leads us."

"Ruin? We've lived in peace for five long years. And which of that pack of his brothers or sisters would you raise if you could? No, it's far better to let Gobro remain king. The chaos of King Galin's time could come again if he fell from the ladder."

"King's Man," Narrion said. It was an old insult.

Val shrugged. "It suits me to live under Gobro's rule."

"Suits you! It suits you to write poems to every beauty at court, never lifting your nose from the paper you write on. Great things are about to happen, and you—you'll never notice them unless they interfere with your pleasures."

"What great things?"

Narrion paused, seemed to weigh what he was about to say. "What if you could rise by Gobro's fall?" he asked.

"I won't speak treason, Narrion," Val said quietly.

They were coming to the river, and the Darra Bridge. What did Narrion have planned for this night? "Where are we going?" Val asked.

"The lower city," Narrion said.

They crossed the bridge into the lower city. The air changed as they went; it smelled of rot here, of too many people living in too small a space.

Almost immediately they passed a criminal in a hanging iron cage. The man's hair and beard had grown to nearly cover his face, and there was a pile of excrement beneath his cage. "Some food, please, my fine lords?" he said. "Some food, good sirs?"

Val and Narrion went past him. The caged criminals relied on the kindness of their neighbors to stay alive: if they had been unpopular, or if they had committed a particularly horrible crime, they could not hope to get fed. They would die, and their bodies could remain caged for weeks as a warning, until the watch decided to take them down.

"I stole a crust of bread for my child," the man in the cage called after them. "That was my only crime, to keep my child from hunger. Please, my kind lords!"

Val knew that couldn't be true. Still, he cursed himself for not remembering to bring food for the criminals. He wondered what the man had done.

Darkened taverns and gaming houses edged the street. The wooden ladders of the Ascending God were here too, sometimes dozens of them, leaning against the sides of the buildings. After the Feast of the Ascending God, when Callabrion had arrived safely in heaven, the ladders would come down; the children of the city would add them to the bonfires lit on every street.

Val started to whistle. Narrion turned, frowning. "You'll rouse all the dogs within miles," he said.

In answer Val began to sing. "She told me she would love me, forever and a day," he sang. "But then one day in winter, she said she could not stay." It was a cheery tune, despite the subject.

Narrion moved on ahead. A man stepped from the gloom between two buildings and came toward them. Val stopped his singing. Narrion put his hand on his sword and edged past the man. Val walked closer to his cousin, his hand to his own sword, then turned to watch as the man made his way unsteadily down the street.

At last Narrion stopped at a tavern and then, seeming to come to a decision, opened the door. Val saw a wedge of light, heard laughter and a quoted line of poetry. Narrion shouldered his way into the room.

Val followed, standing by the door and studying the crowd. He could see none of the noblemen and women who usually frequented the taverns, and he wondered again what business Narrion had among these people of the lower rungs.

His cousin was studying the people too. He called to a man across the room and the man broke off his conversation and hurried over. Then he bent his head toward Narrion's and said something Val couldn't hear.

Narrion returned. "He's not here," he said.

"Who?" Val asked.

Narrion seemed not to hear him. They went outside and into another tavern, and then left that one too. The wind had returned; rags and bits of paper gusted down the street. Val was growing weary. Why had he agreed to come?

A well-dressed young man appeared out of the darkness. "Good fortune to you, my lord," the man said. "I wonder if you could direct me to the Street of Roses."

"The Street of Roses?" Val said. "Go back across the bridge and turn right at the university—"

"I met a young woman there once. She had been jostled by the crowd—she dropped her purse, and I helped her pick it up. She looked at me in gratitude. Her eyes were light brown, like leaves in the fall— Do you know the way to the Street of Roses?"

Val turned away abruptly. He had met several of the ghosts that walked the streets of Etrara; he should have been prepared, should have looked to see if the man's irises shone silver in the darkness.

He looked back to see the young man accost someone else. The ghost's memories were still bound up with the sight of the woman on the Street of Roses, Val knew, and he was condemned to repeat his question until he finally forgot her. And what would my memories be? Val thought. Court banquets and sonnets? Have I ever loved anyone as that ghost loves a woman he barely knew?

Narrion had gone on ahead while he had stood there like a fool, having a witless discussion with a phantom. He could barely see his cousin's torch. He hurried up to him, intending to tell the other man what had happened. They should rid the city of its plague of ghosts, he thought, irritated. That's something for Arion to do during Gobro's peace. There's honor enough.

Someone called from a window overhanging the street; Val stepped aside quickly as a woman emptied a chamber pot.

Somewhere a dog barked. Narrion went into one of the gaming houses down the street and Val followed.

Narrion was already deep in conversation when Val entered. He yawned. This business of Narrion's was as tedious as court philosophy. He longed to be home, out of the cold.

He stepped toward the gaming tables. The sight of the flat conjuring sticks being used as counters made him uneasy for a moment, but then he spied an actor friend of Tamra's and went over to talk to her. The men and women turned toward him for his wager. "A gold sovereign on a summer cast," he said, taking the coin from his purse.

Loud voices came from the other side of the room. Val turned quickly. Lord Carrow, the King's Coin, stood up from one of the gaming boards, his hands brushing his fur-lined cloak. "Look what you've done, you stupid oaf!" he said to Narrion.

"Play the sovereign for me," Val said to Tamra's friend, dropping his counters. "If it wins give the money to Tamra." He moved to join his cousin, his hand ready at the hilt of his sword. "Good fortune!" the woman called.

The King's Coin was surrounded by a group of finely dressed men and women, all of them standing in his defense. He was a fat, dignified-looking man, his fingers nearly covered by heavy golden rings signifying his holdings. His hand dropped to his sword, then moved upward to stroke the chain of office at his throat. His rings glittered in the candlelight.

"Are you picking a quarrel with me?" Narrion said, his dark eyes shining. He sounded amused.

"I?" Lord Carrow said. "It was you who spilled your ale over me, and deliberately too. I'll teach you to respect those who stand higher than you on the ladder."

"Will you?" Narrion said. "What makes you think you stand high on the ladder? The king showed his displeasure with you at the banquet tonight, and that was only the beginning. I'm surprised you think you can walk freely in the king's city."

One of the men around Carrow was looking at Narrion

curiously. After a moment Val recognized him; he was Lord Damath, the treasurer's friend. There had been some court gossip about Damath, but Val could not remember what it was. "I saw you the other day," Damath said to Narrion. "At the apothecary's, I think—"

"Where I go is my own business," the King's Coin said, interrupting him.

"Is it?" Narrion said softly. "Your behavior has gone beyond mere insolence, I think. I wouldn't be surprised if the king had you executed for treason."

Carrow's hand fell to his sword again. His wife grasped his arm, restraining him, then bent close to whisper in his ear. Val could hear the words "Maegrim" and "fortune."

"No," Carrow said angrily, shaking off her hand. "I won't leave this—this puppy unchallenged. Do you call me a traitor?"

"Yes."

It was Carrow Narrion had been searching for, Val realized. What could his cousin want? Narrion was one of the best men with a sword in all of Etrara; if he fought with Carrow, a much older man, he would almost certainly win. Did he think the king wanted his treasurer dead? Or had Gobro himself given orders for the execution of the King's Coin? But surely Narrion would not cast his lot with Gobro; his cousin had never spoken well of the king.

The owner of the gaming house hurried over to them and elbowed his way through the crowd. "If you're going to duel, then do it outside," he said.

"Ah," Narrion said, looking at the King's Coin. His expression was unreadable. "And are we going to duel?"

"Of course," Carrow said.

Somehow news of the fight spread through the gaming house; folks were already jostling each other to make a path for Narrion and Carrow as they moved toward the door. Others left the boards and tables, their wagers uncompleted, to follow the men outside. By the time Val made it to the street the crowd had cleared a space for the two men.

Carrow attacked first. Several people cried out, and someone near Val offered a wager of ten to one for Narrion. Narrion stood his ground and parried the other man's thrust easily. Carrow lunged forward again. Val realized that Narrion planned to tire the man out before he went on the offensive, that he was playing with him.

Carrow raised his sword awkwardly, his breath coming in short gasps. Narrion had barely moved except to raise his sword and brush his long black hair out of his eyes. There was a cruel smile on his lips that Val had never seen before.

Suddenly Lord Damath, the treasurer's friend, drew his sword. Val touched the charm at his throat and drew his own sword. Narrion motioned him back. At the same time Damath took the offensive, forcing Narrion down the street with driving blows. The treasurer dropped back to catch his breath.

Narrion returned blow for blow. His sword rang like a bell in the cold air. For a long moment Damath did nothing but defend himself, and Val wondered if he was like so many gallants in the city who depended on one or two tricks to frighten their opponents away. Sweat coursed down Damath's cheeks. He began to counter Narrion's thrusts, but his moves seemed sluggish, uninspired, as if he had lost heart.

His expression changed suddenly; he looked withdrawn, almost unearthly. Narrion's sword protruded from his chest. The final stroke had been so fast that Val hadn't even seen it. Someone screamed; a few people backed away.

Narrion held on to the sword as Damath fell to the street, then pulled it from the other man's chest. He wiped it on the man's clothing and grinned up at the circle of people surrounding him.

Before any of them could react he sheathed the sword and grabbed Val by his arm. "Quickly!" he said. For a horrible moment Val thought he could smell the blood on his cousin's sword.

They ran south down the Street of Stones, farther into the lower city. Two or three of Lord Carrow's friends called after them, perhaps only now beginning to understand what had happened. Val heard footsteps behind them and put on speed.

Past more taverns, more hanging cages. The footsteps dropped back. The moon had gone behind a cloud and the city ahead of them looked deserted; for a moment it seemed a ruin long dead. Then the face of the moon reappeared and by its light Val could see the city wall ahead of him. A gate in the wall stood open.

Two

• • • • • • • •

NARRION HURRIED THROUGH THE GATE and Val followed. He had rarely been out of the city, and had never left by this way, through the Gate of Stones. "Where are we going?" he asked.

"South," Narrion said. He had slowed but was still moving quickly; in a few minutes they had put the seven-gated city behind them.

"Why?"

Narrion turned impatiently. "Do you know who it was we just killed?"

"Lord Damath. Carrow's friend." It was only after he had given his answer that Val realized Narrion had said "we."

"King Gobro once took Damath's wife as his mistress," Narrion said. Val nodded; that had been the court gossip he had forgotten. "What do you think the king's thoughts will be when he finds Damath dead? People will start whispering that Gobro hired us to do it. No husband would willingly let his wife sleep with the king again."

"The king will look for someone to blame," Val said.

Narrion nodded. "He can't let it be said that he kills husbands—he's noted for rewarding them with money and land. We're the ones who killed him. We're the ones who should be punished."

"I didn't kill anyone."

"Do you think that matters? You drew your sword in front of witnesses. You'll be charged along with me."

The path before them narrowed. Something bulked in front of them; as they came closer Val saw a forest, a great dense stand of trees. "We're leaving Etrara," he said. "We're going into exile."

Narrion nodded again.

Val stopped. "This was the business you had tonight," he said bitterly.

"No. No—my errand had nothing to do with Damath. I didn't mean to kill him."

"Should I believe that? Very well, I'll believe you. But I'm certain you planned something as dangerous, as deceitful. You spoke treason earlier—"

"I said nothing—"

"You said I could rise by Gobro's fall. I don't know what game it is you're playing—"

"I spoke of possibilities, nothing else. Grant me the sense not to speak treason to a King's Man, at least."

"I'll grant you nothing. I'm in no mood to be reasonable. With one stroke of your sword you killed all my future in Etrara. How long will I have to wait before my exile is ended?"

"I'm certain it won't be long. I have friends at court, as you do—I'm certain Gobro can be persuaded that we killed Damath in our own defense."

"You killed Damath," Val said. "I did nothing."

They walked in silence for a while. Val touched the charm at his throat, a silver heron. He had spent his entire life in Etrara, the center of the world, the crowded, exciting, treacherous, ghost-ridden city. When would he be able to return?

The Maegrim had come for him after all. Three summer casts in a winter month—an ill omen indeed. He had thought that he could fall no lower on the ladder, but he had been wrong. He had had a long way to fall, a long way indeed. "Where are we going?" he asked again.

"Tobol An," Narrion said. He had moved ahead on the path; Val could barely hear him.

"Where?"

Narrion said nothing. Tobol An. What had he heard about the place? "Is that where the library is?"

Narrion turned. His teeth shone in the moonlight as he grinned. "It is indeed," he said.

A few paces later he stopped. Val saw that they had come to the beginning of the forest; dark trees stood before them, tangled together, a few stars shining through their bare branches. "We'll spend the night here," Narrion said. "We can continue on in the morning."

They took off their cloaks and spread them on the path. The air before them seemed stale, like an attic long unvisited, and no sounds came from the forest. Val stretched out on the dirt path and fell asleep.

It seemed only a few moments later when he felt the sun through his closed eyelids. Narrion stirred beside him. "Time to go," his cousin said, standing in a single movement. "Carrow must have brought word to the king by now. Come—we have to hurry."

Val stood. His back had cramped in the night and he stretched to ease it. The ranked trees of the forest stood silently before them, casting long shadows. He remembered their hurried flight from Etrara, remembered too Narrion's decision to go into exile. He turned and looked back the way they had come, toward Etrara and the Gate of Stones. "What if I choose not to go with you?" he asked.

"What?" Narrion said.

"I'm innocent—I had no part in your plans. I told you that last night. Suppose Carrow tells the king you killed Damath but says nothing about me. You would have to go into exile, yes, but I could stay in Etrara."

Narrion studied him a moment. For the first time Val thought he saw doubt in his cousin's eyes. "Can you afford to take that chance?" Narrion asked softly. The doubt was gone; it might have been a trick of the pale light. "Gobro could have you put to death, you know. Or have you caged, and all your property confiscated. Come—it will only be for a little while, as I told you yesterday."

Narrion turned and began to walk. Val stood for a moment and then followed him down the path and into the forest. As the sun rose its light began to filter through the branches, too thin and cold to warm them. A thick fall of leaves lay on the ground.

He had a lesson with his fencing master in the morning, Val remembered, and later in the day he was to meet with his gardener to plan an herb garden. When would they begin to miss him? When would they realize that he was not coming back?

It was true, as Narrion had said, that King Gobro had the power to sentence him in his absence, to confiscate his property and goods. His friends might never learn the truth, that he had killed no one, had never even raised his sword. But surely Narrion was right, surely their allies at court would convince the king to be lenient.

He sighed. When they were children Narrion had been able to make him agree to almost any scheme; they had climbed the clock tower together, stolen a priest's robe, been chased by the watch. It seemed that he had spent his life following his cousin in one adventure or another.

They walked on. The place felt unnatural, haunted by something more than the harmless ghosts of Etrara. But the forest was not hostile; it seemed to be entirely indifferent to the two figures entering at its gates, as if they were no more than the beetles scurrying over the forest floor.

Val remembered the banquet the night before, and the herald calling out King Gobro's titles—King of Etrara and the Southern Marches. Were these the southern marches? He had never thought of them as an actual place before; they had seemed just another piece of ritual surrounding the king. Did Gobro rule in these parts too, then? He would wager all his wealth that the king had never been here. How strange to rule over a place and a people you had never seen.

But were there people in this wood? Val could see nothing ahead of him but the path pillared by the great trees. The sun had climbed higher in the sky and cast a strange hazy light through the wood. A dry leaf fell before him, rustling like paper.

The silence felt oppressive. Val whistled a few notes; they sounded thin and off-key. Suddenly he realized he was hungry. "When will we get there?" he asked.

Narrion did not turn around. "It's a while yet," he said.

Val thought of the poet Cosro, who had been sent away from Etrara for writing sharp satires against King Tariel I. Perhaps he too could use his time in exile to write poetry; perhaps he could write sonnets to Tamra.

Tamra. He hadn't thought of her since they had started on their journey. He found, to his surprise, that he missed her. What would she think when she heard of his exile? Would she believe the proclamations King Gobro would surely issue, telling all Etrara of his supposed crime?

Did he love her, then? Would future generations sing songs of the love he felt for her, lost in his exile? Or was he simply adopting another courtly pose, the distant lover longing for his mistress?

Past midday the path turned east and they followed it, walking in silence for a long time. Slowly the forest around them grew dark; Val turned and saw streaks of the red and copper sunset through the trees behind them. They stopped and made camp for the night. The trees stood silent around them.

Another day of walking took them to the outskirts of the forest. The trees here grew farther apart; Val saw light ahead of them. "Look," his cousin said, pointing.

A knight on horseback blocked their path. A standard Val had never seen before was planted in the earth in front of him, and a trumpet lay across the knight's lap. As Val watched he noticed motes of sunlight drifting through the man and his horse, and he realized that they were ghosts.

"Legend says he's sworn to protect Tobol An from her enemies," Narrion said.

"What enemies?" Val said, thinking that the knight must not have stirred for centuries. Who would want to attack a place as insignificant as Tobol An?

They continued on. The knight made no move to stop them, though his standard fluttered a little in a wind long gone. We're not enemies, then, Val thought. He certainly intended no harm to the people of Tobol An, but he could not speak for his cousin. Narrion had killed someone he barely knew and had no quarrel with; Val was starting to think he didn't know the other man at all.

The knight apparently marked the border of Tobol An. The trees thinned out, and Val could see the village beyond. His heart sank. The place was nothing but a few stone cottages clustered together in the middle of a windy plain. A large white building, shaped a little like a chambered shell, stood in the distance. A thin rain fell. How long would he and Narrion have to spend in this forsaken place?

"Come," Narrion said. "Let's find lodgings."

They went forward into the village. Narrion knocked at one of the cottages, and an old man opened the door. The man frowned when he saw them; probably the people of Tobol An didn't see many strangers.

"Yes?" he said.

"I was wondering if you have a room to let," Narrion said. "My cousin needs a place to stay."

Val looked at Narrion sharply. Wasn't Narrion going to stay here as well? His cousin shook his head; something in his eyes warned Val to say nothing.

The old man watched them carefully. Val had an idea that little escaped him. "Yes, I have a room," he said slowly. "But I'll need to know who you two fine gentlemen are before I rent it out."

"Who is it, Uncle?"

The man turned. A young woman came up behind him. "Did I hear you say you wanted a room?" she asked Narrion.

"I do, my lady. Not for myself but for my cousin here."

Val saw that Narrion was paying court to this simple country woman, treating her as if she stood high in the king's favor. He had to admit that, as always, Narrion's eye was good; the woman, dressed in a dark blue skirt and loose white blouse, both homespun, was not unattractive. She was small, fine-boned, with closely cropped black hair. Her eyes held Narrion's in a forthright gaze. She seemed so different from the women of the court that Val thought she might almost be a foreigner, someone from Shai or a barbarian from beyond the seas.

"Ah," she said. "And why would your cousin want a room?"

"Let me take care of this, Taja," her uncle said.

"I want to get away from court for a while, my lady," Val said to the young woman. No woman, however lowborn, would have cause to say that he was less courteous than his cousin.

"Why?" the old man asked.

"I need a place to write poetry," Val said. Taja was looking at him with interest, and he went on. "I want to put the distractions of the court behind me, to find a quiet place where the goddess Sbona might speak to me more clearly."

"A poet," the old man said. "And did the king send you into exile, as King Tariel sent Cosro?"

Confronted with erudition in a place where he had expected only backwardness, Val could think of nothing to say. For once, he saw, his cousin Narrion was speechless as well. "No," Val said finally. "No, it's nothing like that."

The old man grinned at their discomfiture. "Well, come in, then, come in. I'll show you the room. As long as you're sure the king isn't displeased with you. We're fond of our life here—we wouldn't want to see the peace of Tobol An destroyed."

Could the old man have guessed something? But no, he would not have allowed them into his house if he had.

The man and Taja led them to a small room at the back

of the cottage. The place was obviously used for storage; Val saw tightly stoppered pottery jars, a broom made of straw and twigs, wool blankets, a purple fishing net, a broken butter churn. "We'll put a bed in," the old man said. "And we can sweep it out a bit. As for rent, well—I suppose I can let you have it for a sovereign."

"A sovereign a month?" Val asked, surprised.

"A sovereign a year," the old man said. He grinned again. "You'll find that things are less expensive here than they are in the city. It'll be a good place to work."

Val opened his purse. How much money had he brought with him? He remembered throwing down the gold sovereign in the gaming house—could that have been his last coin? No—he had several more sovereigns, most stamped with the head of King Tariel III; only two or three were the debased coins from Gobro's reign.

"I hope so," Val said. "I'll take it."

"That's settled then," Narrion said. "Come see me off, Val."

They went outside and stood a little away from the old man and his niece. "I don't think we should send letters for a while," Narrion said softly. "At least not until we know—"

"I thought you were going to stay here with me," Val said.

"I can't," Narrion said. "We have to split up. That way if the king finds one of us he won't find the other. Trust me—this is the best way."

"Where are you going?"

"I don't know yet. I'll write you when it's safe."

Val looked around him. After the noise and crowds of Etrara the silence of the village seemed oppressive. Two or three faces had appeared at the windows of the other cottages, studying them with open curiosity. Wind blew, bending down the knotted grasses growing along the path, turning the thin rain into small gusts. "What in Callabrion's name am I to do here?" he asked.

Narrion turned to go. "I thought you said you'd write poetry," he said.

Narrion went south, walking slowly until he was certain that Val had gone inside the house. Then he stopped at the last cottage on the road and knocked at the door.

Another villager came to answer it. "I'm here for the horse," Narrion said.

"Of course, my lord," the man said. They walked together to the back of the cottage; the man went into the stable and returned with a chestnut gelding. It seemed a little too magnificent for its surroundings, a duke's horse at the very least.

Narrion thanked the man and mounted, throwing him a purse of coins as he left. Then he turned back and rode into Thole Forest, making the long journey north to Etrara alone.

As soon as he came to the city he rode to the palace, gave his horse to a stablehand and knocked on the palace's outer door. The porter had orders to admit him, and he was brought to the king's Presence Chamber immediately.

Gobro paced the chamber, stopping every so often to look out the window. Narrion would wager his place on the ladder that the king saw nothing of the city spread out below him.

"Good fortune, my lord," Narrion said to Gobro's back. "I brought Val safely to Tobol An, as we agreed."

The king turned. "Why in the name of the Wandering God did you kill Damath?" he said. He was as close to anger as Narrion had ever seen him.

"Your orders were to bring Val to Tobol An. I did that. You didn't mention how I was to get him there. Do you really think that a courtier of Etrara would willingly give up his place here to go off to the ends of the earth? I needed something dramatic, something that would convince him to go into exile."

"It was certainly dramatic. If I didn't need you and Val I

would have had you both executed—yes, executed on the same day. What a show that would have been!"

"Val is innocent, my lord. He did nothing."

The king walked the length of the Presence Chamber, turned and came back. "It's my ill luck that my fortune is tied to yours at the moment. But by Callabrion's big toe, why Damath? Do you have any idea how badly I need Lord Carrow's favor? With his friend dead I can forget about seeing any money from the treasury at all."

"I thought you didn't need Carrow. I thought he was out of favor. You sat him at the opposite end of the hall the night of the banquet."

"I did, yes. I was angry with him and I wanted him to know it." The king began to pace again. "And all the while I should have been currying favor with him. I'm so deeply in debt I have no idea how to get out of it."

"Replace him."

"Don't you think I've thought of that? I can't—everyone loves him. He hasn't raised taxes since I ascended to the throne." Gobro looked directly at the other man. "What made you kill Damath? He was one of my strongest supporters, especially after I made him a lord. I don't trust you, Narrion. You had some reason—"

"I didn't like the man. I owed him a gaming debt."

"I wish I could believe you."

"Why did you want Val sent to Tobol An?"

"Are you questioning my orders now?"

Narrion had never heard that note in the king's voice before. Gobro sounded authoritative, used to obedience. What had the king learned to make him send Val away?

"Leave me," Gobro said.

It was a dismissal; Narrion would get no more information today. He bowed and left the chamber.

How much did Gobro know, or guess? Had someone overheard Narrion and Mariel and Callia whispering together a week before the banquet? Narrion went over his conversation with Gobro carefully, studying each phrase for hidden meanings, looking for clues.

He began to hurry through the halls of the palace, searching for Mariel. There were too many plots here, he thought; the threads might come unraveled before the whole thing was done.

Val woke the next day to the smell of hot oatcakes and tea. He left his room and sat with Taja and the old man, whose name he discovered was Pebr, and they ate in comfortable silence. After Taja cleared the breakfast things away she returned to her place opposite him at the white oak table. "How do you write poetry?" she asked.

Val looked up at her, remembering only then his deception of the day before.

"Do you plan the entire poem in your head and then write it down?" Taja asked.

"No. No, I don't do it that way."

"Would the library have some of your poetry?"

"I doubt it. I've never published any."

"Never— Why not?"

"A gentleman doesn't write for publication." He saw the looks of disbelief on the other faces and smiled wryly. Much of his life at court, he saw, was going to be incomprehensible here.

"Well, then, what does he write for?" Taja asked.

"Other gentlemen, I suppose. But that's not why I write. Poetry is the voice of Sbona. It's a way to ascend, to become like a god. And sometimes—sometimes you write a poem to a lady, and she reads it."

"Ah. And is there a lady who reads your poems?"

"One or two. The subject of a poem must be beautiful, of course—as beautiful as you, my lady."

Taja looked startled. What had he done? He was so used to the conventions of the court, to empty flattery, that he had not considered the effect his words might have in such a simple place.

Pebr was frowning. Val cast around for another topic and remembered the question he had asked Narrion the day before. "Why is there a library here in this"—he nearly said "forsaken," caught himself in time—"place?"

"Tobol An was once a great city, a place that rivaled Etrara itself," Pebr said, taking a sip of his tea. "More poet-mages lived in the two cities than walk Sbona's earth today. But the wizards of Tobol An quarreled with the king in Etrara, and he sent his sorcerers against them. Tobol An was ruined, all but the library, but the victory went to us—all the poet-mages of Etrara died. The survivors in Tobol An caused the forest of Thole to grow up between here and Etrara, as a message and a warning to the king—they would not be subject to his command any longer."

Val nodded, understanding now why the forest had felt so still, so haunted. "What did they fight about?" he asked.

"No one knows."

"But the king—some of the kings—still have magicians. The last king did."

Pebr looked at him sharply. "What do you know about that?" he asked.

"Only what everyone knows. The wizards died. They were killed, people say."

Pebr nodded. "Aye, they were killed. That's what happens to magicians, that's why it's unsafe to meddle in their art."

"You shouldn't have started him on the subject," Taja said, laughing a little. "He hates it that I work in the library."

"I have enough money to support us both," Pebr said. It had the sound of an oft-repeated argument. "There's no need for you to work."

"About a third of the library was destroyed in the war," Taja said. "Books of magic, mostly. He's got it into his head that it isn't safe to work there."

"What other books do you have?" Val asked.

"Oh, everything. History, poetry, languages, old stories."

"I'd love to see it."

"Why don't you come with me? Oh—but I wouldn't want to interrupt your work."

"You won't," Val said. "Perhaps I can find inspiration in the library."

"Good," Taja said. She said farewell to Pebr and they went outside.

She led Val down the village path, heading toward the tall white building he had noticed earlier. Fog shrouded the building, clung white as cobwebs to the stone cottages. As they walked he saw dozens of ladders leaning against the houses, and his heart lifted a little to see them: so they celebrated the Feast of the Ascending God here too.

"What do the other people in the village do?" he asked. "They don't all work in the library, do they?"

"No. They're fisher-folk, mostly."

"Fisher-folk?"

"Aye. We're on the coast here. Or don't gentlemen read maps either?"

He frowned; he didn't like the teasing in her tone.

"Look, I'll show you," she said, and turned off the path that led to the library. They came to a steep cliff; looking down Val could see a cobblestone harbor and tiny, fragile-looking boats bobbing in the water. Waves hissed in to shore. The fog had started to lift and he noticed that the ocean was a dull gray, nothing at all like the color of Tamra's eyes. A fisherman mended a purple net stretched out on the sand. A heron preened nearby; without thinking about it Val put his hand to the charm at his throat.

A huge stone arch, nearly covered with moss and weeds, stood on the cliff overlooking the ocean. Taja followed Val's gaze. "That's the arch of Sleeping Koregath," she said.

"Sleeping—"

"Legend says that the arch is the giant Koregath, turned to stone during the war of the poet-mages."

A giant, Val thought, trying to imagine that much power. A gull cried in a shrill voice above them.

They headed back toward the library. Someone called out to Taja, and she turned.

At first Val thought the thin old woman coming toward them was one of the Maegrim. She wore the same black, shapeless rags, and her gray hair hung lank to her shoulders. His heart began to beat loudly. What prediction did this woman have for him?

As she came closer, though, he saw that she had no hood of badger skin, and he breathed easier. And now that he had time to think he realized that no one he had heard of had ever been approached by a single Maegra; there were always six of them, and then seven. But the hint of something uncanny still clung to this woman. He wondered who she was, what she wanted.

"Good morning, Taja," she said. One of her eyes was brown, Val saw, and the other webbed white with cataracts. "Good morning, my young lord."

"Good morning, aunt," Taja said.

Val nodded to the old woman. For a moment he had the feeling that she knew everything about him, his place on the ladder, his reasons for coming to Tobol An, all his innermost thoughts.

She tilted her head back and looked at the sun. The fog was completely gone now; Tobol An seemed a little warmer than the cold-locked city to the north. "A good day," the old woman said, looking back at them with her brown eye, nodding toward him shrewdly. "A good day to work, to search, to discover one's fortune."

Some answer seemed to be required of him, but he had no idea what it could be. Taja saved him by saying, "Thank you for the salve, aunt. Uncle Pebr says his arm is much better."

The old woman nodded again, briskly, and pushed past them down the path. They continued on toward the library.

"Who in Callabrion's name is that?" Val said when he was certain she could no longer hear them. "Is she really your aunt?"

"No," Taja said, laughing a little. "Her real name is Mathary, but everyone in the village calls her aunt. Everyone except Pebr, who won't speak to her."

"Why not?"

"I don't know. I think he thinks she's one of the ancient wizards, the last survivor of the great battle."

"But she would have to be—"

"Hundreds of years old, I know. Pebr has some strange ideas. To be honest—" She began to whisper, though the old woman couldn't possibly hear her. "—he threw out the salve I gave him. He said he'd rather live with the pain in his arm than use anything that has the taint of magic on it. She knows that, of course—did you see the way she looked at me when I thanked her?"

"Do you think she's a wizard?"

"No, of course not. She's a harmless old woman who knows something about plants, that's all."

The library had grown closer as they walked. Now Val could see that his first impression had been correct: it had been built in the shape of a shell, spiraling out from an unseen center. Taja unlocked a door set into the wall and they went inside.

They stepped into a corridor lined with books. The corridor seemed to turn in slightly. "It leads inward," she said, pointing.

He had never seen so many books in one place; not even the library at the university had had so many. Their deep musty smell was not unpleasant, the moldy odor of scholarship and discipline. "Do you have to walk through the entire building if you want a book all the way inside?" he asked.

She laughed. "There are entrances and exits all over the library," she said. "And there are stairs leading to higher levels. Tell me where you want to go and I'll show you how to get there."

"I don't know. I don't know what's here."

"Well, this book for example," she said, taking one off the shelf. "It's an old story about a man who dreams about the same woman every night. Every night he struggles to free her from danger and every morning he wakes exhausted from his efforts. But finally, after seven years, he rescues her. And when he wakes up that morning she's lying in his bed next to him."

Now Val could see that the shelves held more than books; unbound manuscripts and loose rotting pages and scrolls competed for space with books bound in brass and iron and jewels. "This one," Taja said, replacing the book she had shown him and taking another. "The book itself is completely worthless. But here—" She opened the rotting pages; Val saw lists of words filling the margins. "It was owned by the wizard Hanra, and her commentary is on every page."

Suddenly Val realized that he hadn't seen her strike a flint or light a candle, yet the library had no windows. "Where does the light come from?" he asked.

"From the floor and ceiling," she said.

"How is that possible?"

"We don't know."

The light was clear, he saw, and brighter and steadier than that of candles or oil. "I'll tell you what I want," he said. "Do you have a book of Cosro's poetry?"

"If we do I haven't seen it. I don't know every book here—just the ones I've added to the catalogue. I calculated once that if I live to be five hundred I'll be able to list them all." She looked around her. "Sometimes I imagine all the old librarians and poet-mages working here, walking the corridors, studying, whispering to each other over an old book. There must have been dozens of them, hundreds perhaps. And now there's just me. Don't you feel it?"

Val stood still for a moment, trying to see the ghosts she had summoned up. But no one walked the corridor lined with books; the library remained empty, silent. He shook his head.

Someone knocked on the door to the outside, and Taja opened it. A woman stood there, her arms filled with notebooks and manuscripts and a pen case. "Good fortune," she said. "I'd like to look at the birth records, please."

"Of course," Taja said. "This way. You'd better come along too, Val—it's easy to get lost here."

They started up the corridor. The other woman was probably a natalist, Val thought, someone who sought to predict a person's future place on the ladder from his or her birth date. "Do you have birth records here too?" Val asked.

"The king sends us the records of birth and marriage and death every year, along with a small subsidy for our work." Taja opened a door; it led to a flight of stairs and they began to climb. "He's late with this year's subsidy."

"He's had a lot of expenses," Val said.

If Taja was impressed that Val knew court gossip she didn't show it. They went down another corridor, through a door leading inward and another door opening on another flight of stairs.

Finally they came to a small room off the main corridor. A polished wooden table stood in the middle of the room, and cabinets lined the walls. "Is everyone's birth recorded here?" Val asked.

"Of course," Taja said. "When were you born?"

"The seventh year of the reign of Tariel III."

She directed him to one of the cabinets and pulled out a drawer. "You'd be here," she said, turning to help the other woman.

Val opened the drawer. Almost immediately he found names he recognized, schoolmates, fencing partners, men and women he had met at court, all of them mixed indiscriminately with people from the lower rungs. Here was Narrion, Val saw, and Tamra, and Dorio, his friend from the university who had become an astronomer-priest.

He came to the end of the births for that year. He had not seen his name anywhere. Puzzled, he searched through the records again. The natalist had settled herself at the table, surrounded by records and charts and pens and inkstands holding ink of different colors. "I can't find my name here," he said to Taja.

"Are you certain of the year of your birth?" Taja asked.

"Of course."

"Well, the scribe may have made a mistake. Check the years before and after it."

He turned back to the cabinet. Taja searched with him, perhaps intrigued by the mystery, but neither could find the missing record.

He laughed, trying to make light of it. "Perhaps I don't exist," he said. He shivered; he had spoken truer than he knew. No place at court, no hope of rising on the ladder, no birth record. He shivered again and touched his charm to ward off evil.

"I have to start work now," Taja said. "I'll show you the way back."

He followed her, trying to forget his disquieting thoughts. Probably it was nothing, a scribe's mistake, as Taja had said.

They came to the outer door. "You can stay if you want," Taja said. "I'll find you something to read."

Val shook his head; he had had enough of the library.

"A good day to discover one's fortune," old Mathary had said. Whatever Pebr might think, the woman was certainly no wizard; she could not have been more wrong. It would be a good day for someone else, maybe; he was starting to think that he might have no fortune to discover.

Three
· · · · · · ·

B Y THE TIME HE RETURNED TO THE STONE cottage he had managed to put all thoughts of the library behind him. He borrowed paper from Pebr and began a sonnet to Tamra.

A few hours later he read what he had done and set the poem aside in disgust. He had written that Tamra was the daughter of Scathiel, the winter god; that explained her beauty, he said, and her coldness to him. But she was not cold; she had simply not decided among the dozen or so courtiers that vied for her hand. Would he marry her if she wanted him? Or was it only the chase that mattered, and not the conquest itself?

He stood and began to pace the small room. He had been in Tobol An less than a day, and already he was starting to question his old life, the artifice of the court. He laughed harshly. Perhaps he would marry Taja. They would live together with Pebr in the stone cottage; he would become a fisherman, and bring up the silver wealth of the sea in his purple net.

Why in Callabrion's name had Narrion killed Lord Damath? When would he be allowed to return to Etrara? He was not suited for a life spent in solitude, for endless questions.

Restless now, he left the cottage. He walked along the

cliffs, watching the waves below. As evening fell the sky turned rose red over the water and dark blue farther up, with a thin line of blue-gray separating the two. Clouds drifted overhead, archipelagoes in the vast blue gulfs of the sky. A seagull called; another answered. The colors deepened, becoming the same dark mass as the sea, and he turned to go.

When he got to the cottage Taja and Pebr were already eating. Fish—he should have guessed. He served himself and sat at the table with them.

"I have a few ideas about your birth record, Val," Taja said. "Could your parents have been out of Etrara when you were born?"

Val shook his head. "They would have told me if they had been, surely," he said.

"Can you write to them?"

"They died a while ago," Val said. "The plague."

"Oh. I'm sorry. I'm sorry, Val."

"Don't be." Their deaths, which had been an aching grief to him for several years, had given him less sorrow as he grew older. Still, he would remember them at odd hours, and the old sadness would catch at his throat.

"My parents died too," Taja said. "In a storm at sea, when I was very young. They lived in Mirro An, down the coast. Pebr brought me here and raised me—I don't remember them at all."

"I'm sorry," Val said.

"Well," Taja said. "I didn't mean to make us so gloomy. Here—I brought you a book."

Val took it from her. It was faded, and there was no title on the cover or spine. He opened it and saw poems by a number of people, some of whom he recognized as contemporaries of Cosro. "Thank you," he said, genuinely pleased. "Thank you very much."

So the days passed. Val began a number of poems in the morning, but by noon he would always lay them aside and read one of the books Taja brought him from the library.

A day came when he finished a book and had no more to read, and he went by himself to the library. He met with no one while he was there, though at first the sound of his own footsteps alarmed him.

He was astonished to find such richness. Hours passed as he took down book after book from the shelves: plays he had never seen and poems he had never read and accounts of voyages to lands on no current map. There were books on natalism, on chemistry, on the science of watching the stars. And in every third book he saw long lists of words in the margins: sun and leaf, sea and stone. Wizards' commentary.

A week after he had come to Tobol An he went for a walk by the cliffs. A cold wind blew around him. "She told me she would love me, forever and a day," he sang. The ocean's rush answered below him.

Taja came toward him from the library. "But then one day in winter, she said she could not stay," he sang.

"Good fortune, Val," Taja said. She was smiling; did she enjoy his singing?

"Good fortune."

"I saw you out walking. It's getting late—I thought we might go home together."

He looked at the sky. It was not only late but overcast, with clouds like sodden gray wool. A harsh wind bent back the grasses of the cliff and roughened the waves beneath him. He shivered.

Heavy rain began to fall. Val took Taja's hand and headed toward the stone cottage. "Wait," Taja said.

"Come—the storm will only get worse."

She studied the fishing boats drawn up in the harbor, then looked out to sea. The ocean had turned slate-gray, almost black. "What is it?" he asked.

"One of the boats hasn't come back."

She hurried down the slanted path that led to the harbor. He followed her, wondering what she thought she would do. Against a storm like this, he thought, they would almost certainly be powerless.

More people joined them on the path, which was slick with rain. "Who is it?" someone asked.

"Dochno," Taja said, her voice blown back by the wind. "His boat hasn't returned."

The crash of the ocean was louder as they came closer. The fisher-folk studied the sea as Taja had, clearly wondering if they could venture out and survive. Pebr stood among them, huddled against the wind.

"Look!" someone said. "It's Dochno. He's swimming back!"

A small figure appeared above the waves and then was tossed under. A few of the fisher-folk hurried toward their boats. Val ran down to the sea, taking off his boots as he went. "Val!" Taja called. "What are you doing?"

He could not stop to explain. He had swum in the races in the Darra River for the last three years, and had won the last one. He touched the amulet at his throat and plunged into the waves.

The water was chilling, as cold as the rain. He surfaced, brushed hair and water from his eyes, and looked around for Dochno. There. He swam toward him, his strokes cutting through the water.

A wave battered him, turned him around. He struggled to the water's surface, took a deep breath, searched for Dochno again. The drowning man seemed no closer.

He renewed his efforts to reach him. His muscles felt like lead. He looked around a third time, saw Dochno almost on top of him. The man seemed to make one final effort to reach him. Val held out his hand and Dochno grasped it.

Val pulled him closer, got an arm around him, then turned back to the shore. He had come farther out than he thought. Using his free arm, he began to swim wearily toward land.

Halfway there his leg began to cramp. He nearly cried aloud with the pain. And Dochno had grown heavier; his eyes were closed and he made no effort to dodge the beating of the waves.

Val struggled against the water again. A wave caught him, filled his mouth with water, pulled him down. He fought his way toward the surface. His chest burned. He gained the surface and breathed deeply.

"Val!" someone called.

It's Sbona, mother of all, he thought. She's calling me home. I'll feast in heaven tonight.

He began to relax. "Val!" He raised his head to look up out of the water; it was the hardest thing he had ever done. Taja sat in one of the fishing boats. She tossed him a net.

He grasped it. Someone drew him into the boat, and pulled Dochno in after him. He fell like a catch of fish to the bottom of the boat and lay there gasping.

"Val, you innocent," Taja said. "We use the boats to go after drowning folk."

"I got him, didn't I?" Val said, and closed his eyes.

He woke. He was in Pebr's cottage; they had wrapped him in warm blankets and laid him next to the fire. His clothes were drying on the hearthstones beside him, but he saw that they need not have bothered; the clothes were so tattered that the poorest man in Etrara would not want them now. The ruin of his court finery did not upset him; he had worn them for weeks, having come to Tobol An with nothing else.

What worried him was the question of who had undressed him. He sat carefully. Pebr stood by the fire.

"How is Dochno?" Val asked.

"He's well, praise the gods," Pebr said.

"How did I— What—"

"Taja and I brought you in, and I undressed you. I never knew one man could wear so many different kinds of clothing. You'll have to wear my trousers and shirt now, until we can get you to Soria and buy you something new."

"Thank you," Val said. He put his hand to his amulet; it was still there, Callabrion be thanked. He lay back among the blankets, suddenly tired.

"Good night," Pebr said. Then, grudgingly, "You were very brave. And perhaps the boats would not have reached him in time."

A few weeks later Val found himself talking about Etrara to Taja and Pebr. The three of them had finished their dinner and had drawn closer to the hearth for warmth.

"The city has seven gates," Val said. "The Gate of Stones, the Gate of Roses, of Shadows, Fire, Agates, Keys. And God's Gate, which has been closed since the time of Queen Ellara the Good. Legend says that when she was very old she walked out that gate to meet Callabrion, who had been her lover when she was a young woman. The people of Etrara closed it in mourning for her—they say that no ruler of Etrara since that time has been worthy to walk through God's Gate."

Pebr stirred impatiently. Val had already noticed that the other man didn't like to hear talk about Etrara. "Callabrion will ascend to heaven this week," Pebr said, rubbing his thin arms. "Praise the gods—this winter has been the coldest that I can remember."

"Praise the gods," Val said. "How do people in Tobol An celebrate the Feast of the Ascending God?"

"We—" Pebr said, but Taja laughed and said, interrupting him, "It's not very exciting. What do you do in Etrara?"

"We set up a great arena in the palace courtyard," Val said. "The strongest wrestlers in the city fight one another, and at the end two men who represent Callabrion and Scathiel come out and challenge each other. Callabrion always wins, of course, but sometimes Scathiel gives him a good fight."

"We don't have anything like that," Taja said. "The children light the bonfires, and then at midnight the priest announces that Callabrion has ascended to heaven and the days will start to get longer. And everyone wishes everyone else good fortune in the coming year and we go off to sleep."

"But don't you want to see Callabrion win the fight?" Val asked.

"The gods don't fight in Tobol An," Pebr said, lighting his pipe. "I told you—we're a peaceful people here."

"They don't fight? What do they do?"

"They pass each other on the ladder. Callabrion ascends to wed the goddess Sbona, and Scathiel descends to lose himself on earth, to become the Wandering God. And six months later they change places."

Val nodded impatiently. "Of course. But are you saying that Scathiel gives up his place in heaven willingly?"

Pebr nodded. Smoke plumed around his face. "He misses the earth. He's anxious to lose himself here among us."

Val thought of Arion, and the young duke's insistence that valor was the chief of the Virtues. And wasn't there something, well, womanish about the people of Tobol An? Didn't Gobro's long peace mean that no one's mettle would ever be tested, that the brave could never be told apart from the cowardly? The gods would never shrink from a fight, he felt certain of that.

He had studied courtly politeness for so long that he could not bring himself to say any of this, for fear of insulting his hosts. But Taja must have seen something in his face, because she said, "Why don't you go back to Etrara for the feast?"

"I can't," he said. Pebr watched him shrewdly; he had to come up with some story. "I've taken a vow not to return until I finish my poem."

"Well," Taja said, "you can go in disguise."

He looked at her. Why not, after all? Everyone in the city would be masked on the night of the Ascending God, and there would be crowds coming from the provinces and farmlands. He had gotten homespun clothing in the neighboring town of Soria; to the people in Etrara he would be just another rustic.

What would Narrion say? But there was no way to know;

Narrion hadn't written in the weeks since they'd fled the city.

"Where would I get a mask?" he asked.

"We have a few somewhere, don't we, Uncle?"

Pebr nodded. He stood and left the room, rubbing his arms, and returned a moment later. "They're not what you're used to in the city, I'm sure," he said, holding out two masks. "We don't go in much for disguising here."

Val took them, disappointed. One had been crudely fashioned out of wood and cloth; he thought it was supposed to be the god Callabrion but it looked more like the pictures of Gobro's grandfather, a fat man with a face like a toad. The other was even worse, a half-mask made of disintegrating lace and moth-eaten feathers.

He fitted the wooden mask over his head, thinking with longing of the mask maker he knew on the Street of Apricots. Taja laughed, delighted, and took the other mask from him. Even before she put it on he could see that it was too big for her. It slipped forward immediately, revealing her dark eyes.

"Here, let me tie it," Val said. "No one will mistake you for a great lady, you can be certain of that."

"Do you mean— Can I come to Etrara with you?"

He hadn't meant that at all. Still, why shouldn't she?

"No," Pebr said.

"Why not?" Taja said. She took off the mask and looked at her uncle. "What are you worried about?"

"Everything," Pebr said. "You know nothing about the city, nothing at all."

"Then it's time I learned, isn't it?" Taja said.

"I'll see that no harm comes to her," Val said.

"I can take care of myself," Taja said sharply.

"Oh no, you can't," Pebr said. "I'll let you go, but only if you stay with Val. Promise me that."

Taja looked between Val and Pebr, then nodded slowly. "No one would mistake you for a great lord either," she said to Val.

He still had the mask on. Feeling foolish, he lifted it over his head and nodded toward her in a bow. He *was* a lord, though, if not a great one. That was the difference between them. Or was he? What was a courtier, without the court to surround him?

A few days later he and Taja stood in the great courtyard at the palace in Etrara, struggling to keep their footing among the vast numbers of people. The crowd swayed like a tide, pushing a woman in a dress of silk and gauze against him. She looked up, the smile under her velvet half-mask fading as she caught sight of his mask. On his other side he saw Taja step nimbly backward as a torch threatened to set her woolen cloak on fire.

He had been trying to make his way toward the arena for the last half-hour. The wrestlers hadn't arrived yet; on the stage acrobats tumbled and balanced on ropes and tossed brands of fire to one another.

He and Taja had moved near the edge of the crowd now; he could see the golden light rising from the bonfires. The fires and the press of people made him feel almost hot. He welcomed the sensation; this season winter seemed to have lasted for years. All praise to Callabrion, he thought, who would ascend this night.

He smelled roasting chestnuts and hot cider, heard a group of people singing hymns to Callabrion. A silver mask glimmered in the light from the bonfires, a mask very like the one he had worn to his last banquet in Etrara. The man wearing it was tall and lean, with long dark hair—could that be Narrion? He remembered he had given his cousin the name of the artificer who had made his mask. Could Narrion have had the same idea he had, to come to Etrara in disguise?

The crowd shifted, moved between him and the other man. He shook his head and turned his attention back to the arena. When would Narrion have had time to commission a mask?

"We don't need to see the wrestlers," Taja said, standing on her toes and shouting to make herself heard over the noise of the crowd. "Let's see if we can get some roasted chestnuts instead."

"Oh, you're wrong," Val said. "People in the city wait all year to see these men."

She laughed and headed toward the chestnut vendors on the edge of the crowd. She was surprisingly self-possessed for a woman who had never been out of Tobol An in her life, Val thought, and he wondered for a moment what Pebr feared would happen to her.

They passed a man selling ale, then a woman offering to tell fortunes. The woman was dressed in a black mask and a hood made of black rags; Val thought of the Maegrim and then wondered if he would always be haunted by those grim reminders of fate. But even the Maegrim, he thought, would not dare bring bad news to the Feast of the Ascending God.

A juggler dropped a wooden spoon at his feet and picked it up, looking sheepish. Taja returned with a paper cone filled with hot chestnuts. The crowd closest to the arena cried out; the wrestlers had arrived. Val looked out over the heads of the people around him.

The fortune-teller took his hand. Val glanced down quickly and pulled his hand away. "I see a marriage for you soon, my young lord," the fortune-teller said.

"I don't want my fortune told," he said sharply.

"Oh, why not?" Taja said. "Tell mine, please."

"I'm not finished with this young man," the woman said. Her voice sounded low, croaking, but something told Val that she was acting, that he might have known her in his earlier life at court. She took his hand again. "You will have great fortune and rise high on the ladder. And you will marry soon—you will marry a woman whose name begins with—begins with T."

The mask slipped from Taja's face. She pushed it back quickly.

"Callia," Val said.

"How did you know?" Duchess Callia said. She sounded disappointed.

"Tell me how you knew who I was first."

"Come, Val—I know all the charming young men at

court. You wrote me a sonnet once, don't you remember? I always thought it was a pity you became so distracted by that actor, that Tamra."

"And you wanted me to believe that I'd marry her. That wasn't very amusing, Callia."

"Yes, it was. It would have been, if you hadn't recognized me. How—"

"Your voice gave you away. You're no actor."

"I'll have to study with Tamra, then. But what have you been doing? Something exciting, I hope."

How much did she know? She had never been an intimate of the king, her half-brother; she didn't appear to have heard that Narrion had killed one of Gobro's favorites. Her ignorance made his role much easier to play. "I've been in Tobol An," he said.

"Where?"

"A fishing village on the coast. I became tired of the court—I left to write poetry."

"That isn't very flattering to us."

"Oh, I'll be back."

She didn't seem to have heard him. "Tobol An—that's where the library is, isn't it?"

He nodded, realizing only then how much he had missed the company of the men and women of the court. He had been raised to take his place among them, after all; no wonder he had felt so restless with just Taja and her uncle for company. "Do you know," he said, "they have the records of everyone's birth in the library. Everyone's but mine. I couldn't find mine anywhere."

"Really?" she said. The crowd roared again and she turned in the direction of the noise. One of the wrestlers seemed to have won.

He had hoped she'd show more interest. Had he lived among dull fisher-folk so long that he had become like them, incapable of courtly conversation? "How's Gobro?"

She looked back. "What? Oh, Gobro's the same as ever."

"And the others at court?"

"Sorry," Callia said. "Sorry, I think I see someone I know. Good fortune, Val!" She hurried off and was lost in the crowd.

He looked at Taja. She appeared tired; her mouth, under the half-mask, looked drawn. Perhaps she didn't know who Callia was; she didn't seem at all impressed by the duchess, one of the contenders for the throne. "Do you want to go back to the inn?" he asked.

"No. No, let's stay. Look—I think they're starting."

She pointed toward the arena. A man wearing the gold and green colors of Callabrion had climbed to the stage and stood facing another wrestler dressed in the blue and silver of Scathiel. An astronomer-priest gave the signal and the two men grappled together.

The crowd called out encouragement to the Summer God. The wrestlers struggled back and forth across the arena. They had found exceptionally good men this year, Val thought; for a brief and terrifying moment it looked as if the Winter God would triumph. Then Callabrion threw Scathiel to the floor.

The Winter God lay still. Callabrion stood. A cheer went up from every throat; the man who had played Callabrion was pelted with coins and masks and rare fruit from the tropical south.

The priest stepped forward and raised his hand. The crowd quieted. The priest looked into the sky. "Look where he comes, the Ascending God!" he called.

Callabrion had been received into heaven again this year. All around Val the crowd went wild, strangers hugging and kissing and clasping hands. Trumpets blew, and drums answered. The children, on edge from having stayed up so late, ran off screaming to collect the ladders and throw them on the bonfires. Val turned to Taja. "Good fortune, Val," she said.

"Good fortune!" he said, hugging her. His luck would change this year, he knew it. He would be called back from his exile; he would return to Etrara.

They made their way through the crowd. Earlier in the

day they had been fortunate enough to find an inn with a few spaces on the floor still free, and they headed toward it. On the streets around them they saw people pouring coins into the outstretched hands of Etrara's beggars; Scathiel had descended to the earth in the guise of a beggar and could be any one of these ragged men and women. The beggars made the most of it; they would not receive so much bounty for six more months, when Scathiel ascended and Callabrion came to earth to assume the aspect of the Wandering God.

Val took a sovereign from his purse and pushed it into the hand of an old man. "Good fortune, my young lord," the man said.

Lord? How did the man know? "Val!" Taja said urgently.

Val turned. Someone fell into him, punching him hard in the stomach and knocking him to the cobblestoned street. He struggled to rise, to draw breath, to call out. He heard one or two people laugh and realized that no one around him knew what had happened; probably they thought the man drunk on too much excitement and ale.

The man hit him again. He pushed out with his hands and elbows but the other man had him on the ground now and would not let him up. "So, Val," the man said.

"Who—" Val said. He struggled to see his opponent's face but the mask covered it completely.

The man reached for the dagger at his belt. Only one arm pinioned Val now; Val twisted and managed to force his opponent to the ground. They had traded places, gods of summer and winter. But the man had drawn his dagger and was pointing it at Val's throat.

"Help!" someone said. "Help! Murder! Help!" It was Taja.

The crowd parted. Hands lifted him from the ground. "The wrestling matches are over, my good lord," someone said, and one or two people laughed.

Val stood carefully. He heard the sound of cloth tearing and watched as his opponent ran off into the crowd. His hands shook as he fastened his cloak. He took a deep breath, another. Someone had wanted to kill him.

"Should we follow him?" someone asked.

"No," Val said. His breathing was steadier now. The crowd had closed over the retreating figure. "No, we'll never be able to find him now."

A young man handed him a piece of cloth and he studied it for a moment, but he could make nothing of it save that it was finely woven and dyed. "This came from his cloak?" he asked.

"Aye, my lord," the young man said.

That made the second time someone knew him for one of the nobility. He rubbed his hand wearily over his eyes and realized that his mask had disappeared. "You called the other man 'my lord,'" he said. "Do you know who he was?"

"No, but he seemed noble. He wore fine clothes, and rings, and he carried himself like a highborn man. Like you, my lord." Sometime during this recital the other man had taken in Val's tattered, homespun clothing and his lack of land-rings, and his voice trailed off doubtfully.

Val nodded. "Thank you," he said. He felt for his purse, intending to give the young man a coin for his trouble, and then changed his mind. It would be better to keep the other man uncertain of his identity, unsure even whether he was noble or not. Far too many people knew he had come to the festival as it was. He had behaved foolishly, very foolishly.

"Do you want to call the watch?" the young man asked.

The last thing he wanted was to come to the attention of the law. "No. I'm sure the watch has better things to do tonight."

He turned to go. The crowd was thinning out; parents were calling for their children and preparing to go home. He barely saw them. Callia had recognized him, and so, apparently, had the nobleman who had attacked him. And who else?

As if guessing his thoughts Taja said, "Do you have any enemies?"

He laughed harshly. All he had, it seemed, were enemies. Even the king was his enemy. But the king would not have done this, not with the entire body of the law behind him. "I don't know," he said. "I don't know." He rubbed his hand over his eyes again and realized that without his mask he was still in danger. "Lend me your mask," he said.

She looked at him appraisingly. He could see the questions in her eyes, the realization that he might be different from what he seemed. Finally she took off her mask and handed it to him wordlessly.

They spent the night at the inn and rode through the forest of Thole the next day, saying little. Val wondered if Taja would tell her uncle about the attack. But when they came to Tobol An and Pebr's house the next day she said nothing about it. He was grateful for her silence; he did not want Pebr's shrewd eyes measuring him, guessing his secrets.

A week after Callabrion ascended, Val went with Taja and Pebr to the house of one of the villagers. All the village, it seemed, had crowded into the small stone cottage to hear the elders read from the Book of Sbona. Only three or four people had been able to find seats, and the place smelled strongly of fish.

Val thought of his aunt and uncle, Narrion's parents, who would even now be getting together with others from his house to read from the same book. All over the mapped world, in Etrara and the provinces, in the barbaric country of Shai, people were telling the story of the goddess Sbona. Even in the colonies across the seas, in Udriel and Astrion, they would light candles against the vast loneliness around them and read to each other about the creation of the world.

"Sbona ruled alone in heaven," one of the villagers read. "Then she gave birth to the twins Callabrion and Scathiel, and she created the world we live in and she gave it to them. But the two sons quarreled over who was to have her favor, and they carried their fight to the newly created world, using it as a battleground. For hundreds of years they fought each other, and their struggles made the hills and valleys and mountains, and in the end each killed the other."

The villager passed the Book of Sbona to Pebr. But Pebr did not consult the book at all as he continued the story, reciting solely from memory.

"Sbona wept for her sons in heaven, and her tears fell to earth and created the seas," Pebr said. "She descended to the world she had made and searched for their scattered limbs, and she created men and women to help her in her quest. Finally she gathered together the bodies of her two sons, and she breathed life into them. But Callabrion had lost forever his right toe, and Scathiel his left, and for their disobedience Sbona sent each of them into exile for six months out of the year."

Pebr handed the book to the next villager, Dochno, the man Val had saved from the sea. "Every year in winter Callabrion ascends to heaven, and so things grow, and become strong. And every year in summer Callabrion comes back to earth and his brother Scathiel ascends to heaven, and so things are reaped, and they die. Each is brother to the other, as summer is brother to winter, as life is brother to death. Every year the seasons change, but from year to year the seasons remain the same."

Dochno closed the book. In Etrara at this time Val would spend the evening with Narrion's family, his closest relatives since his parents died. Narrion's father would bring out the golden goblets used only twice a year, and his mother would pour the good Shai wine they had saved for this occasion. Val hoped . . . And there, to his delight, he saw their host setting out clay mugs and pouring ale. He reached for a cup and then, seeing Mathary come up next to him, he gave it to her and turned back for another. She drank it down gratefully.

The villagers settled in for stories. All around the room they went, telling the legends of Callabrion and Scathiel on earth, their lovers, their quarrels, the disguises each had used and how they were unmasked, the gifts they had given and the justice they had dispensed.

When his turn came Val repeated a story he had heard in Etrara about Andosto, said to be the grandson of the god Callabrion, and how he had routed the Shai during the reign of King Tariel III. The villagers listened quietly, rapt, but when Val said that he knew Andosto, that he had spoken to him, they roared with disbelief. The more he protested the more they laughed, until finally one of them slapped Val on the back and claimed he was the finest storyteller of all.

Since they were still laughing, the next speaker, an old woman, began a humorous tale of Scathiel in disguise, of mistaken identity and misunderstanding. The night grew older; everyone vowed to stay awake, to encourage Callabrion by their example to make the days longer and longer. Then the parents with small children went home, and the old people. Val leaned against the wall and fell asleep in the middle of the famous tale of how Callabrion had taken his leave of Queen Ellara the Good.

Someone shook his shoulder. Val opened his eyes, surprised to find himself in a small dim room reeking of coal-smoke and fish. "Narrion?" he said. What had his cousin gotten him into this time?

"Pebr," the old man said. His eyes were bright and alert despite the late hour. "It's time to go home."

"Oh." Someone opened the door and a blast of cold air blew in, chilling Val to the bone. He rubbed his eyes. He had missed the story that was always saved for last, how the goddess Sbona came to earth and gave birth to the ancestor of the ruling family of Etrara. "Good fortune, Pebr," Val said.

"Good fortune to you, my lord," Pebr said, his tone more kindly than usual, and he and Val and Taja set off under the black night sky for home.

The days returned to what they had been before the feast. Taja went to work in the library, and Val sat alone in his room or went for walks by the cliffs. The weather stayed bitterly cold, the sky so dull and overcast that on some days the sun could not be seen. Some folks wondered if Callabrion had ascended after all.

A month after he had come back from Etrara Val sat at his desk, studying the clutter of papers around him. He was no poet; he had learned that much from his stay in Tobol An, if nothing else.

His candles guttered. A sudden movement made him look up. Taja came into the room, carrying a lamp in her hand like Sbona bringing light to the heavens. "I've made dinner," she said.

For a moment he could not say anything, overcome by the strange sight, a goddess dwelling in a humble stone cottage. Then he shook his head, dismissing his fancies, and followed her.

Evening had fallen while he had sat dreaming at his desk; the sky through the windows was black, with no star to light the darkness. Taja lit candles and built up the fire while her uncle brought their supper to the table. Fish again, Val saw. He was starting to long for the oversweet food of the court, for anything that hadn't come out of the sea.

In the past few weeks he had started to tell Taja and Pebr about his life in Etrara. Taking a bite of his fish he began to describe King Gobro's great banquets, and the gatherings that took place afterward in Duchess Sbarra's apartments. "All the court meets there in the evenings," he said. "The lady, and her husband the Duke Talenor, and her poet—"

"Her poet? Why does she have a poet?" Taja asked.

"Why?" Val said. He had never realized how strange his life at court must seem to an outsider. "Everyone high on the ladder has a poet. If someone's poet writes a satire about you then your poet has to respond."

"What if he doesn't?"

"I can't think of one that didn't. If your poet doesn't respond then I suppose you lose the respect of other noblemen. You lose your standing at court."

Pebr scowled. He disapproved of the court, though Val didn't know why. "You would think people would have better things to do," he said. "Dancing and hawking and music and poetry—not one of you has ever done anything important."

"Of course not," Val said. "It's important to seem frivolous, to appear to occupy yourself with the games and fashions of court. But at the same time most courtiers spend their time scheming, plotting ways to rise on the ladder."

"Bah," Pebr said. "That's even worse. Hypocrites, all of them. Do you do this? Are you as cunning as the rest?"

"I suppose not. Life at King Gobro's court suits me. I have to admit I'm as frivolous as everyone thinks I am."

Pebr scowled again. A horse whinnied outside the cottage, and a few moments later someone knocked loudly at the door.

Pebr went to the door. A man stood there, shivering in the cold. He handed Pebr a letter. "For my lord Valemar," he said.

Val took the letter from Pebr as he returned to the table. It was sealed with a willow tree, the crest of his house. A message from Narrion, at last. He broke it open and began to read.

"My dear Cousin," the letter said. "Our exile is at an end. The reign of King Gobro is over, and we have achieved everything we have hoped for. Come to Etrara."

He read it again to make certain there was no mistake. Then he looked up; the other two were watching him closely. "Good news?" Taja asked.

"The best," Val said. "I'm going home."

"Ah," Pebr said. His shrewd eyes did not leave Val's face, and Val remembered that Pebr thought he had come to Tobol An voluntarily. It didn't matter; he would never see these people again. Nothing mattered, nothing but the fact that he would be gone soon, traveling through the haunted forest and then home.

The next morning at dawn he bought a horse with the remainder of his money and bade farewell to Pebr and Taja. His premonition on the night of the feast had been a true one. His fortune had changed; he had ascended with Callabrion.

As he entered the forest he began to think about Narrion's letter. How had Gobro's reign ended? Gobro must have died, of course, but how had it happened? Who ruled in Etrara now? And what did Narrion mean when he said they had achieved everything they had hoped for? Val hadn't hoped for anything but a return to Etrara. What plot did Narrion spin now?

The shadows of the trees began to lengthen around him. His apprehension grew. Would he be safe in Etrara? The last time he had returned to the city someone had tried to kill him. Narrion's letter no longer had the power to cheer him; his cousin's news might be a two-sided coin.

When the sun set he stopped to eat the bread and cheese Taja had given him, then spread his cloak a little ways off the path. He stretched out on the ground and watched as the first stars appeared among the trees.

Moments later he heard horses' hooves, and the chiming of bridles. "Ho!" a man's voice said. "How much longer before we make camp?"

Val sat up in the darkness. Who were they? Should he greet them?

"We'll go a ways yet," another voice said. "Our orders are to get there as soon as possible."

"Are you frightened of the wood?" said a third.

"Not at all," the first man said. "Only tired."

The second man said something Val could not hear, and then they were gone. Who had they been? They had been wrong not to fear the wood; Val had learned that much at least about wizardry. He was glad he had not hailed them.

He reached the Gate of Stones by midmorning the next day. As he rode through the lower city he was surprised at how little had changed in his absence. The ladders he had seen before were gone, burned in the great bonfires on the Feast of the Ascending God, but already several new ladders had been raised to commemorate one piece of good fortune or another. He urged his horse through the Street of Stones.

He saw no one he recognized in the lower city. He

crossed the Darra River, passed the crowded marketplace
where the Street of Stones and the Street of Roses met. He
hurried on; he wanted to know what folks said about him
before he took part in the idle gossip and political discussions
of the marketplace.

The street widened. Statues of the Seven Virtues and
Seven Vices stood to either side of him. The whitewashed
houses with their timbered roofs became taller, two and even
three stories high. On his left he saw the theater and the
university, the tall clock tower capped with gold. Bells rang
out eleven times as he passed.

The street grew steeper as he neared the hill and his
house. His apprehension returned. What would he find when
he returned? Had Gobro confiscated all his wealth?

As he reached the hill he saw an old friend from the
university. "Dorio!" he called.

Dorio turned. He was wearing the green and gold of
Callabrion; after graduation he had apprenticed himself to
the astronomer-priests. Val had not seen him often since
then; the priests were not allowed to leave the observatory
except on business. "Val!" he said. "Good fortune!"

Val dismounted, and they embraced. "I hear the king was
angry with you," Dorio said.

"Aye," Val said warily. How much had Dorio learned,
cloistered within the observatory?

"But Narrion told me he'd taken you to a safe place,"
Dorio said.

"Narrion? Is Narrion back already?"

"What do you mean? He never left."

Never left. Val rubbed his eyes; he was tired from the long
journey through the forest, and tired of treachery as well.
"What did Narrion tell you about me?" he asked carefully.

"He said that you had done something to anger Gobro,
but that you were safe and out of the king's reach. That he was
working hard to bring you back."

"Did he tell you what I was supposed to have done?"

"No. He assured me it was not treason, and I know you

would not have done anything to harm the royal house—
What was it?"

"Nothing," Val said. His weariness gave way to anger.
Narrion had used him, had played with his life as casually as
a man might throw down a conjuring stick. "I've done nothing. Narrion killed a favorite of the king and told me I was in
danger. He convinced me to go into exile. And now you tell
me that he never even left the city."

"Damath," Dorio said. "Narrion killed Damath. But he
convinced the king that it was self-defense. Gobro never punished him for it at all. Val? Is there something wrong?"

"Something, yes. I have a few things to say to Narrion
when I see him next." He thought quickly. He had been right
to be careful; he was not yet out of danger. "Who rules Etrara
now?"

"Queen Callia."

"Callia?" Val said, surprised. Any one of Gobro's half-
brothers or half-sisters would be more suited to rule.

"Duchess Mariel supported her, and she convinced Duke
Arion to join them. I suppose Arion thinks Callia will be easy
to overthrow, just as Gobro was. Only Duke Talenor opposed
them."

"What happened to Gobro?"

"He was poisoned."

"Who—"

"No one knows. Everyone suspects Mariel, of course."

"Mariel? Not Callia?"

"Mariel's the real ruler. Callia does what her sister tells
her. But you'll see it all for yourself soon enough—I hear the
Duchess Sbarra still holds gatherings in her apartments."

Good, Val thought. He could confront Narrion then. He
would be interested in hearing the man's excuses.

He sighed. He had become unused to intrigue in the
quiet months he had spent in Tobol An. Suddenly he longed
for the peace of the fishing village, the nights by the fire
talking with Taja and her uncle. But no—he had forgotten

how tedious that life was. He wondered what sort of place he was suited for, if he would ever be happy anywhere.

"How is Tamra?" he asked.

"Oh, aye," Dorio said. "That's an interesting thing. She and Narrion got married."

Four

· · · · · · ·

TAJA WAS WALKING TO THE LIBRARY WHEN the trumpet sounded. At first she didn't know what it was: she had never heard the trumpet of Thole. Then she saw people leave their houses and hurry down the path, and she realized that the ghost of the forest had been roused. Someone threatened the peace of Tobol An.

The trumpet blew again. Taja joined a group of people heading toward the forest. She saw Pebr ahead of her, and Mathary, and she realized that the crowd consisted of old men and women and children. Everyone else would be out on the fishing boats. She laughed a little to hide her fear. What could this sad little band hope to accomplish against—against what?

The ghost-knight had blocked the forest path with his standard. Three riders dressed in the gold livery of the royal family stood before him, each mounted on a horse with gold trappings. The trumpet sounded again.

The crowd pushed forward as far as the standard. Their brown, lined faces showed little but stubbornness, but here and there a few had given way, almost against their wills, to wonderment. No one living could remember a delegation from Etrara.

Taja felt a great love for them, for their stolid, hopeless determination to protect Tobol An against these armed and armored men. She sought out and found Pebr near the front of the crowd. If trouble came she could at least see to it that he was safe.

"We bring greetings from Queen Callia," one of the mounted men said.

A few in the crowd murmured. Taja had known that things had changed in Etrara; something had called Val away from their village and back to court. But word of a new queen had not yet reached as far as Tobol An. Why should it have, after all? The kings and queens of Etrara had ignored Tobol An since the wizards' war.

"Tell Queen Callia that we pledge to serve her as we have served all the royal family of Etrara," Pebr said. He made a slight bow, and Taja smiled. She hadn't thought her uncle knew that much about court etiquette.

"She wishes us to consult some records at the library," the queen's man said. He seemed to be the leader.

Pebr looked lost. By law everyone had a right to consult the library, but these men could not mean the people of Tobol An any good. "We—I'm afraid we cannot let you—"

"But this is insolence!" another of Callia's men said, his hand moving to the hilt of his sword. He rode forward as far as the knight's standard and stopped, clearly afraid to continue. "Why are we standing here bandying words with these peasants? We're not asking their permission. We're giving them a command from their lawful queen. Any more obstruction and we'll charge them with treason—tell them that."

Mathary pushed her way through the crowd toward Taja. "Let them pass, dear," she whispered. "But see to it that they don't find what they came for."

Taja looked at the old woman, startled. "Do it, child," Mathary said.

Taja moved forward. "Let them through," she said. "I'll show them to the library."

Pebr and a few others looked doubtful. Mathary whispered to another old man, who nodded and signaled to the crowd to fall back.

"Good," the queen's man said. The hand that grasped his sword hilt fell back to his side. "At least one of you has some sense. Call off your guard dog."

"He's not mine to command," Taja said. "Step through him—he can't hurt you."

For the space of a heartbeat the man did nothing. Then he closed his eyes and urged his horse forward. The colors of the knight's standard played over him like ripples of firelight.

The man opened his eyes and looked around him. "He's like the ghosts in the city!" he called back to his companions, looking relieved. "He can't hurt you. Don't believe everything you hear about the haunted forest!"

The leader pushed his way forward. The third man, who had hung back a little, walked his horse gently through the standing ghost. Taja thought that he might be a little embarrassed by the rudeness of his companions.

The knight returned to his accustomed place on the road. Taja set off toward the library and the men followed.

She walked slowly, knowing that the riders would be anxious to finish their task, that it galled them to have to rein in their mounts. When they saw the white spire of the library in the distance they galloped on ahead of her. By the time she reached the library they had dismounted and were waiting impatiently.

She unlocked the door to the library and led them in. "Where's the librarian?" the leader asked.

"Here," she said. "I'm the librarian."

The man who had threatened them laughed. "Everyone else is out guarding the forest, I suppose," he said, and the leader laughed with him.

"What are you looking for?" she asked.

"The queen wants the records of the royal family," the leader said.

She nodded, and as she did so she saw in her mind the location of the records, a wooden box on the third level near the library's center. She could not recall ever seeing the box before.

Lately she had been able to find all sorts of things, from Pebr's lost drinking cup to a child's mittens. Pebr always looked fierce whenever she did it; no doubt he thought it was sorcery.

But she was beginning to fear that there was magic in it as well; she thought that no one could live long in the city of wizards without coming to understand a few tricks. Witchcraft was in the air they breathed, the food they ate. She had even consulted a few of the old books of magic, trying to understand what was happening to her; she had stared hard at the long lists of words, but the books refused to give up their secrets.

She put aside her worries for the moment and concentrated on the men before her. Mathary had told her not to give them what they wanted. "The records, yes," she said. "Follow me."

She started up the corridor, then opened a door leading to a flight of stairs. The third man caught up with her as she started to climb. "That knight in the forest," the man said. "Who was he?"

"Legend says that he betrayed the village to a king of Etrara," Taja said. "The king had him put to death, quoting the old proverb that a man who was false once would show himself to be false again. The knight swore that he would prove his loyalty, and he vowed to defend the village against all its enemies forever." They left the stairs and came out on another corridor.

"Why did he think we were enemies?"

"I don't know," Taja said. She looked at him. "Are you?"

The man seemed startled. Taja tried not to laugh. Val had told her the women of the court were not usually so direct.

The man said nothing more as she led him and the others through the library and into the room with the birth records. "This is everything the king sent us from Etrara," she said.

"Where are the records of the royal family?" the leader asked.

"I don't know. Somewhere in this room, I imagine."

"You don't know? What kind of librarian are you?"

"A very busy one. If you don't mind, I should be getting to my work."

"You won't be going anywhere. You'll stay here and wait until we find what we came for, and then you'll escort us back. Or did you think to lose us in the library?"

She heard the fear in his voice, and knew the other men had heard it as well. Probably he was unused to libraries and scholarship, and uneasy in a place with a reputation for sorcery.

She sat at the table and watched as he and his men opened drawer after drawer. The leader grew angrier and angrier, and the man who had insulted the people of Tobol An began to frown as he rifled through the records. Only the third man remained calm as he studied the papers in front of him, the lists of children born to shoemakers and nobility, merchants and scholars.

"It's not here," the leader said finally. "By the Burning Ladder, you've brought us to the wrong place. Where are the records we want?"

"I thought they were here," Taja said. The picture of the wooden box was strong in her mind.

"Do you know the penalty for lying to the queen's men? I could have you hung for treason."

"I'm not lying. If the royal records aren't with the rest of them I don't know where they are."

The leader slammed a drawer shut. "Let's go," he said. "Show us the way back."

Taja stood. She had not been afraid to exchange words with him, but now that it was over and they were leaving she felt herself trembling. She took a deep breath to steady herself and led the men out of the library.

After they had gone she walked through the library. She came to a room filled with uncatalogued books; they lined the shelves and were piled unsteadily on the floor. A scarred table stood in the middle of the room, and a small alcove opened off to the side. She went into the alcove and took a dusty wooden box from a shelf. The box was locked, but the same vision that had directed her to it now showed her where to find the key.

She took the box back to the table and sat for a moment, studying it. She knew, as strongly as she had ever known anything, what she would find if she opened it. For a moment she considered putting it back in its alcove and continuing on as though nothing had happened. But she could not do that; Callia would not stop until she learned the truth, and it was better that Val learned it from her than from the queen.

And what would he say? She had liked Val at first, thought him handsome, with his gray eyes and brown hair. He had been very brave the night of the storm, but the memory that would stay with her was the sight of him walking along the cliffs, his carefree singing. He must have been so pampered at court, so protected; he knew nothing of the harshness of the world. There was an innocence at the heart of his sophistication.

But as she grew to know him she had come to see his unthinking arrogance, his conviction that because he was from the higher rungs he was somehow superior to Taja, whose parents had been fisher-folk. She remembered the feast night in Etrara, and how he had never thought to introduce her to Duchess Callia. And she remembered his surprise whenever she or Pebr understood one of his literary references. What did he think they did in the evenings, with a library the largest thing within miles? Even the fisher-folk had been known to read a book or two.

Still, he deserved to be told the truth. More than that, he needed to know. Taja had only met Callia for a moment, but in that brief time she had seen that the woman would be a dangerous enemy. Val should be warned about the new queen, and about other things as well.

Taja took a deep breath, stood and found the key behind one of the books on the shelf. She unlocked the box and saw the papers she had been expecting. Then she left the library and went into the village to borrow a horse.

As she rode into Thole Forest she saw what looked like diamonds falling from the sky in front of her. The diamonds touched her hands on the reins and melted, and she realized that she was seeing snow. She had never encountered it before, not so far south, though she had read about it in books.

The severe winter had not lessened after the Feast of the Ascending God. She said a brief prayer to the Summer God and pulled her cloak closer around her.

As fortune would have it Narrion was the first person Val saw on his way to Sbarra's apartments. "Narrion!" Val said. "What game are you playing now?"

"Hush," Narrion said, looking at the men and women heading toward Sbarra's rooms. He pulled Val down a deserted corridor. "I did nothing."

"Nothing? You forced me into exile—because of your devious plots I spent weeks eating fish and listening to unlettered rustics." He was being unfair to Taja and her uncle, he knew; at the moment he didn't care. "And all the while you sat at your ease in Etrara. Why? Because you wanted to marry Tamra? Surely you could have worked out a less complicated scheme—surely you could have accomplished your ends without disrupting my life quite so much."

"The king wanted you in Tobol An."

"Gobro? Why?"

"I don't know. He told me—"

"You don't know! Why in Callabrion's name should I believe anything you say now? Gobro wanted me in Tobol An? Come—you've never been a King's Man."

"Hush," Narrion said again. He was whispering, though no one in the corridor could possibly overhear him. This was the Narrion Val remembered, subtle, secretive, conspiratorial. "I swear by the Burning Ladder that what I'm telling you is true. Gobro wanted you in Tobol An for some reason. He paid me, paid me well, to see that you got there."

"What are you telling me? That you killed Damath just to make certain I went to Tobol An?"

Narrion grinned. "Well, I have to admit I didn't like the man very much. But yes—killing him was the only way I could think of to get you out of Etrara."

"And Tamra had nothing to do with it."

"Listen. Listen, Val. I've ascended very high on the ladder. Callia could not have become queen without the help I gave her. I'm in a position to do you good—you can rise with me. What do you want? Do you want Tobol An? Lord of Tobol An—it sounds fine, doesn't it?"

Once again his cousin had caught him off balance. He thought of the stories and laughter of the fisher-folk the night they had read from the Book of Sbona, of their faces flushed with ale and firelight. What would they think of him if he returned with the land-ring of Tobol An on his finger?

He looked down at his cousin's hands. Narrion wore three land-rings on his fingers; he had had only one when Val had left Etrara. It was true then; Callia and Mariel had rewarded him with land and titles. But how had he helped them?

Suddenly Val remembered something Damath had said the night Narrion killed him: "I saw you at the apothecary's . . ."

Gobro had been poisoned. Narrion had gotten the poison at the apothecary's; that had been the help he had given Callia. Perhaps he had fought with Damath to force Val to leave Etrara, but by killing the man he had also gotten rid of a dangerous witness. And with Val out of the way he had been free to marry Tamra.

There was no end to his cousin's deviousness, Val thought; the man never did anything without having three or four reasons for it. If the plot to kill Gobro hadn't succeeded Narrion would still be high in the king's favor because he had sent Val to Tobol An. He had worked for both sides.

"Val?" Narrion said. "Did you hear what I said?"

"I don't want any gift of yours," Val said. "You killed Gobro, didn't you?"

"Quiet—"

"No, I won't keep quiet! You committed treason against your lawful king—"

"I didn't kill him."

"You bought the poison to kill him, then. Do you deny that?"

"Mariel and Callia asked me to find the poison. Mariel is a powerful woman, and even Callia has her supporters. A request from the royal family has the weight of a command—surely you understand that."

"But you did well out of it. You rose by Gobro's fall, just as you said you would."

"I couldn't disobey them. Even you can see that I didn't have a choice."

Val studied his cousin for a moment. "Of course you had a choice," he said softly. "You could have gone into exile." He turned and left the corridor without looking back.

"Val!" three or four people said as he entered Sbarra's apartments. "Good fortune, Val, and welcome back. Tell us—"

"Come sit next to me," someone said, and the others fell silent. Val looked in the direction of the voice and saw Queen Callia, dressed in royal gold and black and white. So the new queen was serving notice that she would not tolerate any conspiracies begun in Duchess Sbarra's rooms; she would not retire discreetly as King Gobro had. "I want to hear all about the wonderful poetry you wrote," Callia said, playing with the black pearls at her throat.

He took a seat next to her, noticing the golden land-ring of Etrara on her hand as he did so. Should he tell her what had happened? With Gobro dead he no longer had to hide the truth. But Narrion stood very high in the queen's favor, and it would not do to accuse his cousin in front of Callia on his first night at court.

"I'm afraid I have no poetry to show you," he said. "All I learned in Tobol An is that I'm no poet."

He looked out over the faces around him, all of them eager for something to break the tedium of the court. Perhaps he would start a fashion; perhaps now every young courtier would travel to distant places and write poetry. He hoped their quests would prove more successful than his had been.

Tamra and Narrion came into the room and sat near the queen. Narrion put his arm around Tamra and she leaned closer to him. Val felt nothing. It had all been a pose, then: he had not loved Tamra. The knowledge was bitter to him; it would almost have been better if he could have written her reams of poetry, or challenged Narrion to a duel.

But did Narrion care for her? Or had he only married her to rise higher on the ladder? Tamra had high birth, and her family's wealth was far greater than that of the house of the willow tree.

The talk swirled around him. Listening to them Val realized how quickly fashions at court changed; he did not know half the people they mentioned. Gobro had apparently made a secret treaty with Shai, their old enemy to the east. Callia and her faction—Duchess Mariel, Narrion and others— thought the treaty shameful, and had broken it as soon as Callia ascended to the throne.

"It's no wonder Gobro's peace lasted so long," Arion said. "The man was a coward, anxious to placate anyone who rattled a sword in its scabbard. Imagine—he was about to give the Shai access to our ports! Did he truly think no one among us would object?"

"As if we'd let them have our riches," Callia said, playing with her ring. "As if we'd share the wealth of the colonies across the sea with them."

"What does the Shai ambassador say?" someone asked.

"Oh, he's gone home," Callia said. "Silly man. He said I'd broken a peace of five years' standing." She giggled. "He didn't understand that that was exactly what I wanted. And they say the Shai are subtle folk!"

"Who says they're subtle? They have no pageants, no court amusements—they're nothing but barbarians."

"But they have great poet-mages among them. People say they speak in poetry."

"Will they declare war, do you think?"

"I hope so. If they don't I'll have to do it myself." Callia giggled again.

War, Val thought. So it's come to that. The world he knew seemed to have turned upside down while he had sat at his ease in Tobol An.

The man sitting at his side turned to him. "And will you fight in Callia's war?" he asked.

"Oh, aye," Val said.

"Ah. But do you think valor is the greatest of the Virtues?"

Val remembered him now; he was the man who had argued in favor of love the night before Val's exile. His appearance had not improved since then; his tunic was, if anything, more threadbare than before, and his breeches had a hole at the knee. His thick white hair rayed out from his head, making him look like an image of the Summer God.

"No, I agree with you," Val said. "The greatest of all the Virtues is love."

"Of course it is, my lord," the man said forcefully. "Of course it is."

Suddenly Val thought he recognized the other man; he had been the beggar at the Feast of the Ascending God, the one who had thanked Val for the sovereign and called him "my young lord." But no, that was impossible. Although Duchess Sbarra was known for her charity to beggars she would certainly not have invited one to her gatherings.

The other man watched Val shrewdly. For a moment he seemed to become what he resembled, the Summer God, the Wandering God. Gold sparked from his eyes. The room grew warmer, seemed to pulse with heat. Val felt dazed, unanchored. Could this man be a god? Was Val blessed by a god's nearness?

He had never encountered one of the gods, though he knew people who claimed they had. He glanced down at the man's right foot to see if he had lost his big toe, but the other man wore old leather boots that came to his calves.

Val shook his head. This man could not be Callabrion; Callabrion had ascended. "I'm sorry—I'm afraid I don't know your name," he said.

A noise came from the corridor outside. Duchess Sbarra motioned to her poet, who stood and went to the door. "It's a woman," the poet said when he came back. He cast a knowing smile over the gathering. "She says she's looking for Valemar."

Val stood, puzzled, and went to the door. "He'll ascend to heaven tonight," someone in the room said, and the others laughed. He closed the door behind him.

Taja waited for him in the corridor.

"Taja," Val said, bowing slightly. "Good fortune." He understood the poet's amusement now; the man had no doubt seen immediately that Taja was from the lower rungs.

"We can't talk in the hallway," Taja said. "Is there somewhere we can go?"

"Of course," Val said. Almost all the rooms in the palace would be empty; everyone had gone to the gathering in Duchess Sbarra's apartments. He led her down the corridor. A cold draft blew through the stone and marble halls, and he shivered.

They came to Duke Arion's rooms. Val glanced inside and then motioned her to follow him. She looked around as they entered, but if she was impressed by the opulence, the tapestries and carved beams and huge hearth, she didn't show it. Candles burned in front of displays of gold plate, casting a warm glow over the room.

"What brings you to Etrara?" Val asked.

"Queen Callia sent her men to Tobol An," Taja said. "She wanted to consult some records in the library. Records of the royal family."

Val nodded, wondering why she was telling him this. Certainly Callia had the right to use the library.

"I found the records after they had gone," Taja said. "They . . . Here. You'd better read it yourself."

She took three folded pages from her purse and gave them to him. The first recorded a marriage between King Tariel III and a woman named Marea. The second showed that a child had been born to them in the seventh year of Tariel's reign. The child had been named Valemar.

He held the records loosely, uncertain what she wanted of him. Surely she didn't think—

"You're the lawful king," she said, whispering. "See, here—it says they had to keep the marriage secret because the king had so many illegitimate children. The mothers of these children were ambitious, and would have had Marea or the child killed. Would have had you killed. Etrara was at war with Shai then, and at least one of the mothers sided with Shai against Tariel. And look here—" She pointed to the third page. "Marea eventually died. Of unknown causes, it says. Usually whenever that appears in the records it means poison."

"What are you saying?"

"Here. Look here. There's a description of the charm King Tariel gave his son—a heron, it says. You're wearing it now. You've worn it every day since I've known you."

Without thinking, Val put his hand to the charm at his throat. "My mother gave me this," he said. "My parents—are you saying the king gave me to them to raise?"

"I don't know. Your parents might not have known who you are. They could have been childless, and one of the king's men could have given you to them. It's happened before—an unmarried woman of the court has a child, and someone finds a place for it. Maybe that's what your parents thought."

Val shook his head slowly. He remembered his parents' discretion, their unwillingness to push themselves forward, and he thought that they might have been trying to hide him, to keep him and themselves from coming to the attention of the royal family. It would be dangerous to claim the throne, whoever ruled.

His heart beat loudly against his chest. The throne, he thought. King of Etrara. Son of Tariel. Son of Sbona.

"Callia tried to have you killed that night, at the Feast of the Ascending God," Taja said. "She knew that the royal birth records are kept separate from the rest, and she guessed who you must be. When she became queen she tried to make certain. But she still doesn't know."

Val said nothing. Only an hour ago Narrion had offered him Tobol An. Taja's news seemed fantastic, a dream that would fade on waking. But at the same time it felt more real than anything that had gone before, the truth beneath the glittering deceptions of the court. King of Etrara. The rightful king.

What should he do? His parents had been right; it would be dangerous to act. But if Callia knew his secret it would be dangerous not to.

"What will you do?" Taja asked.

"Nothing."

Was that the truth? He thought that it was. He could hide his knowledge from Callia, remain a minor nobleman at court. But he would watch very carefully as the counters of fortune fell. Perhaps he could rise to the highest rung a mortal might attain, just below the gods in heaven.

"Your life is in danger," Taja said. "Callia's tried to have you killed once already."

"I'll be safe. The queen will see that I have no desire to rule. But I thank you for coming all this way on such a cold night."

"Well, then—give me the records back."

"What will you do with them?"

"They'll be safe."

He studied the records again before he gave them to her. Three pages, and his life and fortune were changed utterly. Had the Maegrim come for him on that dark night? But then why had they predicted ill fortune? "Do you have a place to stay?" he asked.

She nodded. "I have a room at an inn. Good fortune, Val."

He bowed to her as she left. It was too late to return to Sbarra's gathering, and he needed time alone to think. He walked down the darkened hill to his house. His parents, his real parents, had been a king and queen; he was king of Etrara.

Halfway down the hill he understood why King Gobro had sent him to Tobol An. Gobro had wanted him to discover the truth about his birth. The king had known his place on the ladder was uncertain and had wanted to abdicate, but could not risk favoring one brother or sister over another. Perhaps he thought that if Val learned the truth through his own efforts he would return to Etrara with an army. Poor man, poor doomed man. He had not understood Val's caution; he had guessed wrong in this as in so much else.

Taja led the horse she had borrowed through the streets of Etrara, looking for the inn she and Val had visited the night of the feast. The streets wound beneath her feet like a skein of yarn, and she wondered how anyone in the city managed to get from one place to another. Tobol An was an honest place compared to the cunning of Etrara; everything there was open, in plain sight.

A group of people came out of the house in front of her, singing and laughing. She cursed and reined in the horse. She felt angry with Val, angry with herself for coming all this long way on a fruitless errand. And it had started to snow again; she shivered in her light homespun clothing.

He was hiding something from her, she felt certain of it. "I have to admit I'm as frivolous as everyone thinks I am," he had said once. But she had seen the shadow that came over his face as she talked to him, the watchful, guarded expression in his eyes; he had lost a little of his innocence.

She cursed again. She had lost her way in Etrara; there

could no longer be any doubt of it. Her talent for finding things seemed to have deserted her in this strange place. She had been unable to reach to Val's heart, to discover what he planned.

Well, it was her own fault, after all. No one could receive such astonishing news and remain unchanged; she should have expected that. But already she found she missed the lighthearted courtier who had come singing to Tobol An.

She would have to rest soon; she was weary from her long journey. Up ahead she saw the signboard of an unfamiliar inn, and she urged the horse forward.

What these fine men and women did was none of her business, she knew that. But she remembered the frivolous woman she had met at the Feast of the Ascending God, and she could not help but think that Callia's reign would be disastrous.

Five

· · · · · · ·

A FEW DAYS LATER VAL WENT TO A LADder maker on the Street of Spiders. As he carried his ladder through the streets of Etrara folks smiled to see him, and a few called out "Good fortune!" as though to share in his luck. People in the city bought ladders to commemorate especially fortunate days, birthdays or weddings or festivals. Val had gotten his to thank the god Callabrion for ending his exile.

He set the ladder against the wall of his house and stepped back to look at it. The first ladder of the new year, the first piece of good fortune to come to the house of the willow tree. Later he would plan how to decorate it. He said a brief prayer to Callabrion and then went off to the Street of Apricots to take care of some errands. The food in his buttery had rotted in his absence, and his clothes were several months out of date.

Taja had told him that there was no ladder maker in Tobol An, that the villagers made their own ladders. But already the flat, dreary plain of the village was fading from his mind like a dream, replaced by the bustle and color and clamor of his city. Nothing could stop the business of Etrara, he thought as he went, not even the lowering sky and the threat of snow.

A group of actors dressed in the costumes of *The Sorcerer's Tragedy* stood outside the theater, arguing heatedly. A merchant drove his cart toward them without stopping, and they scattered, turning to shout curses at him. Past them a broom seller called out her wares, and beyond her Val saw a solitary student leaning against a statue of Patience, the scholar's Virtue.

But all the time Val made his way through the streets of Etrara, he was conscious of the extraordinary news Taja had brought him. King of Etrara. King of the actors, and the broom sellers, and the students. He would have to be careful now, as cunning as Narrion. Did Callia suspect he knew? Did Taja guess his ambitions? It was best for the moment to remain hidden, to remain Val.

A battalion of soldiers on horseback blocked the road in front of him. "Good fortune!" the passersby called to the soldiers as they passed, and one or two grinned back and made the sign of the Ascending God. They looked shockingly young, almost like children.

The soldiers continued toward the river and across Darra Bridge. People lined the road now, forced to stop until the procession had passed. A few cheered. "They're going to fight in the border wars with Shai," one woman said to another. "We'll show those king-killers they can't have our ports," a man near Val said.

Val watched the soldiers go. He frowned. He had heard enough court news to know that the war with the Shai had not begun yet. And if the soldiers were on their way to Shai then why were they riding south, toward the Gate of Stones and Thole Forest? Shouldn't they be headed east?

The soldiers reached Tobol An late in the afternoon. The ghost-knight sounded his trumpet but the commander had been told what to expect and rode through him with only a barely perceptible shiver of fear. His men followed.

Taja had returned to Tobol An several hours earlier. She had hidden the records of Val's birth in the library and then gone home to tell Pebr what had happened in the city. "He said he doesn't want to be king," she said.

"Do you think he's telling the truth?" Pebr asked.

"I don't know. He's hiding something, I'm certain of that much. He's become like the courtiers he used to talk about, the ones who say one thing and mean another. I'm afraid for him—he's never really learned to be deceitful."

Pebr shrugged. "It's none of our business what those grand folks get up to at court."

Now, hearing the trumpet of Thole Forest, Taja knew exactly what had happened. The queen's men had returned for the records. Would they be able to find them where she had hidden them, among tax registries from the reign of King Gobro II? She didn't think so. She and Pebr hurried out and watched as the soldiers rode toward the cluster of cottages.

"Citizens of Tobol An," the commander said to the people who had gathered in the dirt road between the cottages. A thin rain fell. Wind blew across the plain, bending the hardy grasses that grew in the dirt, and Taja shivered. "We are here by the queen's command to protect you from the Shai. We are here to see that these barbarians do not gain access to the port of Tobol An, or to any of our lands beyond the seas. By the power of the queen I am authorized to garrison my troops in your houses, and to requisition any food that they may need. Are there any questions?"

"Aye," someone said, an old woman whose husband had died in the great storm the year before. "We're not one of the great ports here—no one has ever set off from Tobol An to any of the lands beyond the seas. Why do we need protection?"

The commander motioned to two of his men, who dismounted and took the old woman by the arms. The men looked very young, almost like boys. "Mother of light!" Pebr said, moving forward. A few of the others came forward with him.

The expression on the commander's face stopped them. "It is treason to question the commands of your lawful queen," the commander said. "I'm going to cage her, as a warning to the rest of you. Do you understand?"

"No," an old man said. The commander signaled to his soldiers again, but before they could move the old man said quickly, "What does that mean, to cage someone?"

"Watch," the commander said. Taja, who had twice seen the caged criminals in lower Etrara, thought there was a slight smile on the man's face; he seemed to be enjoying himself.

Other soldiers went to the provision carts and took out an iron cage, and the old woman's guards forced her into it. There were none of the cage supports in Tobol An that Taja had seen in the city; the soldiers looked around for a moment before they found a tree whose branches looked high enough and strong enough. One of the soldiers lifted the cage by himself, and he and the others joked about how light the woman must be.

Another man set up a ladder near the tree. Taja saw with shock that the man carrying the cage paused to say a prayer to the Ascending God before he climbed the ladder, and she wondered how in Callabrion's name he could possibly consider himself godly. And these people called the Shai barbarians!

After the soldiers had hooked the cage on a tree branch, the commander addressed the people again. "If you think that this woman's dreadful crime—and treason is a dreadful crime—merits her punishment, then you will avoid her until she has served her sentence."

"How—how long will her sentence be?" someone asked. The woman in the cage had not spoken a word since the soldiers had pinioned her arms, but her face had turned the color of bleached linen.

"As long as I want it to be," the commander said.

"But—" someone else said, and was hushed.

The commander looked around at the assembled faces. Taja saw that he didn't understand the villagers of Tobol An, that of course the woman's friends and kinfolk would feed her while she remained in the cage. Even people who had quarreled with her, who hadn't spoken to her in months, would band together against the invaders from Etrara. Folks did things differently here.

She watched stolidly as the commander assigned a soldier to the house she shared with Pebr. Pebr opened his mouth as if to protest, then closed it.

Taja went with him to their house, intending to see that he kept out of trouble. She knew that the old woman, now swaying above them in her cage as if in judgment of them all, had been right. The soldiers hadn't come to Tobol An to protect the harbor against the Shai. They had come for the birth records. Callia intended to make certain that her claim to the throne was secure.

The proclamations appeared in Etrara within the first months of Callia's reign, large sheets of paper glued to the walls of the city and to houses and merchants' shops and stalls. It was forbidden to stay out-of-doors past a certain hour, except on feast days. All visitors to the city must register with the watch, stating where they came from and how long they intended to stay. Anyone overhearing treason against the queen had to report what they heard to the watch. All the Maegrim must come forward and give their names to the Queen's Pen.

This last proclamation caused the most surprise, and some outrage, when the queen's men posted it on the walls, when those who were literate read it aloud to people from the lower rungs. No one knew for certain who the Maegrim were. Most folks thought them ordinary women—seamstresses and actors, laundresses and noblewomen—who heard the call of the gods and came to dance. There were always six of them; the seventh was summoned during the dance and disappeared when the dance ended.

Val had heard people guess that they must be unmarried; no one with a husband or children could hide their calling so successfully. But others thought that they might have married especially discreet men, people who could keep the secret entrusted to them.

Within a few days the astronomer-priests had formed a delegation to protest the decree. The Maegrim were holy women, the priests claimed in their petition, bound to the goddess Sbona herself. Their rituals were older than recorded history. Acting, they said, had developed from these rituals, just as the custom of poets' feuds had grown out of the wars of the poet-wizards.

Queen Callia kept the priests waiting in the palace ante-chamber for three days before finally letting them see an official, who turned out to be the assistant to the undersecretary to the Queen's Pen. The assistant would not take their petition, explaining that Callia's decree could not be changed. "We can't allow magic to flourish unchecked in this city," he said. "Those who are not directly under the queen's control might someday turn against her, don't you think?"

"It's not that simple—"

"Do you remember the king's banquet last year, when the Maegrim prophesied ill fortune?" the assistant said. A few of the priests made as if to speak, but the official raised his voice and spoke over them. "Yes, we know about that last cast, that it was a summer cast instead of a winter one. You see, that's my point. Everyone knew, or had heard rumors. People panicked—some even packed up and left the city. With the Maegrim speaking only for the queen this sort of thing won't happen in banquet halls or public streets anymore. No one need worry about things that don't concern them."

"But you can't regulate magic," one of the priests said. "The Maegrim can't control when their call comes, or who it's intended for."

The assistant smiled. "You priests think you know all about magic," he said, showing them out.

As they left, one of the priests turned and said, "That last cast, the one that predicted ill fortune—that was meant for all of us, for the city of Etrara."

This priest and some of the others were arrested and caged a few days later. The cages grew more numerous, and the queen's men began building cage supports north of the river, in upper Etrara. Women suspected of being Maegrim appeared in the cages too, and people living next door to unmarried women began to distrust their neighbors. But none of the Maegrim ever came forward.

Officers began impressing young men into Callia's army, and the sight of soldiers became a common one on the streets of Etrara. Excitement grew; it was an open secret that the army would invade the country of Shai soon. But at one of Duchess Sbarra's gatherings the Queen's Axe told Val, in whispers, that Callia had no money to pay the soldiers, that Gobro had emptied the treasury.

Perhaps it was this that caused the people to turn against their queen. Folks began to feed the caged criminals, openly at first and then, when ordered to desist by the watch, at night and in secret. Satires about the queen and Duchess Mariel, about the Queen's Coin, Pen and Axe, appeared overnight on the walls of the city, but despite the edict Callia issued against the satirists they were never caught.

Callia took a poet-mage into her service. Folks laughed when they saw him, a pompous-looking man in an overlarge cloak. The age of magic is past, people said, nodding to one another sagely. It ended when King Tariel's wizards died.

And through it all Val watched and waited. As Callia grew more unpopular he thought it would soon be time to act, to speak to a few trusted men and women. If Callia fell from the ladder, he himself might rise.

Callia waited at the council-chamber door as the herald announced her. She had ordered him to add "Queen of Shai" to her list of titles, and she listened with satisfaction as he spoke all the sonorous-sounding phrases, all the lands she owned. When he had finished she stepped into the council chamber.

Everyone else, of course, had already arrived and was waiting for her. Mariel sat to the right of Callia's chair at the head of the table, Arion and Talenor to the left. The Queen's Pen, Coin and Axe were farther down the table. Penriel, the poet-mage, had taken a seat next to the Queen's Axe and was bent toward him, deep in conversation.

Callia nodded to Penriel as she sat. Gobro had been a fool not to have taken a wizard into his service, she thought.

At the foot of the table sat Narrion and a few of the others who had helped Callia come to power. A scribe had taken his station at a small side table, ready to record whatever was said at the meeting.

Arion looked at her expectantly. "When are we going to invade Shai?" he asked.

"Soon," she said. "But we need money to raise an army, and there, I think, Lord Carrow can help us."

The Queen's Coin looked up from his notes and she smiled at him. Callia knew that he approved of her; she did not waste money on spectacle as Gobro had. And if the invasion of Shai succeeded they would all be far wealthier; Shai's vineyards and vast silver mines would be theirs.

"We can raise the taxes on the ships returning from the colonies in Astrion and Udriel," the Queen's Coin said. "And I have a list here of other items that can be taxed as well."

Carrow began to read. Arion stirred restlessly in his seat. He had always been impatient; when he and Callia had been small children together he had hated the pageantry and ritual of King Tariel's court. "I don't understand why we can't invade now," he said when Carrow had finished. "Gobro had a standing army, after all."

"Some of the army has been sent south," Callia said.

Mariel looked at her in alarm. Callia knew that Mariel thought her as stupid as Gobro, that her half-sister had intended to rule the country even though Callia wore the land-ring of Etrara. But Callia had proved less malleable than Mariel had hoped, and more capable of taking care of herself.

"South?" Arion said. "What's in the south?"

"There's been an uprising," Callia said. "In Tobol—"

"In several of the sea villages," Mariel said, interrupting her. "Nothing important, but we have to see that we keep control of the ports. It would be ironic, wouldn't it, if we won the war against the Shai but let the very ports we fought over slip from our grasp."

Arion was frowning. "But why wasn't I told?" he said. "If there's war—"

"It's not a war," Mariel said. "Those villagers have never fought anyone in their lives. We could have sent the watch to take care of it, if we could have spared them. There's no honor in battle there, if that's what you're looking for."

Arion seemed satisfied. Callia sat back, relieved; it could prove disastrous if Arion went to Tobol An.

She wondered why the men she had sent were taking so long to find the records she had asked for. The commander wrote her letters complaining about the stubbornness of the villagers, but she knew that there was always a remedy for stubbornness—the cage, and then, if that yielded nothing, torture on the ladder.

Did Val know that he was the rightful heir? He'd been a little distant since he'd come back from Tobol An, but Mariel had said that that might be the result of exile, and of seeing his cousin marry the woman he had courted. Callia knew, as all the king's children had known, that the records of the royal house were kept separate from the others, and she had heard rumors since she was a small child of a legitimate heir. But Mariel had assured her that those rumors had never left the palace; there was no reason to believe that Val had heard them too.

Still, she would have to deal with Val sooner or later. He represented too great a danger to her throne.

Lord Varra, the Queen's Pen, was looking at her expectantly. She realized that he had asked her a question and was waiting for her reply. "I'm sorry?" she said.

"I was told that several astronomer-priests came to see me the other day," the Queen's Pen said. "They wanted to protest your latest decree, the one about the Maegrim. It seems to me that challenging the Maegrim might not be wise at this time, that you might want to reconsider. . . ."

"We want to know who the Maegrim are," she said, smiling at the King's Pen. "Uncontrolled magic is a danger to the throne."

"Why do you say that?" Varra asked. "The Maegrim are ordinary women, nothing more."

"How ordinary can women be who are possessed by the gods?" Callia asked.

"This isn't a fit subject for a council meeting," Mariel said.

"I would like to go on record—" Varra said.

"Very well," Callia said. "Lord Varra is on record as protesting our decree." She smiled again. She would have to find another Pen, someone less argumentative. She certainly couldn't rescind her decree now; she could not let the people think her weak.

But even if she could back down she wouldn't do it. Ever since she was a girl her mother, Lady Godemar, had stressed the importance of magic to a ruler. And there was no doubt in Callia's mind that Godemar believed what she taught; she had been the one to poison Tariel's wizards, though no one but Callia knew that. Her mother would have gone on to poison Tariel himself if she hadn't died of the plague.

What would Lady Godemar think if she could see her daughter now, wearing the land-ring of Etrara and presiding over her council meeting? Callia studied her councilors. "Is there anything else?" she asked.

"Yes," someone said.

Callia looked down at the foot of the table. Narrion. She frowned a little; she had made him a council member because of the help he had given them, but she had intended the position to be an honorary one. She certainly hadn't expected him to speak in council. "Yes, what is it?" she asked.

"As you know, my lady, I am a member of the Society of Fools, sworn to Scathiel, the winter god."

"Yes, yes," Callia said impatiently.

"I've talked to several members of the Society, and all of them say the same thing. The days continue to grow shorter. Callabrion did not ascend this year."

Penriel looked startled, Carrow thoughtful. Arion said, "Are you certain—" and at the same time Varra nodded and said, "Aye, I've heard something of this."

"I'm certain," Narrion said.

"What do you expect us to do about it?" Callia asked.

"I don't know," Narrion said. He spread his fingers on the table. "But I think this news is more pressing than anything we've discussed in council so far. We cannot live without the summer god. If the days continue to grow shorter we will lose everything we've worked for."

"I don't see how this is your concern," Callia said. "You're sworn to the winter god, you said so yourself. If he still rules in heaven, so much the better for you."

"There is a balance here," Narrion said. "Summer and winter, life and death—"

"This is a subject for philosophers at the university, not a council meeting," Callia said. She waved a hand, dismissing him. "I'd like to hear more about the invasion of Shai. What are our plans for that?"

Mariel's head was pounding by the time her sister finally dismissed the council. All around her people were standing and bidding good fortune to their fellows; several council members extended invitations to others to continue some discussion over wine. The Queen's Axe rolled up the parchment maps he had displayed, and her scribe capped his bottles of ink and carefully put his quills back into their pen case.

"Good fortune, sister," Callia said to her.

"You shouldn't let the meeting run away from you like that," Mariel said. She hadn't intended to sound so blunt, but her head hurt far too much for her to be polite. Everyone else had left the council chamber, though; she could say what she wanted without fear of being overheard.

"What do you mean?"

Mariel saw with surprise that Callia seemed pleased with the way the meeting had gone. "You don't have to answer to Lord Varra," Mariel said, rubbing her forehead wearily. "He's your minister—he has to answer to you. When he asked about the Maegrim you should have changed the subject."

"Oh, don't worry about Varra. I'll have a new Pen soon enough."

"Do you think that people will let you? Varra has a great many supporters. And what about Narrion?"

"What about him?"

"Is what he said about Callabrion true? Why have we heard nothing about it?"

"It's a rumor, nothing more. Or a jest of that society of his, the Society of Fools. If it were true, the priests would have brought it to our attention."

"Why did he speak in council at all? We should never have given him a seat. The land we gave him should have been enough."

"He's always tried to rise above his station. He should remember that his house is weak and nearly powerless. His and Val's."

"No, sister," Mariel said. "Not Val's."

"True," Callia said. She giggled. "Not Val's."

"It's fortunate we never told Narrion about Val's birth," Mariel said. "You and I are the only ones who know. But what will we do about Narrion?"

"It's simple. We'll force him off the council."

"We can't—he knows too much about our affairs. He's a dangerous man."

"Well, then, we'll have meetings without him, meetings of the inner council. Don't worry—Narrion has no real power."

"And Talenor—"

"Talenor? He never said a word during the entire meeting."

"That's what I mean. What was he thinking? He's plotting something, there's no doubt of that."

Callia laughed. "He never takes his nose out of his books. Come, Mariel—your imagination's running away with you."

"I don't think so. Remember that he was the one to oppose you—"

"Listen," Callia said. Her voice was hard now. "We agreed that I should take the land-ring when Gobro died. I think you should trust me to act like a queen."

Mariel watched as her sister left the council chamber. That was the problem, she thought; her sister did act like a queen. Only there was no substance behind her actions; she might just as well have been impersonating someone in a history play, a queen long dead.

Mariel leaned back in her chair. The meeting had been one disaster after another. Everyone now knew that Callia had business in the south, and had probably heard the name of the village that had aroused her interest. Not a few people would wonder what had happened there.

And Varra, and Narrion, and Talenor . . . Dangers beset them from every direction. She had never realized how difficult it would be to govern, to protect the throne.

She put her head in her hands and closed her eyes. As soon as she did so she saw Gobro's face as it had looked after they had given him the poison. He had been gasping, struggling for breath, and his hands had reached out to his half-sisters. Callia had giggled a little. Mariel had seen a terrible recognition in his eyes; he had known what was happening to him. And his skin had turned as blue as robins' eggs. Narrion hadn't said anything about his skin turning blue.

She opened her eyes. She wondered if she would see the picture of Gobro dying before she went to sleep, as she had seen it every night since Callia had ascended to the throne. She rubbed her temples again, determined to visit another apothecary. The potion she had gotten from the last one hadn't done her much good.

Narrion walked up Palace Hill toward the observatory. Callia was a simpleton, and that blunt-witted council of hers was worse. Not one of them could face the truth: if Callabrion did not ascend, the crops would die. First the crops, then the people. And everything he had worked for would be lost.

He would be excluded from the council after this, he knew. No one welcomed the bearer of ill news. Everyone on the council was busy planning the invasion of Shai, planning a thousand ways to rise on the ladder; they would take care not to see the approaching darkness. He would have to go his own way.

He stopped at the observatory and knocked loudly. The porter opened the door. "I'd like to see Dorio," Narrion said.

"Wait here," the porter said. He turned and went down the halls of white stone, and came back a few moments later with Dorio, Narrion's friend from the university who had become an astronomer-priest.

"I need to talk to you," Narrion said when the porter had gone. "Where can we go that's private?"

Dorio hesitated. "What do you have to tell me that can't be said here?" he asked.

"Come, Dorio," Narrion said. He stepped inside the observatory and moved closer to the other man. "We're both of us keepers of mysteries, disciples of Scathiel and Callabrion. Surely there are things we might say that should not be overheard by anyone else."

Dorio nodded. "I'd heard you'd joined the Society of Fools. Strange—when we were together at the university I never thought of you as a religious man."

"I am. My god is Scathiel, though—the god of winter and death and misrule, god of the cold wind that whispers at your back. He's very different from yours."

Dorio hesitated. "I'll take you to one of the towers," he said finally. The observatory had a differently shaped tower at each of its four corners; they stood even higher than the palace. "No one uses the telescopes during the day."

Narrion followed Dorio down the corridor, passing other men wearing the green and gold of Callabrion. They went through another corridor, then up a flight of stairs.

They continued to climb. Shallow depressions hollowed

the stone stairs. Generations of priests had come to the towers to study the heavens, at first using only their naked eyes and then, beginning twenty-five years ago, the telescopes.

They gained the top. A wooden telescope bound in brass stood there; its base was at least two feet around and its top broke through the roof of the tower. It was fitted with a brass wheel so it could be moved, and an oak ladder climbed to the eyepiece.

As soon as they reached the top of the stairs Narrion closed the door behind him and turned to face Dorio. "You know, of course, that summer hasn't come," he said. "Callabrion hasn't ascended."

Alarm showed on Dorio's face. Narrion felt gratified to see it. "How—how do you know this?" Dorio asked.

"You and your priests thought the secret safe within the observatory, didn't you? Yet anyone who follows the track of the sun has noticed that it sets earlier each day. The Society of Fools knows this, and so do some of the farmers in the provinces. Callabrion did not wed the goddess Sbona—Scathiel still reigns in the heavens."

Dorio nodded. "We're aware of that."

"Are you? And what will you do about it?"

"Why does that concern you? Winter hasn't ended—the disciples of Scathiel should be pleased. The god of winter rules still in heaven."

"What do they teach you in this place?" Narrion said, suddenly angry. Dorio stepped back a little. "Winter is brother to summer—you of all people should know that. Scathiel cannot rule alone. We have to convince Callabrion to return to the heavens. If he doesn't everything will die. Our world will end."

"Is that what the Society of Fools says?"

"The Society says nothing. We're not an order like the priests, living separately in our observatories. We have no leaders, no followers, only men and women devoted to spreading misrule in the early months of winter. I've spoken to a few friends of mine, and they all agree that something should be done, but none of us knows what. That's why I decided to talk to you. Because the two of us need to discuss such things, and to make certain that summer returns."

"You made this decision on your own?" Dorio asked.

"Yes. Is that so surprising?"

"We don't have that luxury. My order is a strict hierarchy—I'll have to talk over what you've said with my superiors."

"Good," Narrion said. "But you have to hurry."

"Why?"

"Because the queen is about to declare war. Do you hear nothing of the world outside in this great observatory of yours?"

"Very little," Dorio said. "The order does not encourage us to leave the observatory." He looked down at Narrion's hands, at the land-rings on his fingers. "I know that the queen has raised you high on the ladder, that you have the queen's ear. Can't she help you?"

"I've just come from her council. All her thought is on war. I would not put my trust in the queen."

Dorio said nothing for a moment. "Very well," he said. "I'll talk to the priests. You're right—those of us who are bound to the gods should discuss this matter."

"Good."

"When do you think war will come?" Dorio asked.

"Within the week," Narrion said. "I'll let myself out. Good fortune, Dorio."

He turned and left; his boots echoed in the stone stairway as he went. Would Dorio help him? The priests thought themselves inviolate, he knew; they had survived generations of war and plague and treachery hidden behind the walls of their observatory. But no wall in the world could keep out the darkness that was about to come.

Duke Arion went down Palace Hill to visit Valemar. As fortune would have it the other man was just leaving his house when Arion arrived. "Val!" he called. "Valemar!"

Val turned. "Good fortune, Arion," he said.

"I have to ask you something," Arion said. "You went to Tobol An, didn't you? Is there anything there?"

"What do you mean?"

Arion hesitated, not wanting to reveal what he had learned from Callia in the council meeting. "Someone was asking me about it the other day. He wanted to visit the place for a few days and asked me to come along."

Val laughed. "I wouldn't. There's nothing there but a few cottages and some ruins. Fish every night."

"Ah," Arion said. He took his leave and went back to his rooms at the palace. What did his sister want with such an uncivilized place? He frowned, puzzled. Perhaps he should go to Tobol An after all.

Six

· · · · · · · ·

ARION'S JOURNEY THROUGH THE FOR-
est of Thole was uneventful. The ghost-knight in the
path startled him for a moment, but then he saw the
cold rain falling through the man and his horse and he nodded and continued onward. He had heard tales of the wizardry of Thole Forest, but now he thought that these were
stories told to frighten children, nothing more. He did not see
that there was anything here more terrifying than the ghosts
of Etrara.

When he came out of the forest he saw that Val had been
right; Tobol An held nothing but stone cottages and a few
ruins. No—a white spire towered in the distance. What was
that? Should he go there? Or should he see how Callia's
troops fared against the uprising?

One of the Maegrim stood before him on the path. His
pulse quickened and he looked around for the other five, his
heart filled with a strange combination of fear and hope. His
fortune was about to change.

But none of the other women appeared, and after a
moment Arion realized that she was alone. A harmless old
aunt, nothing more, he thought. She came closer and he saw
that her hood was not badger skin but plain black cloth.

"Welcome, my young lord," she said.

"I thank you, aunt," he said. "Could you tell me—"

"Aye. I can tell you many things. You will love a foe and hate a friend, and one will betray you and the other save you. You will have your heart's desire."

"I—I thank you—"

"Do you?" She looked at him shrewdly with her one good eye. "You may not be so grateful when it comes to it."

"Do you know where the queen's commander is?"

She said nothing, but pointed upward.

He looked where she pointed and saw only rain and sky. "What—what do you mean?"

"You asked for the queen's commander. Surely the only one to command the queen is the goddess Sbona, who lives in heaven."

He sighed. The woman had lost her wits, that much was certain. He could not help but feel a little regret at the loss of his heart's desire; none of the fortune-tellers and natalists he had consulted in the city had ever promised him such a marvelous future.

"Good fortune, aunt," he said, and continued on the path toward the village.

He passed a few men and women in cages, and saw that the criminals here were better fed than those in Etrara, almost plump. He frowned. What had the commander been doing? Callia was fortunate that he had decided to come here; he would straighten things out for her.

He saw a man in the queen's uniform and asked the way to the commander's house. To his relief the soldier pointed out one of the small houses along the path; the old woman's madness hadn't infected the entire village, then. He went up to the cottage and knocked.

The guard who came to the door recognized him and let him in immediately. Arion had always taken pains to get to know as many soldiers as he could, and as a result he was very popular with the army. He did not think that Callia could have ascended to the throne without his approval; in effect he, and not the Queen's Axe, commanded the soldiers of Etrara.

"Duke Arion!" the commander said, rising from his chair and coming to greet him. "Good fortune! We are honored, sir, honored indeed. Do you come from Queen Callia?"

"Yes," Arion said. Now he noticed that the commander seemed a little nervous, and he saw how that could be used to his advantage. "What is happening here? The criminals are well fed, and the people won't answer a direct question—"

"These things take time, sir. Tell Queen Callia that we're working hard, and that we'll have the information she wants soon."

"How—how far have you gotten?"

"We're searching the library room by room. It's only a matter of time before we find the birth records."

Library, Arion thought. Birth records. There was no uprising at all, then. By the Ladder, what was Callia playing at?

His face must have shown some surprise, because the commander backed away a little and said smoothly, "I would like nothing better than to help you here, but as you can see I have a great deal of work to do. Should I appoint a man to show you around the village?"

"No. No, I thank you."

Arion left and rode aimlessly down the path, angry at both the commander and himself. He was not clever, like Talenor, or cunning, like Mariel; both of them would have made certain they gave nothing away to the other man. But by all the gods, why did Callia want the birth records?

He could think of only one reason. She wanted to forge them so that she would seem to be Tariel's rightful heir. But if the people accepted Callia he would lose his chance at the throne.

A shrill wind blew, flattening the knotted grasses on the plain. Arion shivered. He remembered when Mariel had come to him, seeking his support. She had been reasonable, persuasive; she had mentioned the chaos of King Galin's time, and had warned him that civil war might come again if all of Tariel's children did not unite behind a single ruler.

And he, stupid fool, he had agreed. Certainly, Mariel, by the Ladder let us have Callia on the throne, he had said. Had Mariel suggested to him that Callia would be easy to overthrow, that he would be the next to wear the land-ring of Etrara? He couldn't remember. She had done something clever, had woven her web around him the way she had always been able to do when they were children. And now she ruled Etrara in Callia's name.

The white spire shone before him. Should he go to the library? No—he knew enough about Callia's plans, and the soldiers would certainly report his movements back to her. He urged his horse back toward the forest.

For a brief moment he wondered why Val hadn't mentioned the library. But Val was guileless, uninterested in court politics. It was his own treacherous brothers and sisters that he had to watch out for.

He reached the forest. The ghost-knight stood before him on the path. He moved through him, grinning a little. He would see to it that Callia fell from the ladder, and Mariel with her, and that he would rise by their ill fortune. Callia was the least clever of all of Tariel's children; surely he could think of a way around her.

The man assigned to watch Arion reported to the commander. "He's gone, sir," the man said. "I saw him ride through the forest."

"Did he go to the library?"

"The library? No."

"Good," the commander said. Duke Arion had lied when he'd said he'd come from Queen Callia, that much was certain. What had the duke wanted? He went over their conversation in his mind, hoping that he hadn't given away any of the queen's secrets. But if Arion hadn't visited the library then he probably had no idea what the queen wanted here.

He dismissed the soldier and went back to his work. Suddenly he looked up at the door, a little frightened. Why hadn't

the ghost's trumpet announced Arion? Did the ghost consider
Arion a friend to Tobol An?

Two days after Arion visited Tobol An the queen declared war
on Shai. Suddenly everyone in Etrara ordered a ladder to
assure their good fortune in battle; the ladder makers on the
Street of Spiders worked day and night to fulfill their commis-
sions. Fortune-tellers and natalists grew rich predicting a rise
on the ladder for anyone who consulted them.

The wine sellers nearly sold out their entire stock as the
people threw one party after another to celebrate the declaration. No one would buy the Shai wines, though, and these
were eventually poured into the Darra River, or finished quietly among the wine sellers and their friends.

The parties spilled out into the streets, and Etrara shone
with torchlight and lantern light as it had not done since the
reign of Tariel III. A few nights after the declaration people
near the Darra River saw a sight to delight and amaze them:
the royal barge floated past, its banners showing the queen's
colors of black and white and gold, its lights reflecting silver
on the water. Folks stood spellbound as it went by, and as it
passed they heard the sound of flutes and drums.

But there were those who complained that taxes were too
high, higher than anyone could remember. And with every
healthy young man impressed into the army it grew harder
and harder for families to meet the demands of the Queen's
Coin, to say nothing of the landlords and shopkeepers. A man
whispered that the army had not had nearly enough time to
train; he was caged for speaking treason a day later. He had
spoken quietly and among people he had thought his friends,
and in the months that followed, hanging above the pageantry that filled the streets below, he had ample time to
wonder who among his friends had turned informer.

Most of the young noblemen at court had joined Callia's
army, and Val was no exception. As he had expected he was
made an officer, and he spent all his time in the fields outside
the Gate of Shadows drilling his men.

But there was another reason he had volunteered. He was eager to see battle, to test himself against an enemy. He wanted to understand the valor that men like Arion spoke of.

He was not yet ready, not seasoned enough in battle, to claim the throne. And if he returned a hero the people would welcome him; he might gain more support among them than Callia had.

Duchess Mariel stood next to the queen on the Street of Roses, watching as the troops filed past them. A fine rain drizzled on soldiers and nobility alike, and she was not the only one who glanced up at the thick clouds enfolding the high towers of the city, the palace and observatory and the clock tower at the university. Folks feared a stronger rain, or even snow.

She shivered in the cold air. She could not forget Narrion's speech in council, his warning that the days were growing shorter. She and Callia had had several council meetings without Narrion since then, had demonstrated to him in a dozen subtle ways that he had not risen as high on the ladder as he had thought. Still, the rumor that Callabrion had not ascended had spread through the city like an infection. Could it be true? Could the gods be displeased with Callia, and with the part she herself had played in Gobro's death?

She rubbed her forehead. No—they had poisoned poor Gobro after the Feast of the Ascending God, not before; there was no need to fear divine retribution. She forced herself to pay attention to the soldiers marching in front of her, trying not to wince as their booted footsteps set up an answering echo in her brain. Folks cheered as the men passed, and the bells of all the towers of the city rang out.

Callia touched her arm as Val rode by, and she waved. "He's not wearing anyone's favor," Callia said.

Of course not—whose favor did Callia think he would wear? Callia seemed to regard war as a kind of game, just another of the pageants and shows put on to entertain the nobility of Etrara. As if to confirm her thoughts the queen said, "I wish we could have sent them off later in the year—we could have showered them with roses then."

In her mind Mariel saw the soldiers pelted with the spiky branches of winter roses. She shivered; she hoped the evil vision was not an omen of ill fortune.

At last the long line of troops came to an end. She watched as they headed east toward the Gate of Roses. Then she left without waiting for Callia, going up the hill to the palace.

Except for a few guards the palace was deserted; everyone was out seeing the soldiers leave for Shai. She walked wearily up the main staircase and along the corridor to her rooms, looking forward to drinking the potion the apothecary had given her. Perhaps she would even be able to sleep.

She opened her door. Something moved at the corner of her vision and she turned toward it quickly. She screamed.

Gobro came toward her, wearing the puzzled look she had seen so often when he was alive. "Do you know where Riel is?" he said. "I can't seem to find her anywhere."

She screamed again. Outside she could hear the guards come pounding toward her room.

Val rode out through the Gate of Roses, his men marching behind him. They passed a few houses clustered around the gate, then farmland and fields enclosed for pasture. A few hours later these gave way to the grassy plain of Wathe.

It felt good to be out of Etrara, away from the close, stifling air of the court. A clear wind blew against his face. In the city they had passed under the arch raised to the heroes of the battle of Arbono, and he had thought, as no doubt many of his company had thought, that before the year was out there might be a new arch on the Street of Roses, one with his name inscribed on it. And what then? Callia could not remain queen forever.

Val could barely see Arion's company up ahead of him. He hoped the duke would not leave him behind in his eagerness to join battle. They and all the other commanders had studied the battle plans the Queen's Axe had drawn up, but Arion had seemed too impatient to pay much attention.

The wind blew over the plain, bending back the tall grasses. He thought it might even be colder here than in Etrara, and he pulled his woolen cloak closer. He turned and saw that the men marching behind him had slowed, and he reined in his horse to let them catch up.

As he waited for stragglers he thought about the men he had been sent to fight. He had heard the stories, of course— that the Shai queen married a man who was crowned as the summer god, and that the priests killed her husband six months later, when she married the god of winter. But he thought that the stories could not possibly be true, that they were tales told to frighten children and to keep the people of Etrara at odds with their age-old enemy.

The last of his men had come up, walking wearily toward the company. Several of them shivered with cold, and he eyed the vast plain before them uneasily. They were at least a week from the blue-white mountains that marked the border of Shai. The Teeth of Tura, the mountains were called, after an ancient hero who had searched for Sbona's children at the beginning of the world.

Val and his men continued on. After a few hours of marching the plain seemed no different, and Val remembered the tales of sorcery that had always been told about the Shai, stories of the power that was loosed with the killing of kings. The people of Shai drank blood, folks whispered, and their children spoke in poetry from the cradle, and every one of them grew up to become a poet-mage.

Val glanced up ahead. Penriel, the queen's wizard, was traveling with Arion, but Arion's company had disappeared. The wind blew stronger now, and seemed to cry out with a voice of its own.

The sun began to set behind him, and Val remembered something he had heard whispered in the streets of Etrara. The days were growing shorter, folks said; Callabrion had not ascended. It seemed to him now that wizardry had been loosed on the land, that something was stirring that had been stilled since the deaths of King Tariel's mages. He thought of Tobol An, the ruins of the wizards' war.

He looked at the plain ahead of him and decided to halt and make camp; his men did not seem to be able to travel much farther. They would catch up with Duke Arion later.

He spread his bedroll on the ground and thought once more of Tobol An. At least Taja was safe, he thought. At least her village was spared the horrors of war, and of so much else. He smiled; she knew so little of the great world around her, after all.

Val hardly slept at all; one of his men had been shivering so violently that Val had shared his blankets with him, and the man had trembled all night. Finally, toward dawn, the man seemed to have found the warmth he sought so desperately, and both he and Val dropped off to an uneasy sleep.

It seemed to Val that he had closed his eyes for a few minutes, but when he woke he saw the sun on the horizon and the long shadows of the grasses in front of him. He cursed; Arion would be far ahead of them by this time. He hurried his men through their small breakfast of hard bread and beer and they continued on.

A few days later they had their first sight of the Teeth of Tura. The peaks ahead of them shone white with snow. The sight heartened the men for a moment, and they pushed on.

A march of two days brought the mountains no closer. But Arion had made it through, certainly. And yet Arion had had the queen's wizard to guide him.

Had the duke used wizardry to reach the mountain range? But if Penriel had helped him then why hadn't they waited?

For the first time Val doubted the duke. He remembered that Arion had asked him about Tobol An, and he wondered why the other man should have been so interested in such an insignificant village. And he remembered too that he had been tricked before by a member of the royal family, and that that had been in connection with Tobol An.

Something had happened to him in the months he had spent in exile; he had grown older, less willing to trust those around him. Narrion had spun his plots and had risen like a spider on the thread he wove, and Val had been enmeshed for a brief time in his cousin's web. He shook his head. The duke was not nearly as cunning as Narrion; there was no reason to suspect treachery from him as well.

A day later the land grew stonier, harder, and the tall grasses gave way to matted weeds and small yellow flowers. They had reached the foothills, but instead of being encouraged by the ground they had gained Val felt tiny, dwarfed by the bulk of the mountains. And it had started to rain, a cold, driving rain that made him shiver despite his warm cloak.

For a long time they climbed over the large rocks that lay at the feet of the range. Val had to dismount and lead his horse over the stony ground, watching closely to see that the animal did not break a leg in the treacherous crevices. Boulders and stunted trees, formed into fantastic shapes by the wind, blocked their way more than once, and several times they had to retrace their steps, giving ground to the mountain.

Finally Val found a path that led upward. He waited for the company to catch up with him, and when they appeared rested enough he mounted his horse and set off.

The sun was setting. It was starting to snow. Behind him he could hear his men complaining, and he stopped to allow one of them to mount up and ride behind him.

Something white beckoned to him from the path. He reined in his horse. But no—it was the snow falling, nothing more. He could barely see in front of him now, and when he glanced over his shoulder the sun was a blur of gold along the horizon.

He turned back. The white figure waved to him again. Its sleeves were long, and billowed outward a little in the wind.

He could almost hear words, and although he didn't understand the language its speech froze him into cold despair.

The figure was right; they should turn back. There was nothing for them here, nothing but cold and aching misery. Slowly, as if moved by a will not his own, he lifted the reins. The man behind him on the horse began to speak.

Val turned, a little annoyed. He did not want his men to panic; he was already doing all that was necessary to protect them by leading them off the mountain. But the man's voice sounded clear and strong, and Val realized with a sort of dull surprise that he was speaking poetry.

Wizardry, Val thought. The Shai wizards had sent the apparition, and this man behind him was trying to counter it with his own halting verse. Now, paying close attention to the words, Val realized that the man had not received any formal training as a poet-mage, that his verses were cobbled together from village songs and chants and barely rhymed.

But the figure in front of them wavered a little, like a flag blown in the wind. The man redoubled his efforts, playing with the names of gods and heroes, repeating one or two of the words he had spoken in the first verse. As he went on he seemed to gain in brilliance, manipulating alliteration and meter as Val had heard the great poet-mages had done.

The figure seemed to fly toward them. Val held the reins tightly and watched as it frayed outward in the wind. It passed over them as a gust of snow. He let out a breath he did not realize he had taken.

He turned to the man behind him. "I didn't know I had brought a poet-mage along with me," he said.

"I learned a few tricks in my village, that's all," the man said, grinning.

"More than a few, I'd say. I'm certain you'll rise on the ladder for this. What's your name?"

"Anthiel." The man grinned again. The snow had stopped, perhaps as a result of Anthiel's efforts, and Val decided that his company had gone far enough for one day.

They went back to where he had seen the road widen and made camp.

It was only when he had eaten and settled into his blankets for the night that Val wondered why he hadn't spoken to the apparition himself. He had written poetry, after all, unlike the man from the lower rungs whose verses had hobbled like a lame horse. But he had not sensed the presence of magic until it had been too late. Perhaps there was more to being a poet-mage than the ability to create poetry. He tried to think what it might be, but confused images whirled in his mind— Pebr's cottage, and tall white mountains, and the sound of the sea—and he found himself drifting off to sleep.

Over the next few days they met with more of the illusions: a giant white bird with a snowy crest, a tree with branches burdened by snow, an icy brook that appeared suddenly in their path. But Anthiel spoke his verses to them and they dispersed, spreading across the wind.

Val wondered if the Shai were toying with them, if they were saving their greatest magic for the battle ahead. It seemed to him that anyone could counter these child's fancies, even a man who had had no formal schooling. But whenever he faced the apparitions he stood as if enchanted, without a rhyme in his head.

As they picked their way along the mountain path Val spoke to Anthiel, trying to understand how he had banished the apparitions. "Why do you repeat the same words over and over again?" he asked.

"Those words hold the spell together," Anthiel said. "A traveling wizard once told me they're called keystones."

Keystones, Val thought. He remembered the lists of words in the ancient books Taja had shown him: wizard's commentary, she had said. And he had seen locked books, bound in brass and iron, that Taja had not been able to open. The mages must have guarded their keystones jealously. How did this man come upon words it had taken the wizards a lifetime to discover?

"How do you choose the words?" Val asked.

"I don't really know. I use solid words—tree and rock, table and door—they seem to stand better against something like those illusions."

Anthiel had had to repeat his keystones, each time in a different context, and weave them in with a spell of banishment, and an invocation to the gods, and keep in his head all the while the meter he had chosen, and the alliteration. . . . It seemed to Val, who sometimes took an entire day to write one sonnet, that what Anthiel had achieved was very nearly impossible.

"Why didn't you apprentice yourself to a mage?" Val asked.

"We were too poor. I grew up in a small village, and my family couldn't afford to lose my labor."

Val nodded. Anthiel was a man to cultivate, someone who might become a great poet-mage. If Anthiel came home alive from the wars Val would reward him generously.

Finally they reached the crest of the mountain range and began to descend. From the path Val could see Etrara's army ranged across the plains, and he wondered how the others had crossed the Teeth of Tura. The uneasiness grew that had started when Arion's company had pulled ahead of his.

They reached the plain a few days later. The sun was setting and he felt cold as the snowdrifts in the mountains, felt as if his bones were made of snow. He told his men to make camp and went in search of Arion, walking quickly to get warm.

The duke was standing before a large bonfire, talking to three of the commanders. "Arion!" Val said.

The duke turned. Even in the fading light Val could see his face go pale, as if he had seen a ghost.

"What in Callabrion's name is happening here?" Val said. "Why didn't you wait for us?"

"I—we thought you lost in the mountains, Val," Arion said. "It's good to see you."

"We encountered magic. It was our good fortune that

there was a sort of poet-mage among us. If he hadn't been there I have no doubt we'd still be wandering in the snow."

"Magic? I saw nothing."

"Come with me," Val said shortly, leading Arion away from the other commanders. When a man came to accuse a member of the royal family of deception, he thought, it was best to have as few witnesses as possible. "Surely you saw the things we did, the white birds and trees—"

"I swear by Scathiel's toe—"

"You're a very poor liar, Arion. Who asked you to kill me? Was it Callia?"

"No—"

"But it might well have been, isn't that so? The Queen's Axe, then?"

Arion said nothing. "You were told to lose us somewhere in the mountains, weren't you?" Val said.

The duke nodded slowly. "Why, Val? Why would Callia want you dead?" he asked.

If Arion didn't know that he certainly wasn't about to tell him. He had seen the capricious gods turn the ladder of fortune on its head so that the high became low and the low high, and he had no doubt that the man in front of him might someday be king. "I don't know," Val said.

"She wants something in Tobol An, I know that much. And you were there, weren't you? But what is she playing at? She has no talent for strategy—"

Val said nothing.

"It's Mariel who's behind her, Mariel who plots Callia's every move," Arion said. "My treacherous half-sister. She warned me about civil war, said that the chaos of King Galin's time would come again if I didn't cast my vote with Callia. We'd be fighting the battle of Arbono all over again, she told me. And at the same time she insinuated that Callia would be easy to overthrow, that I would soon be king in Etrara. But all the while she planned to rule in Callia's name. I should have waited, should have gathered my forces. . . ."

How easily these brothers and sisters disposed of each

other, Val thought. He had been right to be careful, right not to lay immediate claim to the throne. "What about me?" he asked. "Did the Queen's Axe tell you what to do if I came out of the mountains alive?"

"Yes. Yes, he did. I was to see to it that you were sent to wherever the fighting was the thickest. He said that Callia would be very disappointed if you returned to Etrara."

"And will you?"

"No," Arion said slowly. "No, I don't think so. She has spies in my company, men who would tell her if I refused to follow her orders. But a great deal can happen in the confusion of battle. I swear on my honor I'll do everything I can to bring you back alive."

Val thanked him and returned to his men. Arion had not told him everything, he was certain of it. A thoughtful note had come into the duke's voice as he spoke, as though he had made other plans.

Val scowled. He had been used as a counter once before in the great game the brothers and sisters played with one another, and he did not want it to happen again. But what did Arion have planned?

Seven

· · · · · · ·

THE FIGHTING IN SHAI STARTED EARLY the next morning. The men woke to the sound of trumpets, harsh and discordant; they reached for their swords and shields.

A messenger from Arion rode into Val's camp as they were arming themselves. "That's the Shai's poet-mage," the messenger said. "He's calling for Penriel. It'll be a duel of magic, for now."

A duel of magic, Val thought. He remembered the first time he had seen Penriel, remembered wondering why the queen had wanted a sorcerer when magic had died out of the world. But he had been wrong, he realized; magic was very much alive. He had seen that much when he had come over the mountains.

Penriel left his tent and climbed a small grassy rise near Val's camp. He looked small and a little foolish in his cloak. Val saw him stare across the plain at the Shai forces.

The noise of the trumpets grew louder. Clouds formed overhead, obscuring the sun. The clouds thickened, layer on layer of them; the sky became dark as night.

Heavy rain fell to the camp, plummeting like knives. Water drenched the men through to their skin. They wrapped blankets around themselves and brushed the wet hair from their eyes. Drops resounded against the commanders' tents.

Penriel began to speak, raising his voice to be heard above the rain. Val listened as the poet-mage chose his keystones, "sword" and "glass." Penriel recited an invocation to the god Callabrion, playing with the sound of his keystones and with the god's name, weaving in spells of illusion and banishment.

For a moment the rain seemed to lessen. Then the torrents returned, heavier than before. Wind tossed the rain into towers, spires, a city made of water. Land and sea had changed places; Val felt he might drown with the force of the waves.

Penriel spoke again, shouting. A loud wind gusted across the plain, blowing the rain before it. The clouds overhead tore, thinned to rags. The rain began to subside.

Penriel hurried through a few more verses. But the rain did not end, though the sun shone weakly through the remaining clouds.

The drizzle continued all day. The men grumbled and pulled their cloaks around them for warmth. A few whispered against Penriel, but others, loyal to the queen, swore by Scathiel that the rain was natural and no wizard's sending.

Val wondered. Even he could see that Penriel was much more accomplished than the ignorant villager who had brought his company safely out of the mountains. And yet something seemed missing from Penriel's verses; at times he seemed almost lost, unable to understand the Shai's magic.

Over the next few days the Shai's poet-mage sent several apparitions toward their camp. Penriel countered them all, but his verses were weak, uninspired. His illusions would waver and become dispersed, and several times a sending of the Shai's passed over the camp, causing panic and despair.

Val wondered if he should offer Anthiel's services to someone, to Arion, perhaps, since Penriel seemed unapproachable. But as the days wore on he realized that he understood almost nothing about the arts of the wizards, and he decided to keep silent.

As long as the battle was fought between the poet-mages he and his company remained idle. He spent the days drilling his men and going for long walks through the camp. His walks always seemed to end at a small grassy rise overlooking the plain, the place from which Penriel worked his magic.

Five days after the battle began he stood on the rise and gazed out at the Shai camp. The grass of the plain, tall and sharp as swords, bent backward in the wind, shifting color as the wind passed, gray and yellow and green.

Something moved toward him, a line of mounted men riding toward the camp. Horses' hooves beat against the plain. The soldiers held their lances straight in front of them, their golden armor and helmets burning far brighter than anything else in the weak sunlight. As they came closer Val could see that they were very tall, nearly twice the size of ordinary men.

He turned to look for Penriel, but the poet-mage, summoned by the sending of magic, was already climbing the rise to look out over the plains. Penriel hesitated a moment, studying the strength of the illusion sent against him, and began to speak.

He started with a ritual opening verse and then moved quickly to a spell of banishment. Perhaps because of the brightness of the soldiers he chose the word "shining" as his keystone. But the men ranged against them continued onward without slowing. Val could hear the ring of the horses' bridles, the shouts of the men. He braced himself for the horror he would feel when the apparitions rode through the camp.

The illusion began to waver. Penriel spoke louder, faster. He began another verse, chose another keystone—"jewel"— and made the two words dance around each other in intricate patterns. Then Val saw Penriel frown, hesitate for a moment, and he knew that the poet-mage had forgotten something, that he had failed to hold all the vast complicated verse in his head. He spoke another line, but it did not rhyme with the line before it, and it used no alliteration at all.

The mounted men reached the camp. Their forms had started to break up and dissolve; Penriel's verses had been effective enough for that, at least. The soldiers from Etrara ran from the path of the illusion. The touch of a sending was enough to drive men to despair, and already one soldier had died from it.

The apparition reached the camp as a confused blur of color. One of the mounted men formed again for a brief moment and touched a soldier with the point of his lance, and the man fell to the ground, screaming. Then the sending passed over them and dispersed in the mountains.

Val had been out of the path of the illusion but he had felt the bleak hopelessness of their position, the terror at being exposed to such an uncanny power. His heart was pounding loudly. We can't survive much more of this, he thought.

Men came forward to lead Penriel to his tent. Val left the rise and sought out his own tent, drained.

A few hours later he emerged. He had seen some of the tricks Penriel had performed for Queen Callia; the man was doubtless talented enough for court magic. But Penriel could not hold his own against the trained wizards of Shai. Something had happened to the wizardry of Etrara, Val thought; when Tariel's poet-mages died an entire generation of knowledge had died with them.

If Arion agreed Val would offer him Anthiel's services. Penriel wouldn't even need to know that another wizard was helping him against the Shai. Two mages working to counter the illusions might be able to succeed where one, almost certainly, would fail.

But when he came to Arion's tent his second-in-command told him the duke was studying the battlefield, planning strategy. Val returned to his company and ate a light supper with his men.

The next day Val found Anthiel and drew him aside. To his surprise the other man, who had been so quick with his help in the mountains, began to shake his head. "One poet-mage knows another," he said. "If I speak my verses Penriel can't help but be aware of it, just as he's aware of the sendings from Shai."

"Well, then, he'll have to agree," Val said.

Anthiel shook his head. "The poet-mages are jealous people. He may stop his work altogether if he senses someone else speaking verses."

"But he'll die. We'll all die if he backs down."

The other man shrugged. "I know only what I tell you. I've met a few wizards in my life, though none as knowledge-able as Penriel. But I have never heard that any of them was able to work with another mage."

"He may have to. We can't continue on like this."

But that morning no illusions came from the Shai camp across the plain. The duke returned from wherever he had been, but Val could not find a time to get him alone. And then, as the camp was taking the noon meal, the sentry blew the trumpet that meant an attack of men, not magic.

Val put down his bottle of ale and stood quickly. He could barely make out the Shai, specks small as birds riding toward them across the plain. The sun sparked off their golden armor, and as they came nearer he could see the helmets shaped like half-masks that covered their eyes and nose. They had more horses than the men of Etrara, and they rode them in tight formation.

Val mounted his horse and called to his men. Before they had gone halfway across the plain they met with the enemy. A mounted soldier armed with a sword attacked, and he raised his own sword to strike.

The sendings of the wizards began while Val and the other man fought together. Bells and thunder pealed across the plain, and after a while he heard a strange music of trumpets and drums. The music seemed to put heart into his opponent and he fought with desperate strength, urging his horse to advance. Suddenly, before Val could raise his sword to counter the attack, the other man fell, his breast pierced by an arrow. Val turned to see his rescuer but there was no time; another man was upon him.

The lessons of his fencing master came back to him and forced out all other thought. He became like the mechanical figure he had once seen at the palace, capable of a bare half-dozen actions, moving only in response to his opponent. Somewhere on the field men screamed and horses neighed and an unearthly music played, but he managed to hear none of it. His world had narrowed down to the flashing blade of the man before him.

Finally the other man allowed him an opening. He moved forward and drove his sword to the man's heart.

There was no time for a respite, though; more of the Shai were heading toward him. It seemed a long time before he could stop and take stock of his troops, but by the sun it could barely have been an hour. The sendings had ceased for the moment; the field was a little quieter now.

Something shone to his right and he turned. The hero Andosto, said to be the grandson of the god Callabrion, fought his way through a knot of men. The light seemed to radiate outward from the man, and Val wondered if it could be the immanence of the gods he had heard about. The light gladdened him, and he wheeled his horse toward the fighting.

He slew two of the Shai fighting his way toward Andosto. By the time he reached him Andosto had killed the others. The hero grinned at Val, the only one on the battlefield who did not look weary. The light around him was stronger now.

Andosto called out something, but it was drowned out by another loud peal of bells. "What?" Val said.

"Where's Arion?"

"Arion? I don't know."

Val saw Andosto frown. Had the Shai taken Arion prisoner? Could they be trusted to ask for a ransom, like civilized men, or would they put the duke to death?

A half dozen of the Shai rode against them, and Val put the duke out of his mind. He and Andosto faced the enemy at the same moment, and side by side they stood against their attackers, forming a wall the Shai could not pierce. The light that came from Andosto warmed him, moving him to a courage he had never known, making him dare much against the enemy.

They killed four of the Shai between them, and the others fled. Val looked around him. In the distance he could see Arion and his men, near the Shai camp: the duke's standard waved in the chill wind from the mountains. Dozens of soldiers had gathered around the duke, and Val realized with amazement and joy that most of Arion's company had survived the battle. He rode toward them.

As he drew nearer he saw one of Arion's archers fit an arrow to his bow and aim it toward him. "Stop!" Val called across the plain, raising his hand. His voice sounded weak among the confused noises of battle. He saw the arrow leave the bow and managed to turn his horse aside at the last minute. The arrow grazed his thigh.

Had the archer taken him for one of the Shai? Val hurried on toward Arion, intending to berate the man for his stupidity. The archer took another arrow from his quiver.

Val wheeled his horse away from Arion's company. The man was mad. Did he, Val, wear golden armor and a helmet? Was this the sort of discipline Arion kept among his men?

He turned in time to see the archer's second arrow fall several yards short of his horse. But he saw something else as well, something far more chilling than the sight of a lunatic shooting his own men. Arion had lowered his lance and was shaking the hand of one of the helmeted men.

Betrayal, Val thought, feeling cold. We're all betrayed. This is the plan Arion made against Callia.

Arion's company and the Shai turned as one, and they headed toward the soldiers of Etrara.

The men of Etrara began to give ground. Some, probably, did not want to fight against their duke, and others did not yet understand that Arion had changed sides.

The Shai came on. They were close enough that Val could see a man riding near the leader and chanting, the poet-mage who had done them so much damage. A sending formed in the air, a huge wave coming on across the plain, unstoppable.

Where is Penriel? Val thought. His leg throbbed, and he looked down at his wound. Blood had drenched his breeches. He felt the despair of the sending reach him before the actual apparition did. He would die of his wound. They would all die, all the men of Etrara, lost here on a plain far from home. Where is Penriel?

The wave roared over him. His horse reared in fright and he fell to the ground, dazed; he managed to get clear of the animal just in time. Then it seemed as if the wave lessened, began to calm. Callabrion be thanked, Penriel had come at last. Val lifted his head.

But it was not Penriel that Val saw calling out verses against the noise of the water. Anthiel stood on the grassy ridge, his voice barely audible over the rush of the waves. The water of the wave subsided and finally disappeared.

Val looked around him. Did they have enough men to stand against Arion and the Shai? And would the soldiers fight on, against the duke, against such terrible odds?

Anthiel was still speaking. A sending formed in the air above him, a vast forest of moving trees. Val saw the Shai wizard say something, a spell of banishment, probably, but the forest continued on, implacable.

Val laughed, his heart lifting at the sight. Truly the man was an artist, a poet. But as he watched he saw this sending dissolve as the first one had. And the Shai, joined with Arion's forces, had not succumbed to despair but had continued on across the plain.

He got to his feet quickly and looked around for his horse. The animal lay nearby but would not be coaxed up; it had been stunned by the sending or by its own fall.

The Shai were nearly upon him. He raised his sword. Andosto rode up next to him and engaged one of the armored men. Val thought he could hear Andosto reciting poetry and he felt hope grow briefly within him; had the man been trained as a mage?

But as he listened he realized that Andosto was speaking an invocation to his grandfather, the god Callabrion. If Callabrion heard he did not choose to help his grandson; the light around Andosto grew stronger but his enemies did not retreat.

One of the Shai in front of him drew his sword, and Val parried the attack wearily. He heard Andosto call out triumphantly but could not spare the time to look at the other man. At the edge of his vision he saw a man fall from his horse. Arion.

Val doubled his efforts against his opponent, hoping to fight his way toward the duke. But others had seen Arion as well, and a handful of soldiers on both sides pressed toward him. In the confusion Val lost sight of the Shai he had been fighting. Something hit him hard, and he fell.

When he woke it was night. He could not hear the sounds of the battle, and he wondered if it might be over, wondered who had won. Where was he?

He tried to sit up, but a sharp pain in his chest made him lie back. He had probably broken a rib in addition to receiving the wound in his thigh; he was no soldier, that much was certain.

Someone near him spoke in the barbaric accent of the Shai, and the shock was enough to make him sit up despite the pain. He had been taken prisoner, then. He remembered wondering if the Shai ransomed their prisoners or killed them. Suddenly the question did not seem at all theoretical.

There was no moon, and the stars did not provide enough light for him to see anything but the distant bulk of the mountain. He put his hands out and felt grass, and then another body only a foot from where he sat. The other prisoner groaned. Val drew his hand away quickly.

The prisoner groaned again. "Water," he said. "Water, please, before I die."

Val felt thirsty too, and very cold. He listened for the Shai who had spoken before but could not hear him anywhere. In the dark Val felt rather than saw the other prisoner move.

"Who are you?" the man said.

"Arion?" Val said, astonished. "It can't be—Arion?"

"Yes," Arion said hoarsely. "Who are you?"

"Val."

Arion laughed shortly. "Val. Sometimes I think you worry Callia more than the Shai, you and Tobol An. By all the gods, I wish I knew what she's planning. I don't suppose you'll tell me now, now that I'm dying."

"Come—you won't die here."

"I will, though. I can feel my death coming for me—I'll be feasting with Sbona before the night is over. She told me, the old woman. She said I will love a foe and hate a friend, and that one will betray me and the other save me. The Shai betrayed me, that much is certain. They accepted my help, but they never intended to let me live."

"It was Andosto who attacked you."

"Was it?" Val heard the bitterness in the other man's voice. "Then why am I wounded in the back? They killed me, the Shai did, after I had given them the forces of Etrara. And you'll save me, Val, won't you? You'll tell them in Etrara I fought bravely in the defense of my country."

How many people had seen Arion riding at the head of the Shai's forces? It didn't matter; if Val repeated his story often enough no one would question it. And he would do that one favor for Arion, for his brother, would grant the man the heroic death he so desperately wanted. "I will," he said. "Who told you this? Who was the old woman?"

"She said I would have my heart's desire. What is my heart's desire, though?"

"A hero's death," Val said.

"Yes." Arion coughed. "A hero's death. They'll make songs about me in Etrara after I'm dead, won't they?"

"Of course they will. I'll make a few myself."

Arion said nothing for a long moment. Then, "Betrayed," he said finally. "Betrayed by everyone. Penriel left the field after that last sending, did you notice?"

Penriel hadn't fought because Anthiel had made his own verses. The poet-mages are a jealous people, Anthiel had said. "Who won the battle?" Val asked. "Do you know?"

"Oh, the Shai, of course." Arion sounded weary. He coughed again. "Their forces are far better than ours, and their commander, Rakera, is a brilliant man. Callia was over-confident—she knows nothing about the realities of war."

He laughed harshly. "Callia. Valor is nothing without honor, I learned that much. There was no honor in fighting for my sister, and none in fighting against her."

Arion was silent a moment. Then he said, "No, Val, tell them how I died. Tell them that there are better things than a hero's death. Tell them I said that heroes should live, not die uselessly in battle."

"I will, Arion. Come, you shouldn't spend your strength talking. Sleep. I'll tell them."

Arion said nothing. Val slept a little, fitfully, waking when the pain in his side grew worse. It was only when dawn came that he saw Arion stretched out cold on the grass; the duke had died sometime in the night. He feasts with Sbona now, Val thought, and closed his half-brother's eyes.

Taja sat in the central room of the library and worked on the catalogue. The room's great walls curved inward and met in an arch far overhead. Rows of scarred wooden cabinets were bunched together in the center, looking somehow out of place in the vast hollow of the room.

She leafed through a book called *A History of the Battle of Arbono* and, as she had feared, found another book sewn into the binding. She sighed; she would have to catalogue it twice. The second book proved to be a hymn to the goddess Sbona. And there was a third book after that, a treatise on medicine.

When she had finished she put the triple book back on the pile of those already catalogued and opened the next one.

A book by the poet Cosro, according to the title a hymn to the
Ascending God. She read a few lines and nearly laughed out
loud. The book was in fact about a man's first night with a
woman, and used the images of rising and falling to mean
something very different.

Two soldiers came into the room. "We need to get back
to the records room," one of them said. He spoke carefully,
as if he expected his voice to echo in the enormous spaces of
the room. Instead he sounded plain and clear, like the actors
who had once visited Tobol An. Taja tried not to smile. She
had seen people respond this way to the catalogue room
before.

"Take that staircase over there," Taja said. "Turn left
when you come out and—"

"No," the man said. "You show us." He had a large
mustache, which he smoothed after he spoke.

She sighed and put down her pen. As the weeks passed
the soldiers had grown more uncomfortable with the small
traces of wizardry left in Tobol An. They did not go into the
library alone, and they began to avoid the ruined stones left
by the wizards' war. They did not travel into the forest at
all.

As she led the two men to the records room she passed
five more soldiers, who demanded to know the way out of the
library. "By the Wandering God, I think the place changes
shape whenever we come here," one of them said. No one
laughed.

They were actually within two doors of the exit. She directed them to the outer door and then climbed a staircase to
the next level. Since the soldiers had come she seemed to
spend half her time showing them through the library.

She usually didn't mind being helpful; it was part of her
task as a librarian. But like the rest of the villagers she resented
the soldiers for other things, for the men and women—five of
them now—who had been arrested and put in cages, for the
huge amount the soldiers consumed in food every day, for

the fact that they insisted on paying for their meals and lodging with the debased coins of King Gobro III.

They came to the records room and she turned to go. "No, you'll stay with us," the man with the mustache said. "The records have to be somewhere in this room. And I think you know where they are. I think you've lied to us."

She sat and watched as the two soldiers went through the drawers. They worked methodically; unlike the first men she had brought here they studied every name, not just the file headings. It took them more than an hour to finish.

"By the Burning Ladder, the records have to be here somewhere!" one of the men said, slamming the drawer shut. "You know where they are, don't you?"

"No," Taja said. She looked directly at him; she had noticed that the soldiers always turned away whenever her eyes met theirs. Val had done the same thing.

"She's lying, as I said," the other man, the one with the mustache, said. "She's the librarian, after all."

"The queen's getting impatient. The commander said she wants us to try torture on the ladder."

"Aye, sometimes torture's the only way to get to the truth." The second man moved closer to Taja, looked down at her. "Would you give up your secrets then? Your hands stretched over your head, your legs tied, your body hurting in every joint? You'd beg to tell us the truth, wouldn't you?"

The first man seemed uneasy; he had probably mentioned the ladder only to frighten Taja. "We—we should ask the commander first."

"We'll take her with us to the commander, then."

They moved toward her. She was ready for them and managed to hit one in the midriff and knock the wind out of him, but then the second came for her. She tried to fight him off but the first one had recovered and seized her from behind. She struggled and the second hit her across the face.

"How do you suppose you'll get out of here without my help?" she asked.

The second man drew a knife and laid it across her

throat. "We'll kill you if you don't help us," he said. "Your body could lie here for days before anyone found it."

The first man stirred behind her. "Tell us where the records are," he said.

She thought he sounded a little desperate; things had moved too quickly for him, had gotten out of his control. She tried to turn and face him, but the other man pressed the edge of his knife into her throat. "I don't know," she said. "I told you—I don't know."

"Good," the second man said. "Let's take her."

She directed the soldiers out of the library. It was raining hard when they left, but a few people had business out-of-doors and they stared after her in horror. No one said anything; they had already learned their lessons in the months the soldiers had been in Tobol An. She was only glad that Pebr wasn't there to see her.

The commander had taken over the cottage of the first woman he had caged, and the soldiers led her toward it and knocked on the door. A guard let them into the front room. The commander sat behind a desk, studying a few pieces of paper before him.

The second soldier and the commander talked together in low voices, stopping every so often to glance over at Taja. The first soldier had remained to keep watch over her. Finally the commander looked up. "Good," he said. "I was about to suggest something like that myself."

They took her into another room. Everything had happened so quickly that she had had no time to feel fear. Now, seeing the strange ladder against the wall, its rungs spaced only an inch or so apart, she understood what the gods had chosen for her. She said a brief prayer to the goddess Sbona, mother of all.

The soldiers tied her feet to the ladder's rungs, then stretched her arms above her head. "Where are the records?" the commander asked. The soldiers tied her hands to the ladder.

"I don't know," she said.

"I can raise you even higher on the ladder," he said. The soldiers moved out behind him, and the one with the mustache grinned. "Or you can tell me what I want to know. Where are the records?"

"I told you—"

"Well," the commander said. "I'll leave you here for a few hours. When I come back I'll want to know where those records are. And if you don't tell me I'll tie you a few rungs higher. Think about that while I'm gone."

He and the two other men left the room. After only a few minutes she felt the weight of her body pull against her arms. Her joints seemed on fire. What would it feel like to be tied higher on the ladder? They would have to untie her first, and she would have a few moments where she wouldn't feel stretched like a god between earth and sky. But perhaps she would have grown used to the pain by then; perhaps it would hurt even more to be untied.

Rain fell heavily outside. Her hands felt numb. What if she told them what they wanted to know? Val said he hadn't wanted to be king; she wouldn't really betray him if she told the commander where she had hidden the records. And then the soldiers would leave Tobol An, and the cages would come down. . . .

Footsteps sounded in the front room and she tensed, thinking that the commander was about to return and stretch her higher on the ladder. The pain in her joints, which she had managed to ignore for a while, returned stronger than before. She closed her eyes. Why should the entire village suffer for one callow, foolish courtier?

She opened her eyes. Mathary stood in front of her. "How—" she asked.

"Hush, child," Mathary said. "You must not tell the commander where the records are. You must save Val, so that Val may save Tobol An."

"What do you mean?"

"Hush."

"Val won't save Tobol An. Val has never thought of any-one besides himself in his life. How can he—"

But Mathary had gone. Probably the old woman had never been there, Taja thought; probably the pain had caused her to see visions.

The commander came into the room. "What were you saying?" he asked. "Did you want to tell me something?"

"Yes," she said, feeling light-headed from the vision. Her gift for finding things led her to the heart of this man, laid his life and thoughts bare before her. "You don't want to be here. You fear that Callia sent you to this backwater as punishment, that she won't allow you to go with the troops to Shai and so win honor in battle. And you fear the traces of magic left—the poet-wizards haunt your dreams—"

"Quiet! How dare—how *dare* you—"

"You think we'll never surrender—"

The commander moved toward the ladder, but at that moment she heard hoofbeats on the path outside. The commander turned. A messenger hurried into the room.

"I bring you a message from the queen," the man said. "You and your men are to leave Tobol An at once and return to Etrara."

"What? Why?"

"I wasn't told that. There are rumors that the fighting in Shai is going badly for us."

The commander turned toward Taja, a look of great satisfaction on his face. "So much for your prophecies, wizard's get," he said. "You can hang here until I get back."

She must have fainted. When she woke she saw Mathary's face close beside her, and she realized that the other woman had climbed the ladder in order to reach her bonds. Mathary helped her lower her hands.

"Why did you— What did you mean when you said that Val—" Her voice was hoarse.

"Hush," Mathary said. "You must not speak of that."

"Were you really here? Or was it a vision?"

"Shake your hands to get the blood back in them. Do you feel well enough to stand? I'm going to untie your feet next."

"But what—what happened?"

"Great things, child. Great things."

Eight

· · · · · · · ·

VAL STOOD AND WALKED THE CONFINES
of his tiny cell. He stopped once to stare from the
small window set into the side of his room, but he
could see nothing except other featureless buildings, other
cells, he thought. He turned and began to pace again.

Light came from lamps of twisted iron hanging from the
ceiling. A faded rug covered the floor, red with an intricate
pattern of twined gold and blue.

How had it come to this? How had the great army of
Etrara lost the battle, and perhaps the war as well? What
would happen to him, and to Queen Callia, and the rest of
the royal family? We were overconfident, Arion had said. Val
laughed harshly.

A key turned in the lock, and the door opened. The
guard, bringing him his meals. Like all the Shai Val had seen
the man was tall and flaxen-haired. The guard had said nothing when they had marched him and Andosto and the other
captive soldiers to their cells, and had not spoken since.

The guard set Val's tray down on the wooden table. A
brown spider scuttled across the table, and the guard made a
fist and killed it before Val could speak.

"Why did you do that?" Val asked, startled.

"Why not?" the guard said in his strange accent.

So the man had a tongue after all, Val thought. He longed for conversation, even with one of the barbaric Shai. "Why? Because spiders are holy. They ascend to heaven like the gods. It brings ill fortune if you kill one."

To Val's surprise the guard sat and studied him across the table for a long moment. Finally he said, "We don't believe in that."

"Don't believe in the gods?" Val asked.

"We don't believe that men should rise and fall like the gods. Men should know their place and stick to it. My father was a soldier, and my grandfather, and my son will be a soldier after me. That's my place on the ladder—that's what the gods ordained for me. You men of Etrara are far too ambitious."

"But it's good to be ambitious. You might almost call ambition one of the Seven Virtues. If it hadn't been for ambition we would never have sailed for Astrion and Udriel, the lands beyond the seas."

Was he truly discussing philosophy with an unlettered man of the Shai? Did he miss the court that much? But he felt pleased when the guard answered.

"You discovered those lands because your country lies on the sea. If we'd had the ports and our priests had told us to sail west we would have done so, even if we fell off the edge of the earth."

"But—"

"And we'll have your ports soon, and Astrion and Udriel as well." The other man grinned. "We fight border wars with our neighbors to the east—we've learned a great deal about warfare while fat Gobro ate sweets and lean Tariel dallied with his mistresses. It was your ambition that convinced you you could win a war with us. Your ambition will be your downfall."

"Do you truly think you'll win this war? Soldiers with ambition fight harder, and in my country a common soldier can rise to be a knight or a great lord."

"In our country a common man can become a king, and wed a queen. But only for six months, and then he is put to death. That's what happens to men who try to rise on the ladder."

Val said nothing. So it was true, then, that the Shai killed their kings. And what of the magic that was loosed by the shedding of the kings' blood? Were those rumors true as well?

No, that was folly. Folks said magic was so common in Shai that the people spoke in poetry. But this man before him was no poet-mage.

Still, he could not help but wonder about the Shai sorcerers, about the man he had seen riding at the head of the army, chanting his verses as he came. The wizards of Shai seemed to have knowledge that those of Etrara did not. Something had been lost since King Tariel's time.

"Your poet-mage—" Val said cautiously.

"Kotheg," the guard said. "The greatest mage of our time, or perhaps of any time. It's no wonder that your troops could not stand against him."

"But what gives him his power?"

For the first time the guard showed surprise, almost astonishment. "You mean you don't know? Ah, but then your people would have no reason to sing the praises of our poet-mage. Kotheg has spent the night on Wizard's Hill."

"What's that?"

The guard shook his head. "Truly your people are ignorant, very ignorant. If a man wants to be a sorcerer he spends the night on Wizard's Hill. And in the morning he is either dead, or mad, or a poet."

"But our wizard, Penriel—"

"Aye, he has some ability, it's true. And ability counts for something. But to be a true poet-mage a man must risk everything."

"Must be ambitious, then."

"The rules are different for the wizards, you know that. They ascend to heaven by their poetry. Your people had a poet, a famous poet, who went to Wizard's Hill. Cosh-ro."

At first Val could not understand the guard's barbarous accent. Then, "Cosro?" he said. "I never heard that."

"Aye. And when he came back to Etrara he was unable to lie, and so your king sent him into exile."

"But what happened to them there? What did Kotheg see, and Cosro?"

"I don't know. And by all the gods I hope I never find out. I would not on my life go to Wizard's Hill."

The guard left shortly after that. Val sat and ate his dinner in thoughtful silence. He had to agree with the man; although he had long wished he could write like Cosro he did not think he would risk his life for the sake of a sonnet, however beautiful.

Narrion went up Palace Hill toward the observatory. The weak sun glinted from one of the observatory's four towers, a green copper dome. He hurried on.

All the news he heard was bad, very bad. Etrara had lost the battle, and perhaps the war. The Shai had more men and more horses, and their poet-mage, Kotheg, had spread terror among the soldiers of Etrara.

He knocked at the door to the observatory. The porter recognized him, and led him without speaking to Dorio's room.

Dorio looked up from his studies. "Did you talk to your priests?" Narrion asked.

"Yes."

"What did they say? Will they help us?"

"I don't think so."

"What? How long will they pretend that nothing has changed? Why won't they help?"

"They said they are certain Callabrion will return to the heavens in his own time. And that they do not think it is our place to meddle in the affairs of the gods."

"By Scathiel's big toe! Whose business is it, then, if not the disciples of the gods?"

Dorio shook his head. "I don't know."

Narrion was silent a moment. "You'll have to help me on your own, then," he said.

"I? What can I do?"

"Your library has certain books I'll need. Invocations, verses of magic . . ."

"Magic? I can't help you with magic. I'm no sorcerer."

"I didn't say you were. I asked for books, nothing more."

"I can't take books from the library without permission. We're not like your lawless Society."

Narrion said nothing. He had heard rumors that the astronomer-priests had come to an agreement with the Shai: they would give the enemy their support in exchange for safety, sanctuary within the observatory. If that was true then he could look for no further help from Dorio.

"You'll be safe here, for a while," Narrion said softly. "You can cower behind the walls of your observatory, and so avoid the Shai altogether. But the days continue to grow shorter. What will you do when the sun goes out forever, leaving us in eternal darkness?"

He turned and left without waiting for Dorio's answer. In a very short time, he thought, the Shai would be at the Gate of Roses. He had to get himself and Tamra to safety, had to find the books he needed to continue his work. Otherwise what he had told Dorio would become a reality: the sun would disappear forever. And even if, by some miracle, Etrara stood, all he had gained would be worth nothing.

The troops sent from Tobol An were too few and too late. A week after Val had been captured the Shai won a decisive victory, and they marched over the Teeth of Tura toward Etrara. No apparition stopped them, and they reached the city wall and the Gate of Roses a week later.

The Shai saw no one as they rode their horses down the Street of Roses. The commander, Rakera, looked around him uneasily, remembering the stories he had heard about Etrara. Ghosts haunted the city, they said, and there were fortune-tellers who could blight a life with a single glance.

A figure moved out of the shadows. Rakera stopped and put his hand to his sword. "My lord," the figure said, kneeling.

"Rise," Rakera said, startled. It was true, then—these decadent people had no honor. He smiled. A traitor in the city would make his task much simpler. "Who are you?"

"One who wishes only to serve," the man said. Light glinted from the glass before his eyes, and Rakera, who had never seen spectacles before, looked at him in amazement. "Here—I have prepared a small pageant in your honor."

"Your name," Rakera said harshly. "What is your name?"

"My name is Talenor, my lord," the man said.

Duke Talenor, Rakera thought, no longer surprised at the extent of these people's treachery. The traitor waved his hand. Others came forward out of the shadows. Someone played a flute, and a woman began to recite a poem welcoming the Shai to Etrara. As she spoke she motioned him forward, toward a black cloth stretched across the street.

Rakera's hand had never left the hilt of his sword. Now he looked back at the soldiers massed behind him, searching for his poet-mage. Kotheg spurred his horse forward until he was nearly even with his commander, and together they rode toward the cloth. Rakera motioned his men forward.

Two men of Etrara parted the cloth. Rakera almost laughed. The traitors had built a triumphal arch to honor their conquerors. A woman came through the arch, made him a curtsy, and began to speak in praise of valor.

When she had finished another woman joined her, this one reciting verses about honor. Rakera listened, puzzled. Why did these people speak of valor and honor when they had none? "The Seven Virtues, my lord," Talenor said near him.

Rakera nodded. He had heard about these, the frivolous court games of Etrara. He tried not to show his impatience.

Finally all seven Virtues had spoken, and an eighth woman came through the arch. She repeated the names of the Virtues and recited a short poem praising Rakera; the Shai commander, she said, combined all seven Virtues in his person. All the women curtsied once more, and then the eighth woman invited the Shai to the palace, where more entertainment awaited them.

Rakera motioned the troops forward again. Talenor moved to Rakera's side. "Any of these women would be pleased to share your bed," the traitor said.

"Where is the queen?" Rakera asked.

Talenor frowned, as if it pained him to hear questions asked so openly. "She's fled, my lord. Queen Callia and her court went to the countryside. Only a few remain in the palace."

"Where in the countryside?"

"I don't know. She didn't tell me. My sister the Duchess Mariel also stayed behind—perhaps you could ask her." They passed through the triumphal arch. "What do you think of this arch, my lord? Is it not fine?"

Rakera glanced around him. Every inch of the stone had been carved. The commander shrugged; he had never liked the overelaborate art of Etrara.

A short while later they reached the Street of Stones, and Rakera motioned the troops toward Palace Hill. At the courtyard the commander sent Kotheg and some of his men into the palace to make certain that they were not walking into a trap. But even here the people of Etrara proved themselves cowards; the soldiers returned to say that the palace was almost deserted.

Rakera dismounted and sent his horse to the stables. Talenor walked before him and knocked at the outer door. A porter opened the door to them, bowing deeply.

Talenor led Rakera and his men through the entrance room and into the banquet hall. The traitor waved his hand. The tables in the banquet hall were set with linen and crystal and silver. Candles burned at every table, and more shone in sconces on the walls. Talenor clapped his hands. "We will have more entertainment here, and then a banquet. Does that please you, my lord?"

"If you will taste every dish first," Rakera said.

Talenor looked pained again, then smiled grimly. "Certainly, my lord," he said.

"Good."

Rakera's men began to find seats at the tables. Talenor led the commander to the dais and turned their chairs around so that they faced the stage. They sat. The traitor clapped his hands again, and gestured in front of them.

Women danced to the stage. "A play, my lord," Talenor said. He smiled again. *"The Comedy of Hendo and Hendist."*

A woman stepped to the front of the stage and began to speak the Prologue. Rakera frowned. Of all the things he had seen so far in Etrara the strangest was this, that these women should display themselves so openly in front of men. He himself was not as strict as some in the matter of women; he even let his own wife come with him to the major festivals. But he felt with conviction that here the people of Etrara had gone too far. Disgust and displeasure rose so strongly within him that he missed the sense of the Prologue.

The actor who had recited the Prologue left the stage. Two women dressed as men came out. They spoke slowly and with broad gestures; Rakera understood that their speeches were intended to be humorous, but he could not follow them any more than he had understood the Prologue. For the first time he wondered if this entertainment was a jest at his expense, if he had underestimated the subtlety of these people.

A woman in black rags climbed heavily to the stage. One of the actors clapped her hand to her mouth; she seemed to be suppressing a scream. Another woman in black appeared on the stage, and another.

Someone finally did scream; Rakera felt almost grateful for it. Here at last was something he could understand. "What are these women?" Rakera asked the traitor. "Surely they're not Virtues?"

Talenor had gone very pale. "Maegrim," he said.

"What?"

"The Maegrim. Someone's fortune is about to change."

The women began to dance, turning slowly so that Rakera saw their hoods of badger skin. These are the fortune-tellers, then, Rakera thought. The ones who can change a life with a glance. He had almost thought they were no more than stories.

The women danced faster. There were six of them, and then seven. One took out a flat bundle of conjuring sticks and sank to the stage; a stick fell from her hand to the floor. "Summer!" the woman said.

"What does that mean?" Rakera asked.

"A summer cast in a summer month," Talenor said. He seemed pleased about something. "Good fortune."

"Summer!" the woman called again.

"Good fortune?" Rakera said. He laughed. "It's still winter—can't you tell? Callabrion hasn't ascended this year."

"Summer!" the woman called out one final time, and then gathered up the conjuring sticks and left the stage.

"Stop them!" Rakera said. He put his hand to his sword and half-stood. Men ran up to the stage. Rakera blinked in confusion. The women had disappeared.

He turned back to Talenor. "Where did they go?"

"I don't know, my lord. They—"

Rakera motioned to his men, who caught the traitor in a ring of swords.

"They come and go as they please," Talenor said. "They are—they are witches, sacred to Sbona—"

"Quiet," Rakera said. He had grown weary of the games of Etrara; he needed time to think. Finally he said, "Someone's fortune is about to change, is that what you told me?"

Talenor nodded.

"In Shai there are only two people whose fortunes change, the king of summer and the king of winter," Rakera said. "We kill the kings at the end of their reigns, to make the crops fertile and to show what happens to people who aspire to more than their place on the ladder permits. Everyone else does exactly what his father did and what his grandfather did before that."

Talenor said nothing.

"The god-king still rules in Shai," Rakera said. "It must be someone from Etrara whose fortune is about to change.

And the only man of Etrara I see in this room is you, traitor."
He scowled. "Tell me why I should not have you killed."

"I—I can be useful to you, my lord," Talenor said.

"You weary me, traitor. I don't want your help. Haven't
you heard the proverb? 'A man who is false to one king will
prove false to another.'"

"It's an honor to be killed by one of our guards," Rakera
went on. "In Shai we put out the eyes of traitors before we kill
them, so that they will not see the honor being done to them.
As for barbarians—"

Talenor moaned. Rakera reached out and gently
removed the duke's spectacles. Talenor shut his eyes. "You've
already proven you have no honor," Rakera said. He motioned to one of his men. "Kill him. And find me the Duchess
Mariel."

The man moved forward and stabbed Talenor to the
heart.

For a week the Shai left Duchess Mariel alone. They hammered their lamps of twisted iron into the ceilings of the
palace, splintering the paintings in the royal suite of the goddess Sbona creating the world. They laid their barbaric rugs
of gold and blue or black and red over the patterned marble
tiles. They burned herbs in the fireplaces that made Mariel's
eyes sting and her head ache, and whenever two or more of
them met in the hallways they beat their swords together,
making the corridors ring hollowly.

A guard was posted at the door of the royal apartments,
but Mariel seemed to be free to walk through her rooms and
those of her brothers and sister. But the rooms were deserted;
she met no one on her wanderings, not even Talenor.

She wondered what had happened to Talenor; he had
told her of his plans to gain favor with the Shai. Even he
had proved to have designs on the throne, she thought. He
had fooled everyone for so long, pretending to be a scholar,
interested only in his books. She had been the only one who
hadn't been taken in.

One day she came upon a man sitting in a pool of shadow. At first she took him for another ghost, but then she recognized Sbarra's poet. "Sorth," she said.

"My lady," Sorth said, standing quickly. "Please—I beg you—take me with you when you go."

So Duchess Sbarra had gone with Callia when she fled, Mariel thought. She could imagine the arguments between Sbarra and her husband, the accusations each had made; Sbarra, unlike Talenor, would not find it so easy to turn traitor.

"I'm afraid I'm not going anywhere," Mariel said dryly. "I seem to be a prisoner here too. Why didn't you leave with the duchess?"

"There was no room for me. She took her personal servants and no one else. And now I—I'm trapped here." He looked into the shadows as if he saw enemies lurking there. Perhaps, Mariel thought, he had ghosts of his own.

"Why do you say that? The Shai have left us alone so far. There's no danger here."

"There's a danger to me. Don't you understand? A masterless poet is a target of scorn for every other poet—their satiric verses could kill me."

She could see that he believed it; he looked gaunt and hollow-eyed, as if he had not slept since Duchess Sbarra had gone. "Don't be ridiculous," she said.

"I beg you—"

"I'll take you into my service. Would that do?"

"Yes," he said immediately, gratefully. "Yes—I thank you, my lady. I'll write a poem praising your generosity—future generations will remember your goodness. But why didn't you leave with the royal family?"

"I don't know," she said.

He looked doubtful, as if he thought her about to do some heroic deed he could set down in verse. But she had told him the truth; although Callia had pleaded with her to go with them she had made up her mind to stay. Leaving the palace would do her no good at all; she could not escape her guilt.

She had thought it would be easy to kill Gobro. It had been she who had raised the idea of poison, who had asked Narrion to visit the apothecary, she and Callia who had given him the poisoned cup. She had not reckoned with his ghost.

A few days later she finished her sleeping potion, but she was not allowed to send a servant to the apothecary's for more. She stopped her wanderings and lay in her rooms with her eyes closed, trying to dispel her headache. In the long hours alone she began to think of her brothers and sister, Tariel's children.

Tariel had been a scrupulously honest tyrant, treating each of his children and their mothers with equal fairness. She remembered walking in some procession or other; she and Talenor, as the oldest, had each held a corner of his train, and Callia and Arion and Gobro, tiny children then, had walked behind them.

Once, though, Callia's mother had displeased Tariel for a reason Mariel could not remember, and Tariel had banished his former mistress to the kitchen and ordered her to do scullery work. The children of the palace servants had understood immediately that Callia could now be taunted without reprisal; they had called her "God's child"—the peasant term for someone who was illegitimate or whose father was not known—and worse names than that. Mariel did not think that Callia had ever forgotten it; from that day forward she would never set foot in a kitchen, not even to give orders to a servant. Perhaps that explained her sister's obsessive need for pageants and finery. Perhaps Callia still thought of herself as somehow less noble than the rest of them.

Poor Gobro was dead now, and Arion too: she had heard about his death when the remnants of the defeated army had come home. Some of the soldiers had whispered that Arion had betrayed them, and Mariel had wondered if that could be true. With Arion dead there were only the three of them left.

And Val, of course, though Val didn't seem to know that

he might be the legitimate heir. Even after coming back from Tobol An he had gone on being Val, courteous and pleasant and a little distant. When Callia had asked her what she thought, Mariel had advised her sister to do nothing.

But Callia had apparently not taken Mariel's advice; Mariel had heard that Val had been sent to where the fighting was the thickest. And Val was another who hadn't come back; perhaps he was dead too, another death on their hands, though she had heard rumors that he had been captured. But who remained to ransom him?

The next day a delegation of the Shai came to her room. She was still lying on her bed, her head having gotten no better after a night's sleep. "Where is Queen Callia?" Rakera said.

"Callia?" Mariel said. She knew quite well where her sister was; the queen and some of her courtiers had fled to relatives in the country. "I have no idea. Surely you asked Talenor."

"Of course. He said his sister refused to talk to him when she found out he intended to turn traitor. He didn't put it that way, of course—no man thinks of himself as a traitor." Rakera paused. "Talenor's dead," he said.

"Dead?" Mariel asked. Fear filled her; the pounding of her head grew worse. It was impossible to think. But she would not ask this man how her brother died; she would not give him the satisfaction.

"Where is Queen Callia?" Rakera asked again.

"My sister comes and goes as she pleases. She's the queen—at least she was. She has no need to ask my leave for her actions."

"Shall we use the ladder then?"

"The—the ladder?"

"Aye. Or did you think your position here would protect you?"

She felt stretched on the ladder already; her head had given her no peace all night. She did not think she could survive torture. "I have no position here," she said.

"That's true, quite true. The ladder, then. And if you still resist we'll have you put to death."

They would take her out of her cool dark room and force her into the dreadful light of the iron lamps. Then they would bind her arms and legs to the rungs of the ladder. And if she didn't die of the pain they would kill her; they had already proven their cruelty in killing Talenor.

"I don't—" she said feebly.

"Come, come, Duchess Mariel. We've already got your poet tied to the ladder—he'll be a little taller when you see him next. It's only a matter of days, of hours, really, before he tells us what we want to know. Why don't you save his life, and your own, and tell us where she is?"

"She's with her mother's relatives," Mariel said weakly, lying back against her pillows.

"Are you certain?"

"Yes."

"And where is that?"

She told him. As the Shai left she heard one guard say to another, "A decadent people, as we thought. There's no honor left in any of them."

First Gobro and now Callia, she thought, closing her eyes: she marveled that betrayal seemed to grow easier with time. Would they truly kill the queen? They seemed to know all about killing royalty.

Something moved in her room and she opened her eyes cautiously. Gobro stood in front of her, the weak light from the window shining through him. A jewel at his fingers glittered. "Do you know where Riel is?" he asked.

"Go away," she whispered. "Go away—you're dead, go away."

Val heard the key in the lock and his guard came in, bringing him breakfast. Since their conversation about ambition the guard had spent a few minutes of every day talking to him, and Val had begun to look forward to his visits. The man had none of the courtly graces of Duchess Sbarra and her friends, but Val had quickly learned to overlook his shortcomings in exchange for his company, however brief.

"The news from Etrara is good," the guard said now, putting down Val's tray. "The city has fallen without resisting."

"No," Val said, profoundly shocked. "No one fought at all?"

"No one." The guard sat at the table opposite Val. He grinned. "Some of them even turned traitor, making our task that much easier."

"What of Queen Callia? And Talenor, and Mariel?"

"I don't know. My commanders don't tell me such things. Why should they, after all?"

"Do you know—what will happen to me?"

"Ah, that I do know. There's no one left to ransom you— you'll be sent as a slave to Shai. They'll put you to work in the silver mines, perhaps, or the vineyards."

A slave. From king of Etrara to slave. Despair overcame him; he put his head in his hands, saying nothing.

No—he would not sit quietly, waiting to be shackled and bound. He looked up. "It seems that you were right about ambition after all," he said carefully. He stood and went to the window, looked out at the other cells.

"That's true," the guard said. "The gods dislike a man who tries to rise on the ladder."

"Aye. And now the gods have struck me down, as easily as I might cut the thread of that spider there."

The guard turned to see where he pointed. One step brought Val to his side. He drew the other man's sword and moved away quickly.

"Open the door," Val said. The sword was unfamiliar, heavy, but it did not waver as he pointed it toward the guard.

The guard went to the door. "The city you knew is gone," he said. "Where will you go?"

"That's my business. Open the door."

The guard put his hand on the ring of keys at his belt.

Suddenly, so quickly Val did not see him move, the other man drew his dagger. He moved toward Val, the dagger poised.

Val picked up a chair, threw it at the other man. The guard went down, hitting his head against the wall as he fell. Val wrenched the dagger from his hand and took his keys. The guard stirred a little, moaning, but he did not wake.

Val unlocked the cell, fumbling with the keys and the dagger in the same hand, and hurried outside. "Andosto!" he called. "Andosto, it's Val! Where are you?"

Someone answered from another of the cells. Val ran toward the sound and turned one of the keys in the lock. Nothing happened. He tried again, and the door opened.

Andosto came to the door. Val threw him the sword. "Hurry!" he said. "Etrara's fallen. We have to get away, get free."

Two more of the Shai came toward them, moving quickly. Andosto could deal with them, Val thought; he ran to open the other doors.

Men left their rooms, blinking in the unfamiliar light. "Go help Andosto!" Val said, not staying to see if they understood. One cell opened to Anthiel, the untutored poet-mage who had saved them in the mountains. Val unlocked the last cell and looked around him.

More of the Shai had come up; Andosto was holding off two of them, and a third lay dead at his feet. One of the Shai saw Val and broke off to run toward him. Andosto bent, took the dead man's sword, and threw it to Val. Val caught it by the hilt, a trick his fencing teacher had taught him.

As the Shai came closer Val saw that it was his guard, the man who had spoken so eloquently about ambition. He had roused himself, then, and had found another sword.

Once again the lessons of his fencing master came back to him, and he parried the other man's strokes until he found an opening. His opponent, caught off guard by his sudden movement, took two steps backward and stumbled against a rise on the ground. Val thrust his blade forward and the man fell.

Val looked around him. One of the men Andosto fought with was down, and the other seemed to be tiring. Val hurried toward them.

"How—" Andosto asked.

"Not now," Val said. "We have to get away before they realize we've gone."

The second Shai guard turned and ran as Val came up to Andosto. The other men of Etrara joined them. "Hurry!" Val said, leading the men away from the cells.

As they went Val heard Anthiel speak a brief spell of illusion, cloaking them from the Shai, and a spell of protection against whatever evil magic remained. After a short time they topped a rise and Val could see the plain stretch out before them, and the Teeth of Tura in the distance.

They came down to the plain. The grasses, sharp as swords, bent in the cold wind. For the first time since his escape Val felt his wounds, the dull aches in his rib and thigh.

He looked over his shoulder, but no one seemed to be following them. "How did you escape?" Andosto asked.

"I took my guard's sword," Val said.

"And—Etrara's fallen, you say?"

"So my guard said, and I see no reason to doubt him. He said they would not ransom us, that we would be put to work as slaves."

They walked for a time without speaking, passing trampled, muddy earth. He felt very weary. No one in Etrara had thought they would lose; all their talk had been of conquest, of the riches they would find in Shai.

"What will you do now?" he asked Andosto.

"I'll go back to Etrara. Maybe I can help—help somehow—"

For the first time Andosto sounded uncertain. Val saw the other man's future very clearly: he would fight on, waging a hopeless battle against the Shai until he was overcome and killed. He could not exist quietly in a conquered country; it was the nature of heroes to be heroic.

"What about you?" Andosto asked. "Where will you go?"

Val was silent a moment. Until now, he saw, he had been content to follow where others led. He had gone into exile because Narrion had told him to, and had fought in Callia's war because it had been expected of him. But what did he want for himself? Did he want to be king? And could he claim the throne if the Shai ruled Etrara?

No—there were traitors in Etrara, his guard had said, and one or another of them might have given his secret to the Shai. It would be dangerous to return.

Suddenly he thought of Tobol An. He felt a profound desire to see it again, to sit by the hearth drinking tea, to talk with Taja and Pebr about the great world outside. The war had probably left the tiny village untouched; its harbor was certainly too small to interest the Shai. He could stay there until he decided what to do.

"I'm going to Tobol An," he said, and felt relief sweep through him as he said it.

They came to their abandoned camp at the foot of the mountains and stopped to forage for food. Then they began to climb, shivering in the cold wind blowing across the snow. The rumors had been true then, Val thought. Winter had not ended.

No apparitions appeared in the mountains; Val thought that Anthiel's verses might be protecting them. Even so their second journey seemed to be much harder than their first. Without horses they were forced to trudge through the snow on foot, and at night they slept wrapped only in their cloaks. One of the men took sick and could barely continue for the coughing that racked his body. For the first time Val understood what his men had gone through while he had sat at his ease on his horse, and he marveled at their hardiness. There were more ways than one to be a hero, he thought.

On his second day in the mountains the wound in Val's leg began to ache, and by the third it pained him so greatly that he was forced to rest several times. He found a tree branch and used it as a cane, walking carefully along the snow-laden trail; the other men stopped several times to wait for him.

And always, as they picked their way through the snow-drifts, they kept one eye toward Shai in case of pursuit. They could see no one on the trail behind them, but the snow made it impossible to look down into the plain. He hoped that the Shai had decided to let them go; it would not be worth the trouble to follow them when they could have their pick of slaves in Etrara.

Finally they came to the plain of Wathe. On their second day of marching Val bid good fortune to the other men and turned south. The food he had gathered at the camp was running low, but he went a little faster now. He would see Taja again, and Pebr, would sit in their stone cottage while the harsh wind gusted against the door.

He traveled for several days, favoring his injured leg. On his third day alone he came to a bridge made of weathered oak planks. He crossed it, realizing with surprise that the noisy hurrying river beneath him must be the Darra, which had turned south from Etrara.

On the other side of the river, fern and wet green moss climbed the banks and fanned out onto the shore. Tall trees shadowed the path. As he walked he left the sound of water behind; the trees became more massive, silent, oppressive. They seemed dry as paper, the fallen leaves the accumulation of years.

He had reached the Forest of Thole, he realized, and he turned south once more, hoping to leave the forest completely. After a while he saw the weak winter sun breaking through the trees, and he hurried out into the light. He kept the ancient trees on his right, not wanting to return even to search for food. He had had enough of magic, he thought.

Finally the houses of a village appeared ahead of him. For a moment, filled with hope, he thought he had reached Tobol An, but as he came closer he saw that the town was far larger than Taja's village. Soria, he thought, remembering when he had gone there to buy clothes. Pebr and Taja had gotten candles and soap and bolts of cloth at the same time.

Evening had begun to fall, the strange oppressive dusk that seemed to blanket the land earlier and earlier since the Feast of the Ascending God. He did not want to stop, did not want to speak to strangers, but his leg hurt too badly to continue. He went into the village and found an inn.

The common room was crowded. He limped between the trestled tables and called for the innkeeper. A man hurried toward him. "I need a room for the night," Val said.

"Did you fight?" the innkeeper asked. "What news of the war?"

"Etrara's fallen."

A dozen people in the common room began to speak at once. "Fallen, did you say?" one of the men asked, louder than the rest.

"Aye."

Something in the way Val spoke silenced their questions. The innkeeper gave him a key, and he walked slowly up the stairs. They had to hear it sooner or later, he thought. But he was too weary to stay and talk; he wanted only to sleep.

He had an early breakfast and set off the next morning. A day's walking brought him to a ruin from the time of the wizards, a huge black boulder that seemed made of glass. The sight heartened him; he was getting close, then. For the first time in a long while he began to sing.

Two mornings later, as the weak sun lightened the sky, he saw Tobol An, approaching it from the east rather than the north this time. The white spire of the library gleamed against the horizon. As he came closer he saw the familiar stone cottages rising from the barren plain, huddling together as if for warmth. A gull called overhead, and he could smell the complex salty odor of the sea.

He felt hunger and weariness strongly now, and the wound in his thigh ached sharply as he walked. It would be good to have a meal by the fire, and a bath, and to sleep for a very long time. . . .

Suddenly he stopped. A group of people dressed in fan-

tastic costumes stood by one of the houses, all of them arguing furiously. Actors, he thought. What in Callabrion's name
were actors doing in Tobol An?

Tamra and her friends had acted for the love of it and
never for pay; their high station forbade it. Their performances were only for the men and women of the court. Other
companies in the city acted professionally, and had the pa-
tronage of one noble or another. But less fortunate, masterless troupes roamed the countryside and put on performances
wherever they could, in barns or alehouses or open fields,
hoping to catch the eye of a rich man or woman and exchange
a play for one night's shelter in a manor house.

These women had to be masterless, Val thought. Why
else would they travel to tiny Tobol An?

He came closer. The women were beautiful, he saw, fairer
by far than the slatterns he had expected. One of them, wearing a dress of blue brocade, turned and looked at him.

His breath stopped. "Taja," he said finally.

"Val?" Taja said, lifting her skirts and hurrying toward
him. "Val—it is you! Where have you been? Did you fight?
What happened to you?"

For a moment he could not speak, amazed by the sight
of her as a noblewoman, a woman of the court. He had
thought of her so often during the war, he realized; it had
been the image of her that had sustained him through all his
pain and hunger and hardship. Now, seeing her, he felt as if
he had come home.

"I fought, yes," he said. "Not very heroically, I'm afraid.
I was captured, and managed to escape. But what of you? The
last place I would have expected to find you is in an acting
troupe."

"They needed someone to play Jerith. Galin's wife, in *The
Tragedy of King Galin.* I have three sentences to speak." She
laughed.

He glanced at the colorful troupe. One of the women
looked like— But no, it couldn't be. "Some friends of yours

are here as well," Taja said evenly. "Narrion and his wife.
Tamra."

"What in Callabrion's name—"

"They had to flee. Narrion was on the Queen's Council—
the Shai would have imprisoned them if they hadn't left.
Narrion came here once before, with you, and he remembered it. Tamra and her friends disguised themselves as traveling actors—they got away just as the city fell."

"What of the others? Callia, and Mariel?"

"I don't know. Callia would know better than to come to
Tobol An."

"What do you mean?"

"She sent troops here," Taja said, speaking quietly. "She
wanted to find your birth records. Don't worry—the records
are safe. But we were caged, and—and tortured. I was tortured
on the ladder."

At first Val thought she was speaking metaphorically.
Poets who had had ill luck often said they had been tortured
on the ladder of fortune. But she continued to look at him
with her level gaze, and he realized that she had truly been
subjected to the ladder. She had been tortured for his sake.

He remembered thinking that Tobol An, at least, was
safe, that Taja would never know the horrors of war. He
cursed himself for his stupidity. "I'm sorry," he said, hearing
as he spoke them how inadequate the words sounded.

"It's all right, Val. It's all right. We came through, and
the troops are gone—"

"What about Narrion? He was on the Queen's Council,
you said. Didn't he have something to do with sending the
troops here?"

"He says that he wasn't in the inner circle, that he had
little power in the council. Pebr believes him, and most people in the village will follow Pebr. They respect him."

Val shook his head. "Narrion could sell wine to the Shai
if he wanted."

"Do you think he's lying?"

"I don't know. Yes. Yes, he's lying, if not about this then about something else. He's a liar. Don't trust him, Taja."

"Don't trust whom?"

Val turned quickly. Narrion stood there, his arm around Tamra. "Good fortune, Narrion, Tamra," Val said, nodding toward them in a slight bow. "Taja tells me you had nothing to do with sending the troops to Tobol An."

"No. No, that was Callia's doing. Why did she want the troops here, by the way? And why did Gobro send you here in the first place?"

Did Narrion truly not know? It would be fortunate if Callia had told no one of her suspicions. "I don't know," he said.

Narrion shook his head. "And you call me a liar, Val."

"Yes, I do. A liar, and a conspirator."

"Gobro told me to bring you to Tobol An—it was no doing of mine. I thought we'd agreed to put that behind us."

"You'd agreed. I haven't agreed to anything. And you bringing me to Tobol An was the least of your treachery."

"I explained everything to you."

"I don't trust you, Narrion. I'd give a lot to know what you're planning now."

"Nothing, Val," Narrion said. "Nothing, I assure you."

One of the actors called out, "We're rehearsing act three now. Tamra, we need you. And Taja—you too."

Taja and Tamra joined the rest of the troupe. Narrion followed them. Val watched him go. Was it just ill luck that had brought Narrion here, to Tobol An? Val would have to be vigilant now; it could prove disastrous if his cousin guessed the secret of his birth.

Taja took her place among the rest of the women. He had never realized how beautiful she was. Val shook his head. Narrion, and Etrara, and the Shai—none of them mattered now. The most important thing in the world was seeing her walk.

*   *   *

Rakera took Mariel with him when he and his men went after Callia. He assigned her two guards but Mariel thought that he might have saved himself the trouble; the pain in her head was so great she could barely move.

They reached the manor house of Lady Godemar's relatives after a half day's ride. The doors were barred against them, but once the Shai battered them down the people of the house offered no further resistance. The Shai hurried inside, spreading out to find all the members of the household.

Within a few moments everyone had been brought into the vast banquet hall. Mariel saw her sister immediately. She had changed into servant's clothing, as had the other members of the court, but the way she walked, holding her head high, was unmistakable. The two women looked at each other and Mariel looked away quickly, worried that the Shai would ask her to identify her sister. Worse, she feared that Callia would guess who had betrayed her. Poor Callia, Mariel thought. All her life she had dreaded becoming a servant.

But Rakera did not even look at Mariel. Instead he took a coin from the purse at his side. A gold sovereign, stamped in the reign of Queen Callia.

He held the coin up to each of the women in the hall, servants and nobility alike. Twice he paused for a moment and then continued on. Finally he came to Callia.

Carefully, almost gently, Rakera pulled back her peasant's hood. Her golden hair shone in the light from the windows. Even her expression was similar to that on the coin, imperious, unyielding.

No one spoke. Rakera led her to another of his men. "I want to know who the rest of her courtiers are," he said. "And anything else she chooses to tell me."

The man took her into another room. After only a few minutes Mariel heard a deep, terrible scream. None of Tariel's children can stand up to torture, Mariel thought in despair. We should all have been drowned at birth.

Another scream came from the next room. Mariel put her hands over her ears.

After what seemed like an eternity the man returned alone to the banquet hall. He went unerringly to Talenor's wife Sbarra, and then moved on to others of the court. Soldiers separated the men and women he had picked out from the servants and peasants of the household.

"Where— What happened to my sister?" Mariel asked.

"Dead," the man said.

Mariel slumped against her guard. Was this why she had been brought with them, so that she could witness the result of her treachery? Would Callia haunt her now as Gobro did? Perhaps her society would consist entirely of ghosts; she did not think she was fit for the company of the living.

"What will happen to us?" Sbarra asked.

"Nothing," Rakera said. "Nothing as long as you do as you're told. We've treated Mariel well, haven't we, Mariel?"

Very well, Mariel thought. Except for killing my brother and sister. She said nothing.

"She said something before she died, sir," Callia's torturer said. "Something about another brother."

"Another brother! How many bastards did this Tariel have?"

"This one might not be a bastard, sir. She thought he could be the rightful heir."

"The rightful heir," Rakera said. He looked thoughtful. "They will not like this news in Shai—it could prove dangerous to us, very dangerous. Was Tariel married, then?"

"He seems to have been. The queen said something about a library, birth records. I didn't fully understand her— she was babbling by then."

"Do you know the brother's name?"

"Yes, sir. Valemar, she said. And she gave me a description, and the name of a village he might have gone to if he isn't in the city. Somewhere called Tobol An."

Nine

· · · · · · ·

W AR BELONGS TO SCATHIEL," OSA,
one of the actors, said. "Everyone feels cold when
war comes."

"No—war is hot and fierce," Tamra said.

"Not for the dead," someone said. "No one is as cold as
the dead."

"I was never so cold as in this last war," Val said. "Scathiel
had this one, if none of the others."

The actors sat before the hearth in Pebr's cottage, along
with Val and Narrion and Taja. Pebr had scowled when he had
seen them coming, and had hurried off to the cottage of a
friend. He had done this every night the actors had visited; his
dislike for the court of Etrara had, if anything, grown stronger
in the months Val had been away.

Val sat on the floor near Taja and stretched his legs out
in front of him, grateful that the pain had gone. Mathary had
given him some salve for his wounds and they had healed
quickly.

"And poetry?" Taja asked. "Who does poetry belong to?"

Val looked at her, pleased. She had never spoken at one
of the gatherings before. Osa and a few of the others were
looking at her as well; probably they hadn't expected a daughter of the fisher-folk to understand court games.

"Poetry?" Osa said. The actor had pale brown hair that fell to her shoulders and curled back toward her face. She wore large round spectacles that she removed before every performance; now they glinted in the firelight. "I don't think—"

A slightly puzzled tone had entered her voice, as if she was uncertain how she had come to address one of the lower rungs. In fact, Val thought, annoyed, Taja's question had been well within the rules of the game.

"Yes, poetry, very good," he said quickly. "Poetry belongs to—to both the gods, of course. Poetry helps us ascend—"

Three or four people cut him off with cries of "Unfair! Unfair!" The point of the game was to assign each attribute to one god or another.

"Poetry is like music—"

"Not at all—poetry is more like magic—"

Val watched them as they argued. He had never seen before how unimportant these games were, how ineffectual all the court was. Etrara had fallen, and still they danced the old measures as though nothing had happened. But then he had done the same; he had even discussed virtue and ambition with one of the barbarous Shai. For the first time he realized that that man was dead now, that he would have no more discussions on any subject again.

How could he have thrown in his lot with these people, all glitter and trifles? How could he have pursued Tamra, and all the other women before her? That day when he had come back to Tobol An he had seen Taja for what she was, and it seemed to him that since then he had seen everything clearly, without pretense. He had never before understood the court's unconcern for others, their disregard for those who stood lower on the ladder. Taja had shown him more of the world in one season than he had learned in all his years in Etrara.

Finally the troupe left, and he was alone with her. They returned the chairs to the storeroom, Val's room, saying nothing. When they had finished Taja said, "Mathary told me you would save Tobol An."

"Did she?" he said, startled. "I wonder why."

"Arion saved us, I think," she said. "He turned the battle against Etrara, and drew the troops away from the village. That's why the ghost-knight didn't warn us about him. Because he was an enemy of Callia, and so were we. So he was our friend."

He did not know what to say. He was unused to her bluntness, her openness about the royal family. No one from the court had mentioned Queen Callia once during their exile. How strange her manner was, after all, how different from the cloying subtleties of the court. How new it all was.

"Taja," he said.

She turned to look at him, one of the mugs left by the company still in her hand.

"Did you get the sonnet I sent you?" he asked.

She nodded.

"Did you—did you like it?"

She set the mug down. "I don't know, Val," she said. "The actors say that you used to write poetry to Tamra, and even to Callia, before she became queen. And how many were there before her?"

How well she knew him, after all: she could strip him bare with a look. She had summed up his life in a phrase, the way the poet-mages did in the old books. "Tamra meant nothing," he said. "The others meant nothing—"

"Then how do I know what I mean to you? If this is a game, something you do for your own amusement—"

"No. No, it's nothing like that."

"If this is a game, then it's one I don't know how to play. And I don't understand why you would want to send me poetry otherwise. I'm a daughter of fisher-folk, and you—you're a lord, a king."

"I send you poetry because you're beautiful. When I came back to Tobol An after the war it was like returning home. I saw you for what you were that day—"

"You saw me dressed in court finery. I'm nothing like that."

"Taja, I swear by Callabrion—"

"Hush," she said. "Don't swear. What would I do now, if I were a lady of the court?"

"You would thank me for the sonnet. But you would leave me in doubt as to your meaning, and I would have to write you another, and probably a few more after that. Then you would chance to drop something of yours while talking to me—a scarf, perhaps, or a handkerchief. And I would wear it on my sleeve, so others would know that I courted you."

She shook her head, smiling a little. "Why is it all so complicated?"

"It's not complicated. It's amusing, enjoyable—"

"A game," she said.

"No—no, it's—"

"Good night, Val," she said, still smiling, and turned to go.

The days ran on, one into the other, and the company created a court in miniature in Tobol An. They talked about the attributes of the gods, about the Virtues and Vices, about the old poetry and plays they were finding in the library. But no one spoke of politics, or the Shai, and no one mentioned what they all surely thought, that they would have to make plans before their money ran out. None of them, Val knew, would be at all suited to the life of the fisher-folk.

Val had not spoken directly to Narrion since his first day in Tobol An, though he had watched him carefully. Was his cousin speaking the truth for once when he said he had nothing planned? How could he trust Narrion after all the other man had done to him?

Rehearsals of *The Tragedy of King Galin* continued. Taja suggested that they stage the play in the library, but a few of the actors disliked the presence of so much magic and the company decided to use the open plain instead. They had one final rehearsal, and then they announced the date of their performance.

On the day of the play Val arrived at the makeshift stage

early. Nearly the entire village had turned out on the plain, and he was hard-pressed to find a place from which to see the stage. Finally he sat on a slight rise at the back of the crowd, close to Mathary.

The Prologue stepped forward. As he watched the woman speak Val felt a superstitious dread; the last play he had seen had been marred by the presence of the Maegrim at just such a moment. He looked at the plain around him, unable to help himself. The sound of the ghost-knight's trumpet came toward them, faint and far away.

The Prologue stopped. "Soldiers!" someone on the stage said, and at the same moment someone in the audience called out, fearfully, "The Shai!"

"They've come for you," Mathary said to Val.

"What?"

"They've come for you. They know who you are."

He did not think to doubt her. "What should I do?" he asked.

"Play a part," she said. "You should be good at that, at least."

He studied her for a moment, not understanding. Then he ran to the stage. "Give me a costume," he said urgently to Osa. "Teach me what to say."

"What?" Osa said. She peered at him nearsightedly.

"The Shai. They're here for me. Find a costume for me— they'll never think to look for me among women."

Taja grinned at him. "You can be the King's Pen," she said. "You'll be on the stage in almost every act, but you only have two sentences to speak. Do you think you can do that?"

Val nodded. "Quickly," he said. Someone handed him a costume of faded velvet and a chain of office, and he hurried behind the stage to change.

The costume had been made for a woman; it was too broad in the hips and chest and too tight at the waist. The breeches, Callabrion be thanked, were almost long enough; he remembered the tall woman who had spoken the Prologue at court. He left them unfastened and tied a belt around his waist; to his relief the tunic came down far enough to cover the belt. He ran his hand over his face, glad that he had shaved that morning in honor of the play. Then he tucked his amulet beneath the tunic, said a brief prayer to Callabrion, and went to find the others.

A few of the Shai stood on the stage; in their gold breast-plates and helmets they looked like actors in a play about strange and fantastic outlanders. "We are looking for a man named Valemar," one of them said.

Val glanced up, then looked away quickly. He had only caught a glimpse, nothing more, but he felt certain that he had seen the man who had shaken Arion's hand the day they had all been betrayed: Rakera, the commander of the Shai. He remembered that Arion had called the commander brilliant, and his heart sank. How could he hope to fool this man?

The troupe of actors clustered by the stage. Val joined them hurriedly, standing near Taja. No one in the audience spoke. With his senses sharpened by fear Val could see Narrion and Pebr and Mathary, and beyond them more soldiers guarding Duchess Mariel.

"Valemar," Rakera said again. "We know he is here. Bring me the lady Mariel."

One of the soldiers led Mariel to the stage. "Where is he?" the commander asked her. "You know him—tell me which one he is."

Mariel looked out at the audience and then at the small group of actors. Despite his apprehension Val felt shocked at the change he saw in her face; she looked haggard, bled white, as if she had been tortured on the ladder. "I don't—I don't see him," she said.

"Come, Lady Mariel. You know what happens when you lie."

"I don't—he's not here."

The soldiers began to move through the audience. Would Mariel betray him? And what of Narrion? The other man had given Val scant reason to trust him.

Two of the soldiers came over to the troupe by the stage

and looked at them closely. "Actors," one of them said. "They pretend to be other people. They're all women."

The other soldier peered at Val. He did not seem to have understood his companion. Could it be that they had no plays at all in Shai?

Finally the second man shrugged and moved away. "Women," he said, sounding doubtful.

"Yes," his companion said. "So I said."

The soldiers returned to the stage. To his horror Val saw the man who had studied him speak to Rakera. Both men turned toward him, and then the commander grinned. "Come," he said. "Let's see a play." He led the soldiers off the stage and they took seats among the audience.

Val looked at Taja. She had not even had time to teach him his lines. "Don't stand like that," she whispered.

"What?" he said. He had been leaning against the stage; his legs were shaking.

"Don't sprawl like that. Women take up less space than men."

"What are my lines?"

She told him. They marched onto the stage and stood ranged behind the king.

For the first few scenes Val saw and heard nothing of what went on around him. He left the stage with the king and court and returned with them, and all the while he wanted only to glance in the soldiers' direction. They must have guessed, he thought; surely he looked nothing like a trained actor.

By the second act, though, he had calmed enough to pay attention to the play. He saw with admiration how Osa, the actor playing the king, commanded most of the space around her, how she became a king in the eyes of the audience. He saw how the wicked councilor managed to suggest disloyalty with a few words and a manner of standing. He heard gasps from the audience when Tamra, dressed as a fortune-teller, spoke her prophecy. And soon, to his great surprise, he began to look forward to saying his lines. He was a man disguised as a woman disguised as a man; the part would call for great subtlety.

Finally he heard his cue. He risked a look into the audience and saw that the Shai were watching him intently. He faltered. What had he been about to say? Taja whispered something but he could hear only the blood pounding in his ears.

"My lord must guard against his treachery," he said finally, warning the king against his evil councilor.

The play continued around him. Val could not bring himself to look directly at the audience but it seemed to him that no one moved, that his deception had been successful. But as they marched off at the end of the scene Taja passed him and whispered, "Too loud."

He nodded, feeling his fear return. Had the Shai noticed?

Nearly everyone appeared in the final scene. The evil councilor poisoned Taja, the king's wife; she lay on the stage and winked at Val with her head turned away from the audience. Finally, too late, the king began to realize the extent of the treachery around him; the nobles had conspired against him, the trap in the garden had been laid, the tragedy continued inexorably to its end.

Despite himself Val began to get caught up in the drama unfolding in front of him. The king and his councilor killed each other in a duel and lay in a heap together. "And so are good and evil strangely mixed," Val said. Then all that remained was to carry the three dead bodies off the stage.

He had never heard any audience applaud so loudly and so long, not even when Callabrion climbed to the heavens at the Feast of the Ascending God. He looked out into the crowd and saw that the Shai had gone. The audience was applauding for him, he realized, for him and for themselves; together they had triumphed over the Shai.

He jumped down from the stage and joined the crowd of actors and villagers. "Val!" three or four people said at once. "We did it, Val. We fooled them!"

Pebr laughed and clapped him on the back; Val had never seen the old man so demonstrative. Even Mathary was looking at him with something that might have been approval. "You did well, Val," someone said. He turned, and saw Narrion.

"Yes, I did, didn't I?" he said, grinning.

"Why were the Shai looking for you?" Narrion said quietly.

"I don't know."

"Come, Val—surely you must have some idea."

"I tell you I don't know," Val said, irritated. He sought Taja in the crowd and waved at her, then pulled away from Narrion.

He had been wrong; he could not be at ease at Tobol An, could not be an idle courtier, ignoring the world around him. He had to spend every moment guarding against his cousin. It seemed as if all the world knew his secret: Taja and Callia and Mariel, and now the Shai knew it as well. It would be only a matter of time before Narrion guessed, or bribed someone to tell him.

And then what? What would Narrion do with the knowledge, Narrion with all his ambition? My lord must guard against his treachery, he thought.

"Why so grim, Val?" Taja said.

At any other time he would have been glad of her concern for him. Now, though, his worry forced all other thoughts from his mind. "Narrion," he said. "He guesses something."

"Why don't you tell him the truth? He might have some idea of what to do."

"I can imagine the kind of idea he'd have. King Narrion the First—he'd like that."

"Do you think so? Is he that ambitious?"

Val laughed harshly. "He'd climb the ladder and storm heaven if he could," he said. "Cast down Callabrion and Scathiel and rule in their place."

Taja looked doubtful.

"He's an ambitious man," Val said. "Do you know why I came to Tobol An the first time? He'd convinced me that our lives were in danger, that we had to flee the anger of the king. And then he returned to Etrara, betrayed Gobro, married Tamra, became a council member. All the while I was in exile he was spinning a web so complex I'm still not certain I've unraveled it all."

"Well, then—what will you do?"

"I don't know. I know only that I have to be on my guard against him. He said he has no plans, but I don't believe him."

"The queen is dead—did you know that?"

"Callia? Dead?"

"Narrion managed to talk to Duchess Mariel during the play. The Shai killed Callia, and Talenor as well. There's only Mariel left now, and she's under guard. She said Talenor turned traitor—that's why they killed him. He tried to offer the Shai a masque."

"Traitor?" Val said. He felt sorrow for the man's death, but there was relief as well. Talenor would surely have pointed him out to the Shai.

They talked a little more, and then Taja left. He would have to decide what to do soon; his few sovereigns would not last much longer. And then what? Perhaps he could join the acting troupe, and travel over the countryside. He laughed. He did not think he was much of an actor.

A week later Val left his room to walk along the cliffside. He had spent the day reading and thinking and had not realized how late it had become until he stepped outside. The strange early dusk had fallen, casting a sooty darkness over the village. Spring had failed to arrive, Val knew; trees which should have been putting forth new green leaves remained stark and bare. Folks in the neighboring countryside had planted their crops but whispered about the possibility of failed harvests, of plants dead in the ground.

He left the path and walked toward the ocean. As he came toward the ruined arch of Sleeping Koregath he heard the sound of voices above the hiss of the waves. At first he thought the women he heard were rehearsing a play. But then a voice spoke louder than the others, and he realized that Narrison was there with them.

Val started to move forward. Then he stopped, and without thinking about it he crouched behind the ruin and listened. Cold wind whistled through the arch.

"Say it again," Narrion said. "It's not like acting, where you can drop a line or two. If you forget a single word here we might as well have done nothing."

"Great king," one of the women said. "Sovereign and ruler, we beseech you—"

"*Our* sovereign. Our sovereign and ruler."

"Our sovereign and ruler—"

"Narrion!" someone said, another woman's voice. The actor broke off. "Is that you?"

"Over here," Narrion said.

"Good fortune, Narrion," the second woman said, coming up to the group of actors. Taja, Val thought. "I found the book you asked for."

"I thank you. And I wanted to ask you about another matter as well. Do you know why the Shai asked for Val?"

Val leaned forward and peered around the arch. The actors were black shapes against the dark gray sky; they looked a little like ruined stone themselves.

"No," Taja said. "No, I wondered that myself."

"Have you asked him?" Narrion said.

"Yes. He says he has no idea. What are you doing out here in the dark? It's cold as Scathiel's heart here."

"We were just going in," Narrion said. "We'll walk you back to the village."

The actors left. After a while Val followed them, walking slowly. What in Callabrion's name had Narrion been doing? Who was the great king? There was no king in Etrara now, nothing but—

He stopped. Nothing but the Shai, and their kings who died each year at the Feasts of the Ascending and Descending

Gods. Narrion had been rehearsing a play to present to them, to the ancient enemy of Etrara. Like Talenor and Arion, he had decided that the quickest way to rise on the ladder was by treachery.

Val continued, barely feeling the wind against his cloak. How much would Narrion do to gain the Shai's favor? Narrion had been there at the play, and had heard them ask for Valemar. Would he betray the man he thought was his cousin in exchange for a little power?

Val thought that he would. Narrion had proved that he had no morals at all; he pretended to work for several sides at once but his true loyalty was to himself alone. He had already killed at least one man, and helped poison another; Val thought he would surely be capable of killing again to get what he wanted.

Val hurried toward the village and Pebr's cottage. Suddenly he felt the cold; he started to shiver and could not stop.

The next day Val went to the cottage Narrion and Tamra rented from one of the fisher-folk. "Val!" Narrion said, looking up from the book he was reading. "I'm glad you've come. I've been thinking about that strange visit the Shai paid us."

"Have you?" Val said.

If Narrion noticed the edge in Val's voice he didn't show it. "Do you have any idea why they were so interested in you?" he asked.

"No, I don't. Why do you want to know? Are you planning to sell the information to the highest bidder?"

"I wish you trusted me more, Val."

"How can I trust you? Look where trust got me—a month in exile, shivering in fear of the king. And all the while you were living comfortably in Etrara—"

"I told you—Gobro said he wanted you in Tobol An."

"Gobro said. And then you helped poison him. Do you see why I can't trust you? What are you plotting now?"

"Nothing."

"Come, Narrion—I'm sick of lies."

"I haven't lied to you since you returned to Etrara."

"You lied the moment I stepped in the door, when you said you were glad I'd come. You weren't glad to see me—you wanted to ask me another of your endless questions. And how can you say you're plotting nothing? I heard you yesterday, rehearsing a play—"

To his surprise Narrion laughed. "Yes, we were rehearsing something," he said. "Is that treasonous?"

"It can be. Talenor offered the Shai a masque—perhaps you had the same idea."

"They killed Talenor for his masque, didn't they? Poor man—he was never very clever, for all his learning." Narrion brushed his black hair out of his eyes and handed the book he had been reading to Val. "Taja got this for me from the library," he said.

Invocations to Callabrion and Scathiel, Val read. "Callabrion and Scathiel!" he said. "What have you to do with the gods?" he asked.

"I'm a member of the Society of Fools," Narrion said. "I thought you knew."

Val nodded. Most people thought of the Fools as little more than jesters; they forgot that the Society was bound to Scathiel in the same way the astronomer-priests were bound to Callabrion.

Despite his mistrust of Narrion Val smiled a little, remembering last year's Feast on the longest day of the year. The sun had shone brightly; it had seemed impossible to believe that Scathiel had ascended and the days would grow shorter again.

The Society of Fools danced and capered through the city. They wore masks shaped like skulls and clothing painted like skeletons; they were there to remind the revelers of the death that lay beneath life, the misrule beneath apparent rule, the coming winter threatening the beautiful summer day.

For one day they had taken over the offices of king and priest, councilor and commander of the army. Riot was let loose in the streets as the Shadow King, the Fool acting in Gobro's place, issued one ludicrous proclamation after another. Val saw a Fool march a battalion of soldiers backward, heard another Fool disguised as a professor give a lecture in praise of mince pies. Long lines had formed in front of the bakeries and wineshops; the Shadow King had decreed that all pastries and wine were free.

The masks of the Fools covered their faces completely but Val thought he saw Narrion at least once in the streets that day. He listened, fascinated, as the man sang the traditional songs, "Bones Brown as Ale" and "The Lord of All Misrule." Like all the male fools he had a dark and melodious voice.

When he had finished singing the Fool picked up a small child and tossed her to another skeleton-clad man. The girl screamed, but with excitement more than fear. The second man put the child down, gave her a sweet and twirled gracefully away.

"Callabrion hasn't ascended this year," Narrion said now. "Surely you must know that, or guess."

Val nodded.

"I want to restore him to the heavens," Narrion said.

"Restore Callabrion?" Val asked. "Why? That hardly seems a fit occupation for a queen's councilor."

"I'm barely a councilor any longer. Mariel and Callia used me to get the poison and then left me to my own devices. I have no support at all on the council."

"So you were a pawn as well, just as I was. Not a very pleasant feeling, is it, Narrion?"

Narrion shrugged. "Mariel is a prisoner, and Callia is dead. The council is gone. But even if they still ruled in Etrara they would soon cease to matter. If Callabrion does not ascend the days will grow darker and darker, and finally the sun itself will go out."

"And you think you can persuade Callabrion to return? With that book?"

"If not with this one then another. I've spent hours in the

library—it's amazing what's hidden there. People have no idea."

That's true, they don't, Val thought, remembering the birth records Taja had found. Was that what his cousin had been searching for? It was difficult to believe that Narrion was concerned with Callabrion. Had he somehow found the records, learned the truth about Val's birth?

He had to get away from the cottage, Val thought, had to get outside and clear his head. Narrion seemed to be telling the truth, but he had sounded as sincere when he had led Val into exile. Surely if Narrion wanted to betray him, to turn him over to the Shai, he would not admit to it. "Good fortune, Narrion," he said.

Heavy rain was falling when Val stepped outside. He wrapped himself tightly in his cloak and walked toward Pebr's cottage. Had Narrion been truthful for once? He couldn't know; he was no poet-mage, able to understand everything in a man's heart. If Narrion was honest then Val could stay in Tobol An. But if the other man had lied then Val's life was in danger.

Val hurried down the path. Could he afford to trust Narrion, to wager his life on nothing but his cousin's promises? If the past was any guide Narrion was treacherous indeed; Val would be open to attack from the Shai every day that he stayed in Tobol An.

No, there was only one way left to him now, the way Taja had shown him when she had come to the palace so long ago. It was time to return to Etrara and claim the kingship, to seek out Andosto and free the city from the tyranny of the Shai.

He was running now. He reached the cottage, but neither Taja nor Pebr was home.

Panic seemed to grip him; the tap of a branch against the window made him start as if the Shai were already in Tobol An. He could not wait for Taja to tell her his plans. He packed his few belongings quickly, putting the heavy Shai sword in with the rest of his things, and left the cottage to hire a horse.

He felt his amulet through the cloth of his tunic. Whatever his shortcomings he was certain he would prove a better ruler than Gobro, or Callia, or the Shai. And if he took the throne he would finally be safe, would no longer have to fear Narrion's treachery or danger from the Shai.

He paid a sovereign for a horse, and rode off into the Forest of Thole. The next face to be minted on a sovereign, he vowed, would be his own.

Taja took a book from the pile in front of her and opened it, then dipped her pen in the inkwell to record the title. It was getting late; she should finish these books and then go home. Pebr worried if she stayed out too long.

Something caused her to look up. A noise? No, she could hear nothing. She glanced around but no one had come into the catalogue room, not villager or soldier or ghost.

The strange feeling returned. It was almost as if she had grown another organ like eyes or ears, something that helped her perceive whatever it was that had happened. She shivered.

She had had this sensation before, but never so strongly. She rested her head on the table helplessly, waiting for the visitation to end.

Val had told her about the Maegrim in Etrara. She had listened entranced, wondering what it would be like to see first six women and then seven, all the while hoping or fearing that her fortune would change. But now, as wave after wave of the unearthly feeling washed over her, the Maegrim did not seem nearly so quaint. Now she felt certain that they were calling her.

She shivered again. She did not want to be one of the Maegrim, did not want to stop her work or leave her family whenever she heard their summons. It was dangerous now, very dangerous, to put on the hood of badger skin and cast people's fortunes. Val said that Callia had demanded the names of all the Maegrim, and the women probably fared even worse under the Shai.

The sending stopped. Taja raised her head and took

several deep breaths. Then she put on her cloak and went to find Mathary.

"The Maegrim?" Mathary said. "No, I don't think it's the Maegrim."

They sat before the fire in Mathary's cottage. Although the old woman had placed lamps and candles on the tables and mantelpiece these did not seem able to penetrate the gloom Taja remembered from her other visits. Shadows gathered in the corners, parting when the fire danced high to reveal shelves and shelves of stoppered ceramic jars. Even in winter Mathary's house smelled of wild growing things, of tangled roots and loamy soil.

"What is it then?" Taja asked.

"Someone is using magic."

"Someone—here? In the village?"

"Aye."

"But who?"

"I don't know. I don't recognize it."

"What are you going to do?"

"Do?" Even in the candlelight Taja could see the web of cataracts covering Mathary's eye. "I'll do nothing, child. He'll reveal himself, whoever he is."

"He?"

Mathary nodded. "It's a man's magic, I can tell that much. You'll learn the difference soon enough."

What did the old woman mean? Taja did not want to learn the old magic; Pebr had warned her about it often enough. "What—"

"I had a dream the night you were born," Mathary said. "It was cold that day, but Callabrion ruled in the heavens—we knew that the days would grow warmer soon. In my dream the wind blew the door open and it seemed that spring had come into the room—I could smell the scent of roses and fresh grasses. My cat walked through the door, the cat that had died, oh, ten years before. And she said to me, 'Take care of this one. She's Sbona's child.' "

Taja shook her head impatiently. She did not want to hear Mathary's dreams; she had come on a far more pressing errand. "But what if the man's dangerous?" she asked. "Shouldn't you—"

"The knight in the forest hasn't warned us of any danger. The best thing we can do now is wait."

Taja nodded, dissatisfied. Did Mathary know what was best for Tobol An, or had she lost her wits, as Pebr thought? Her mind seemed to wander more and more these days; Taja thought she might be too frail to be entrusted with the care of the entire village.

She bid good fortune to the other woman and began to leave. As she put on her cloak Mathary said, "Don't say anything about this to your uncle, child. You know how he feels about wizardry."

The sending returned the next day, while Taja was in the library. She had been sitting with her pen poised over the catalogue, thinking about Val. He had not returned to the cottage the night before, and someone in the village had said he had seen him ride north, toward Etrara.

Val was free to come and go as he liked, of course. Still she could not help but wonder if he had gone to claim the kingship. And if he had, why hadn't he waited for her? She knew that his protestations of love for her were part of a courtly game, nothing more, but she thought that he might at least have told her of his plans.

The sending came again. She forced herself to stand and go outside, and then to follow its source down to the cliffs.

Narrion and the acting troupe stood by the arch of Sleeping Koregath. Taja understood immediately that they had chosen the ruin because it remained from the time of the wizards; they thought that it might still hold magic within it.

"Great king," one of the women said. "Our sovereign and ruler, lord of summer, god of the waxing year . . ."

As she listened, horrified, Taja sensed the presence of magic all around her. The currents were not focused, as she somehow knew they should be, but wild, undisciplined. She felt the invocation as a terrible wrongness, a sickness that invaded her soul.

Narrion began to speak, reciting an invocation to Callabrion. Was he a poet-mage? She had heard that wizards' verses had no power if they were not composed at the very moment of their sending, though of course the mages all used the same ritual names and phrases. But Narrion seemed to have memorized his poem beforehand, and he had anchored his spell badly; he had used an inappropriate ritual verse at the beginning and an ill-chosen word as his keystone.

Magic gusted around them, discordant and fierce as wind. The waves beneath them crashed to shore. Narrion continued, speaking with difficulty, reciting a poem about leaving the pleasures of earth and returning to heaven. What in Sbona's name was he trying to do?

One of the actors cried out in terror. For a moment Taja saw two ruins on the cliffside where there had been one before; the actors were turning to stone like the giant Sleeping Koregath. Her lips began to move, whispering poetry.

Nothing changed. She spoke louder, chanting an opening ritual verse. She chose her keystone, understanding only as she delivered the words how the poem had to be constructed, how to use her meter and alliteration. The poem required another keystone; she found one almost without thinking and hurried on.

Narrion continued to speak. She felt the force of his will, strong as the magic he had called up. The actors were immobile now, caught in stone, but still Narrion refused to stop. Finally she heard his voice slow, saw his hand freeze as he lifted it. He had turned to stone like the others, captured by the magic he had raised.

Suddenly she knew the words she had to speak, saw them as clearly as if they had been written in one of the books of magic in the library. She chanted her verses more easily now, unhampered by Narrion. The wind of magic lessened; the dreadful torrents subsided. The actors began to move slowly, as if waking.

The arch moved too; she had gone too far, had roused the giant. There was the terrible sound of boulders breaking. She spoke her final verse quickly, using both her keystones, and Koregath drifted back into his deep slumber.

Narrion came toward her. She had never seen him look so pale, so uncertain. His long hair had knotted in the wind. "I thank you," he said. His voice was hoarse.

"What—what were you doing?" she asked.

Narrion looked around. She followed his gaze and saw a crowd of old people and children, everyone who hadn't set out to sea that day.

"I tried to summon Callabrion. He hasn't ascended this year—the days grow no lighter, and the trees are bare. I thought to—to convince him to return to the heavens. The book you found for me in the library had some invocations, and I thought—" He moved his arms behind his back and stretched in one supple gesture, as if trying to convince himself that he hadn't turned to stone. "I didn't know you were a poet-mage."

"I'm not," she said abruptly, and turned to go.

She made her way toward her cottage, seeing almost nothing around her. She opened the door cautiously, but Pebr was not at home. He had been among the crowd of people at the arch; she thought that he must be horrified at what she had done. She sat in a chair by the hearth and put her head in her hands.

Not the Maegrim, no. She was something worse than that, far worse: a poet-mage. How else had she known how to speak the invocation, to use the keystones?

Even the soldiers from Etrara had known who she was; the man who had tortured her on the ladder had called her "wizard's get." She remembered a saying Pebr was fond of: "Even a dog might speak a prophecy." Had everyone known, everyone but her?

She shuddered. Pebr had told her that poet-mages never

lived long; their enemies feared their power and found ways to kill them. Someone had killed King Tariel's wizards, and once, long ago, a storm of magic had been loosed in Tobol An. She did not want such terrifying power.

She looked up. Well, then, she would renounce it. There was no call for a poet-mage in Tobol An; Mathary nursed the sick, delivered the babies, made up charms for love or fertility or good fortune. She would assure Pebr that she would never recite another invocation, and convince the villagers that they had not heard her speak a word at the arch. Mathary would know, of course, but Mathary could be trusted to say nothing.

A memory came to her then. She was riding hard through the falling snow in the still forest of Thole; she was hurrying to deliver her message to Val in Etrara. How would he receive the news that he was the true king? What would he think when everything he had ever known proved to be false?

She knew now how he felt; the same thing had happened to her. Only she had learned that she was something far more dangerous: a poet-mage.

Val had gone on to Etrara, she thought now. And suddenly she saw to Val's heart, understood everything that had happened since Val had visited Narrion. He thinks Narrion is his enemy, she thought. He thinks he'll betray him to the Shai. But Narrion had only been trying to summon Callabrion, to return warmth and light to the land. The "great king" had not been a king of the Shai but the summer god.

It was time for her to claim her birthright, whether she wanted to or not. She had to help Val, had go after him and warn him.

Her heart lifted; it would be good to see him again. It seemed to her that he had changed during the war; he had gained in wisdom, become more thoughtful. His innate courtesy had grown to include her, and all the people of Tobol An.

And it would be good to help him claim the throne of Etrara, she thought, remembering all the books filled with heroic deeds that she had read in the library. She put on her cloak and hurried from the room.

*   *   *

The daylight faded almost as soon as Taja entered the forest. She rode hard for several hours more, hoping to reduce the distance between her and Val. Finally the light disappeared altogether, and she knew that if she caught up with him she would pass him all unknowing in the dark. She dismounted and spread her cloak on the ground.

The soft earth, covered with leaves and twigs, felt very cold. She turned and wrapped herself in her cloak, trying to get comfortable. No wonder Narrion wanted to summon Callabrion, she thought, cursing the early darkness. But who would have guessed that he would be so religious? Val had told her that Narrion might be a member of the Society of Fools and sworn to Scathiel—what business did he have with Callabrion? But she was not versed in the mysteries of the Society; misrule needed rule, apparently, as winter needed summer.

She thought of Val, of Narrion and Tamra and the quarrelsome, treacherous royal family of Etrara. And then somehow she was in the city, drifting silently through the streets like one of its famous ghosts. She saw the burned ruins of houses and knew that the Shai had set them on fire to punish the inhabitants for some disobedience or other. She saw soldiers returned from the wars; some had turned to thievery after they had gone through their meager wages, and others, maimed in battle, sat near the fountains and statues with their beggar's bowls in front of them. The sky was edged with smoke and the streets were eerie, silent; other than the soldiers and caged criminals few people ventured out-of-doors.

She was in the palace now, moving through the marble corridors. It was darker than she remembered; the Shai had hung heavy tapestries over the windows and the only light came from iron lamps. She went to the royal apartments, passed the rooms where she had delivered her message to Val. Someone moved through the gloom reciting verses; she thought he must be one of the pet poets Val had mentioned. At the end of the corridor Taja saw the woman the Shai had called Duchess Mariel. "I told you—I don't know where Riel is," Mariel was saying. "Is Callia there with you? Will she torment me next?"

Now Taja could make out the ghost in the corridor with Mariel. His irises shone silver, and his jewels sparkled in the sooty darkness. She had seen his face before, stamped on coins: King Gobro.

"This is why I stayed, isn't it?" Mariel said. "Callia wanted me to go with her, but I knew I had to stay here. To beg your forgiveness."

"She told me she would be here," Gobro said. "But I can't find her anywhere."

"I'm sorry. I'm sorry I killed you. Everything's gone wrong since we gave you the poison. You were right—it would have been better to make peace with the Shai. You were always right—we never saw what a good ruler you were. We never knew."

The ghost said nothing.

"Is it better where you are?" Mariel asked. "Is it simpler? All the complexities of your life, reduced to one foolish riddle: Where is Riel? And what will my question be, I wonder? Where is Gobro?"

"She's never been late before."

"I'm sorry," Mariel said. A dreadful note had come into her voice, a cry of terror and longing and fear. "I'm sorry I killed you—I'm sorry, I'm sorry!"

Taja struggled to come awake. The dream was ending, Callabrion be thanked; if she could only open her eyes she would be out of the dreadful city Etrara had become. She saw a jagged hill, and two figures, small against its bulk, struggling to the top. She woke.

For a moment she did not know where she was. Then she felt the cold around her, saw the cobwebs of fog still clinging to the trees. She was in the haunted Forest of Thole, and she was searching for Val.

She stood and mounted quickly, trying to forget the painful lonely sound of Mariel's screams. She knew beyond any doubt that her dream had shown her what Etrara had become, that the understanding she had gained let her see things as they truly were. And if the city had changed so greatly then the sooner Val ascended to the throne the better.

Val woke from a confused dream of Etrara, of the hot sun striking the green copper dome of the observatory and the golden turrets of the palace. He sat up in the near darkness and rummaged through his traveling bag, finally finding one of the slices of Taja's oatmeal bread he had packed the day before.

As he ate, and later as he mounted his horse and rode through the forest, he struggled to remember his dream. But he saw only the cold white fog and bare outlines of the trees around him, and the last remnants of the dream vanished.

The fog grew thicker; he could barely see the trees in front of him. His horse moved to the left and he let the animal go, trusting in its ability to find the path.

The cold matched his mood; he felt cold within as well. Had Narrion been about to sell him to the Shai? He was alone, in the forest as in the world, with no one but himself to protect him against treachery. He drove his horse forward.

A few moments later the horse moved to the left again, and he looked around him. Hadn't he seen this path before, those three trees together and the bare one near it? The bare tree's limbs splayed outward; he could imagine them as cage supports, or as an anchor for a hangman's noose.

The horse turned left again. There could no longer be any doubt; he remembered this clump of mushrooms growing by the side of the path. He reined in his horse and looked around him.

Fog still shrouded the forest. He dismounted, intending to study the path, and as he did so he knocked his traveling bag from the saddle.

The bag felt light to him, too light. He looked through it and saw to his horror that he had no food left; he had eaten all the bread and hard winter apples he had packed. How long had he been wandering through the forest? It had seemed like a day, a day and a night, but now he thought, terrified, that it might have been longer.

Who had raised this magic? It could have been Narrion or Mariel or the poet-mage of the Shai; he had no shortage of enemies. As he stood, holding the pack in his hands like a witless man, he heard the sound of hoofbeats on the path.

He turned, straining to hear them. In the dense fog the sound seemed to come from every direction. How many horses? He moved off the path quickly.

The fog parted. Taja rode toward him, her eyes finding him unerringly. "Val!" she said, dismounting quickly. "Thank the gods I've found you!"

"Taja?" he said. "Were you behind this magic?"

"Magic?" She studied him for a moment and then nodded. "Oh, I see. You were lost in the forest. No, I think the forest itself did that. It wanted me to find you."

"The forest? Why?"

"Because I have things to tell you. Listen—Narrion tried to use magic yesterday."

He nodded. What mischief had Narrion done now?

"He recited a spell by the arch of Sleeping Koregath," she said. "He was trying to return Callabrion to the heavens. You thought he wanted to betray you, but he didn't."

"He told me something of this," Val said slowly. "But I didn't believe him. I don't think I believe you either. How can I, after all Narrion's done to me?"

"Because I understand him. And I understand you as well. I—I think I'm a poet-mage. Narrion's magic failed, and I spoke the verses to counter it. I knew exactly which words to use, and how to use them, how to find a keystone . . . and I know other things as well. I know why you're returning to Etrara, why you want to claim the kingship."

Once again she seemed to find his heart, to understand him effortlessly. "Do you mean Narrion was telling the truth?" he asked slowly.

Taja nodded. "He would never harm you," she said. "He

would send you into exile, yes, and use you for his own purposes. But even when he brought you to Tobol An he knew you would be safe."

Relief overcame him; his legs nearly gave way under the weight of it. He had thought himself alone, had not understood the strength of Taja's concern for him. "He told the truth," Val said, grinning. He hugged Taja, spun her around on the path. "He told the truth! He broke his long habit of silence and told me everything. And I—I was so used to treachery I could not believe him."

"Do you still want to return to Etrara?" Taja asked. "Or did you only want the throne to revenge yourself against Narrion?"

He thought of Gobro's vast expenses, of Callia's disastrous war. Whatever happened he knew he could rule Etrara better than his half-brother and sister. "I hope my reasons are better than that," he said slowly. He took a deep breath. "I would like to see Etrara free of the Shai. And I would like to return home."

"Well, then," she said. "You'll need a poet-mage."

"You'll come with me?" he asked, surprised.

"Something brought us together, a king and a poet-mage. Narrion may have sent you to Tobol An for King Gobro's sake, but I think that we were meant to meet."

Val nodded slowly. "You may be right," he said. "There are more things working here than even Narrion could know." He thought for a moment. "I learned something while I was a prisoner that might help us. But it's dangerous— It's— No, I won't tell you."

"What do you mean? Is it something that might save Etrara?"

He nodded reluctantly.

"Come, Val—if it can help us—"

"A man in Shai, my jailer—he talked to me about their poet-mage, Kotheg. He said that Kotheg had spent the night on Wizard's Hill in Shai, that to gain power a man—or a woman—must spend the night there. And that by the end of the night they would be either dead, or mad, or a poet."

"That was my dream!" she said. "I dreamt I went up a mountain. And Val, you were there with me. It was a true dream, then, a dream of the future."

"No," Val said. "No, I have no right to ask this of you. You can't know what will happen. Dead, or mad—"

"I know what you're hiding from me, Val. I know that Callia's mage Penriel did not go to Wizard's Hill, and neither did Anthiel. But Kotheg did, and he was able to overcome them both."

Taja hesitated a moment. "Something tells me to go with you," she said. "I think that I will not be whole, will not be a true poet-mage, until I spend the night on Wizard's Hill. I want to claim my birthright, just as you do."

He turned to her. Only an hour ago he had been alone, fleeing Tobol An in fear of Narrion's treachery; now his fear was gone and he had a companion, a poet-mage, at his side. The outcome was still uncertain; it was probably folly to think that they could walk unseen into the enemy's country. But his heart was strangely light. "Well, then," he said. "I thank you."

Val and Taja returned to Tobol An, intending to look for maps of Shai in the library. They decided to tell no one but Pebr about their decision; the Shai might return, Val said, and it would be best if as few people as possible knew where they had gone.

"No," Pebr said. "This is lunacy—I won't let you go."

"We're going anyway, Uncle," Taja said. "We just wanted to tell you first."

"No, you're not. Think about what you're doing—going off into the enemy's country, for one thing, and that isn't even the worst of it. You could be dead at the end of it, isn't that what you told me?"

"Nothing will happen to us."

"You can't promise me that. If you survive this you'll be a—a mage, and mages never live long."

"I have to go, Uncle."

Pebr sighed. He looked frail, defeated, his arms thin as bare branches. "I would have spared you this if I could," she said softly.

"You're the only family I have," he said.

"I know. But I'll come back to you, I promise."

"Your father said the same thing," Pebr said.

"What did Pebr mean?" Val asked Taja. They had spent a few hours in the library but had not found a good map of Shai. Now they were heading back, hurrying toward Pebr's cottage before the light failed. "You promised you'd come back, and he said that your father had said the same thing."

"I don't know," Taja said. "My parents were fisher-folk—they lived in a village to the south, in Mirro An. They drowned in a storm when I was very young, and Pebr brought me here. I suppose my father told Pebr he'd always come back from the sea."

"That's strange," Val said.

"What?"

"Look. Over there. Your uncle's talking to Mathary."

"No!"

"Yes. Near the cliffs."

"By all the gods," Taja said slowly. "I wonder what they found to talk about."

Ten

· · · · · · ·

A WEEK AFTER VAL AND TAJA LEFT TOBOL
An, Narrion and Tamra rode into the Forest of Thole.
The sun had not yet risen, and the trees were blacker
shapes against the darkness. As they picked their way carefully
along the path a strange gloomy light, like the light seen
through stained glass at the palace, began to filter through
the trees, and they could see flakes of snow, small as jewels, fall
from the sky. Their breath ghosted white in the air.

As they rode Narrion thought of his failure. He had
spoken the wrong verses, used the wrong ritual. Doubtless the
library at Tobol An had the invocation he needed, but he
could not find it without Taja; he had no idea how to search
through all the books on his own. And Taja had made it clear
she would not help him. He had to go back to Etrara, had to
talk to others at the observatory and in the Society of Fools.

He had explained his decision to the troupe of actors the
night before, but all but Tamra had refused to follow him. It
would be dangerous to return to Etrara, they had said, and
even more dangerous to try to work magic. They still remembered the terrifying moment by the arch when they had almost turned to stone.

They came to the city by midafternoon. The Gate of
Stones was closed and guarded by two men in the golden

armor of the Shai. Narrion dismounted. He and Tamra wore
the homespun clothing of Tobol An, but his tunic concealed
some of the jewels he had taken when he fled Etrara. It would
be dangerous if the guards stopped them.

"What is your business in Etrara?" one of the guards
asked.

"I'm here to see some of the merchants in the city,"
Narrion said. "I have messages from Tobol An."

"Messages? What sort of messages?" the first guard said,
but the second guard was already opening the gate and motioning them through.

Narrion mounted and followed Tamra through the gate,
his face impassive. He had invented a story about fish merchants and trade but he could not be certain that the guards
would believe him.

Most of the houses on either side of the Street of Stones
had burned to the ground. Men and women lay sprawled in
the street with their begging bowls in front of them, and more
people squatted in cages above them. The air smelled of
smoke. "Please, master," one of the beggars said. "The Shai
burned my home—"

Narrion urged his horse past him. Another man came up
to him. "Scathiel will reward your charity," he said, looking
up at Narrion slyly.

It was the manner of beggars in Etrara to imply that they
were whatever god had descended to earth, Scathiel in summer and Callabrion in winter. Any storyteller could tell a tale
of generosity rewarded a thousandfold by the gods, of people
whose casual gift of alms had caused them to rise high on the
ladder. But Narrion knew that this man could not possibly be
Scathiel; Scathiel still ruled in heaven.

Tamra slowed in front of him. "It's—it's terrible," she
said. "Look—that's where the gaming house was."

He nodded. But he could do nothing against the Shai, he
knew that. His own concerns were far more desperate than
who ruled Etrara: if Callabrion did not ascend to heaven the
harvests would fail.

They came to the Darra River and crossed the bridge, then continued up toward Palace Hill. Even here, in the upper city, Narrion could see beggars and burned houses. Pale winter grass grew up between the cobblestones on the streets. Soldiers marched two and three abreast, and the few people who had ventured out-of-doors fell silent as they passed.

The marketplace at the crossroads was closed, the stalls shuttered and locked, the colorful banners furled. The university was deserted save for a few Shai guards, and one of its buildings had been laid bare by fire. As they passed, the bells from the clock tower rang out. Narrion looked up in surprise. He would have expected the Shai to silence them, along with everything else.

He had hoped to see Val in Etrara; Pebr, when asked, had said that Val had returned to the city. Narrion suspected Pebr of not telling the truth; like Val, the old man was a poor liar. But he could not think of anywhere else Val might have gone. Now, though, studying the streets before him, he saw how vain it had been to expect to meet anyone in this desolate place.

He turned down a crooked way near the theater and halted before one of the houses. Then he dismounted and knocked at the door. No one answered. He knocked again. After a long moment he heard footsteps. The door opened a little, then was flung wide as the man inside saw who stood on his doorstep. "Narrion!" the man said, obviously delighted.

"Good fortune, Noddo," Narrion said.

Noddo laughed. "No one wishes anyone good fortune anymore," he said. "There's so little of it around, after all. But come in, come in. There's a stable at the back."

After they had seen to the horses Noddo led them into the house. He was a small man, with tufts of brown hair growing at the sides and back of his head. He had a way of walking on the balls of his feet that made children laugh, even when he was clothed in the skeleton of the Society of Fools. "It's good to see you," Noddo said. "You hear all sorts of rumors, you know. Some folks said that you'd died."

"No, I'm alive—very much alive. Do you know my wife Tamra?"

Noddo made her an elaborate bow. "I've had the pleasure of seeing her act," he said. "Sit, please." He motioned them to high-backed wooden chairs. "Where have you been?"

"A fishing village called Tobol An. We fled Etrara when the Shai invaded."

"Would you like some tea, or some ale?" Noddo asked. "We can't go to a tavern, you know—it's no longer possible to talk where you can be overheard. And I have the idea that what you want to say is dangerous. You were never one to sit safe at home."

"Dangerous? Everyone knows that Callabrion has not ascended this year, but is it dangerous to say so?"

"It is, yes. The Shai are fearful that the people will panic at the slightest sign. Tell the citizens of Etrara that their crops will fail this year, that they'll have to go hungry as well as homeless, and they're likely to revolt."

"But the days continue to grow shorter. Surely that can't be kept a secret."

Noddo shrugged. "People see what they want to see. If you can be caged for saying the sky is dark rather than light you'll keep your observations to yourself. And who knows?— the sky may even start to look lighter to you."

"Well," Narrion said. He leaned back in his chair and told Noddo what had happened when he had tried to summon Callabrion.

"And you did all this—alone?" Noddo asked when he had finished.

"With the actors' help, yes."

Noddo's slightly foolish expression had vanished; his brown eyes were hooded and he looked serious, almost worried. "I can't say that I can help you, or that any of the Society can help you. Our business is with the rituals of the Descending God, after all. If Callabrion has not ascended it's a matter for the astronomer-priests—or would be, if the priests had not made a treaty with the Shai."

"I've heard rumors of that," Narrion said. "But this is our concern as much as theirs. Scathiel needs Callabrion, as misrule needs rule. You taught me that."

Noddo laughed a little. "Aye. But this is a far cry from my experience as a Fool. If the songs and dances of the Feast of the Descending God could help you I would be the first to offer my services. But I couldn't imagine how you would summon Callabrion."

"I thought the Society might have books, or know of rituals—"

"No—none of our books deals with the summer god. What about the library at the university?"

Narrion shook his head. "They have no books of magic."

"Ah. Books of magic. As to that, you just came from the greatest collection of wizards' books in all the world. Or is the library at Tobol An less than legend says?"

Narrion said nothing. He had no desire to explain how he had run afoul of the librarian of Tobol An.

"Duke Talenor had a library," Noddo said.

"Talenor," Narrion said. "We heard that he turned traitor."

"Aye, he did. Tried to offer the Shai a pageant—he thought he was still a courtier, poor man. They killed him, of course."

"Is his library still in the palace?"

"It should be. But the Shai guard the palace at all times—Mariel is still there."

"And Callia? Mariel said that she died—that she was killed."

"Yes. That was bad, very bad. On the streets you can sometimes hear the Shai sing what sounds like a counting rhyme." Suddenly Noddo began to sing; like all members of the Society he had a beautiful, evocative voice. " 'One is for Gobro, he was poisoned they say. Two is for Arion, his men led astray.' They mean to imply that soon all the royal family will be dead."

Narrion shook his head. "It's worse than I thought. We hear none of this in Tobol An."

"The news is not all bad. Folks say that King Tariel left an heir, a legitimate heir. That a king will come to free us."

Narrion made an impatient gesture. "That's nonsense. What else do they say—that he'll come walking through God's Gate, locked since Queen Ellara's time? No one will free us but ourselves."

"They also say that the hero Andosto is alive, hidden somewhere in Etrara."

"Alive? Where?"

Noddo shook his head. "I don't know. Someone was killing Shai soldiers, secretly and at night, but then the Shai executed ten citizens for every man dead and the killings stopped."

"Andosto," Narrion said. Suddenly he smiled. "I think I know how to get to the palace. Can you find Andosto for me?"

"I don't know."

"I thought the Society knew everything that happened in Etrara."

"We did, once. Things have changed beyond recognition since you left. But I'll try to find him for you."

Taja and Val rode along the southern outskirts of Thole Forest. None of the maps in the library had showed them Wizard's Hill but they had decided to leave anyway; Taja felt certain that she could find her way once they reached Shai.

Sbona fashioned us for finding, she thought. The proverb was meant to refer to the first man and woman, created to help the goddess find her lost dead sons, but Taja understood now that it also spoke of the power of the poet-mages and their gift for finding. She had discovered the right invocation when Narrion had raised his destructive magic, and she had seen immediately which words to use as her keystones. Soon, she thought, she would be able to feel the pull from Wizard's Hill.

She repeated the proverb to Val, hoping to cheer him.

He laughed. "Aye, but did even Sbona think to see two idiots walking recklessly toward their enemy?"

When dusk fell they dismounted near Soria to eat and make camp. Taja took out her tinderbox; they built a fire and cooked some of the fish and vegetables they had brought. After the meal they moved their blankets closer to the fire to get warm. Stars burned overhead, hard and sharp in the crystalline air.

"Is it strange to be returning?" Taja asked.

"Stranger than I can tell you," Val said. "It almost seems as if the young man who went off so cheerfully to war is dead. I've seen so much since then. . . . I've seen that Callia was wrong to war with the Shai, that we were unprepared. Gobro, of all people, was right. We should have never broken the treaty."

"The people wanted war, though," Taja said.

"Aye," Val said. "And what can a king or queen do then?"

He sounded thoughtful; Taja marveled at how much he had changed from the frivolous courtier she had known. Suddenly she desired him, his warmth, the laughter in his voice. What would he do if she moved her blanket next to his? There were probably rules governing that as well in Etrara; the courtiers seemed to make everything far more complicated than it needed to be. And in all the sonnets she had ever read she had never come across a simple description of a man and a woman lying together. He would probably be horrified.

She reached out for him in the dark. Her hand found his, and he drew her toward him. They embraced, holding each other for warmth and comfort as much as for desire. "Taja," he said, kissing her. "Taja." She ran her fingers through his hair.

The next morning they went into Soria to buy food and heavier clothing. His manner toward her had not changed; he was still easy, companionable. She wondered what would happen to them when they returned to Etrara, wondered if Val's fine courtier friends would call him a fool for lying with a daughter of fisher-folk. But for the moment it was enough to know that she had a friend on the road.

A few days later they crossed the weathered bridge over the Darra River. They continued on. Several mornings after that they topped a rise and saw the Teeth of Tura to the east, a dark shape against the gray-black light of dawn. Taja looked up at the mountain range and shivered. "Did you really climb that?" she asked.

"Twice," Val said, grinning. "And we did it to the north of here, where it's steeper."

The sun rose slowly above the Teeth, and they rode on. The next day they came to the foot of the mountains and began to climb.

As they went Val told her a little about the apparitions he had seen in the mountains. Taja looked around uneasily, wondering if she would be forced to battle with monsters appearing out of the snow. She was not yet a poet-mage, she knew; she understood very little about sorcery. But no wizard's sendings disturbed their climb, and a few days later they reached the crest of the mountain.

The snow stopped as they descended; probably, Taja thought, they had traveled even south of Tobol An. But somehow she knew that they were headed in the right direction. Whenever they stopped to eat she could feel the pull of Wizard's Hill, and if she closed her eyes she saw the outline of the mountain, stark against the sky, and two small figures making their way up the side.

As they traveled down toward Shai they saw a town the size of Tobol An lying near the Teeth. "I don't know where we are," Val said. "I've never been this far south before."

Without discussing it they began to take paths leading south, hoping to skirt the village. Anyone coming from Etrara would be an object of suspicion, they knew, especially in a town as small as the one that lay before them.

They reached the flatland. The land around them looked like a desert, parched and wan, the only growing things a few grasses and stunted shrubs. Taja thought that in summer it must be hideously hot, but in this unending winter it was cold, a chill wind blowing constantly from the mountains. No rain fell; the shrubs looked starved for water.

They continued east. During their first day in Shai they met no one on the road, but on the second day Taja, who was in the lead, saw a straggling line of people walking toward them. She pulled her hood closer to her face and motioned Val to do the same. The people of Shai were taller and fairer than those of Etrara, and it would not be wise to pass them uncovered.

As the file came toward them, though, Taja saw that these men and women were citizens of Etrara. Their hands were tied with rope to their neighbors' hands, and their feet hampered by a sort of hobble. Slaves, Taja thought, feeling cold. Slaves from Etrara.

She and Val rode off the path as the line passed. Shai guards with whips rode among the slaves, but only one man spared them a glance. Probably they had been told to do their job and not dawdle, Taja thought; Val had said the Shai had little ambition or initiative of their own.

She let out a breath after they had gone. "Lord Varra," Val said, whispering as if the Shai could still hear them.

"What?" she said, urging her horse along the path, away from the Shai.

"Lord Varra, the Queen's Pen. I saw him among the slaves. He didn't leave Etrara in time."

She shivered. What would the Shai do to one of Queen Callia's advisors? Worse, what would they do to a king, the rightful king of Etrara?

She realized, startled, that she had almost forgotten Val's birthright. The king of Etrara. She remembered how she had desired him, and she felt hot with shame. What would he want with her, a simple woman from Tobol An? All his poems and protestations had been part of an elaborate game, something to occupy him now that Tamra had married; he would forget her as soon as they reached Etrara.

"I never saw him without his finery before," Val said. "He seemed almost naked."

"He might have said the same about you," Taja said.

Without discussing it they began to ride faster, hoping to put as much distance between them and the slaves as they could. Her sense of where Wizard's Hill lay was strong now, as if it were a magnet and she a piece of iron it pulled.

As evening fell they saw more people on the path, all of them traveling east. One man dropped back to ride with Val and Taja. "Are you riding to see the king?" he asked.

At first Taja could not understand his accent. But Val said, nodding, "Oh, aye. The king."

"Where are you from?" the other man asked. "Your accent is strange."

"North."

"North? Did you see the barbarians from Etrara? Did you fight?"

"Aye, I fought."

"I heard they were a weak and decadent people. And I heard that their poet-mage was no match for Kotheg."

"No," Val said. "No, he was not."

The other man would have said more, but Val urged his horse on ahead. When they had gone far enough he turned to Taja. "The barbarians from Etrara," he said, laughing. "He little knew how close he came to a barbarian from Etrara."

"What did he mean about the king?" Taja asked.

Val shook his head. "We'll find out, I'm sure."

The number of people on the road continued to swell; there were soon dozens of men and women traveling with them. When night fell the Shai left the path and pitched tents on level ground. Taja and Val joined them, spreading their blankets on the hard desert floor.

That night she and Val slept apart; none of the folks they traveled with showed much affection toward each other, and they thought it best not to do anything that would call attention to themselves. But for a long time Taja could not get to sleep; as the land around them grew stranger she found herself desiring Val more. She missed the closeness they had shared.

The Shai called to one another in their harsh alien accents; they lit cookfires and prepared their meat with strange-smelling spices. As she drifted off to sleep she heard them start to sing, a ballad in a minor key about the deeds of their heroes. Their wavering voices and laughter were the last things she heard that night.

The Shai rose early the next day. Taja and Val remained wrapped in their blankets, hoping no one would draw them into conversation. But the man who had questioned Val the evening before had been unusual for one of the Shai; even among themselves they did not seem to talk much. Taja noticed that they stayed in the same groups as the day before, and that each group had a different-colored tent, red and black or purple and silver. She thought that they must travel in clans or tribes.

More caravans thronged the roads; they found it impossible to avoid one clan or another. She wondered what they thought of her and Val, two people traveling alone and without a clan, but for the most part the Shai did not even glance at them.

They passed fields that stretched to the horizon on either side of the road. Ancient twisted vines climbed supports built of wood. Vineyards, she thought; the good Shai wine must come from here. But the vines looked as dead as their supports, showing no bloom of leaves or grapes. Even here, so far from Etrara, the spring had not returned.

By midday they came to a few straggling houses. The road widened, became a small street paved with cobblestones. People at the front of the line began to call out in excited voices. Finally she could make out what they had seen; ahead of them stood a city that seemed even larger than Etrara.

The houses were low, one story or two at the most, with sloping roofs; they looked a little like the tents the clans had pitched on their journey. Colored mosaics in dizzying, intricate patterns surrounded the doors and windows, but as the travelers walked through the crooked streets Taja noticed that the same two or three designs repeated themselves over and over. Mirrors set among the tiles winked in the sun as they passed. Caged men and women hung overhead; that at least was no different.

She saw no fountains, no parks. There were no statues or images of any kind, and she remembered from her dream that the Shai had hidden or destroyed the beautiful murals in the palace, covering the walls with patterned rugs and tapestries, and that they had hammered their iron lamps into the painted ceilings.

The street widened again. The travelers stopped, their way blocked by a massive crowd. From her seat on the horse, above the heads of the people, Taja could see a huge low building almost completely covered with designs in gold and silver and black—a temple of some sort, she thought.

A man came out of the temple and stood on the stairs above the crowd. He blew a long wailing note on an instrument made of horn, and the people fell silent. More men came out of the temple, and then a woman, dressed in white with a crown of massy gold on her head.

The horn sounded again. Another man joined the people on the stairs. He wore white as well, and the jewels on his crown were clustered together as thickly as melon seeds.

The king, Taja thought, remembering what she had read in the library about the Shai. He had wed the queen, the woman in white, at Callabrion's feast, and he would be killed a half year later, at the feast of Scathiel.

People bowed their heads. Beside her she saw Val do the same, and she quickly imitated him. When she looked up the king moved near his queen. He was young and muscular, Taja saw now, and she was at least fifty, and very plain. He took the queen's face in his hands and kissed her.

The crowd cheered. Taja shivered, wondering what the two people on the stairs thought of this ceremony. The queen might have wed and bedded these young fine-looking men for thirty years or more, and lived with each of them for six months, only to see them go off at the end to be killed. And the king—although he had great power, his every desire satisfied, he had to know that he would die in a few short months.

But perhaps they didn't think of it that way. Perhaps they had taken on the roles assigned to them, so that the woman became Sbona, creator-goddess, mother of light, and the man her son and consort, the god Callabrion. The king and queen raised their hands over the crowd in blessing. The people cheered again, and the horn blew, and the ceremony ended.

The crowd dispersed. For the first time since she had come to Shai Taja heard groups of people speaking at once. Several of the Shai looked around as if fearing to be overheard, and they lowered their voices when they saw Taja and Val. Still, she managed to catch fragments of their conversations: ". . . should have killed . . ." ". . . the old ways . . ." ". . . bought him time, at least."

What did they mean? Did they want the priests to kill the young summer god now, before the Feast of the Descending God? Why?

The people they had traveled with now journeyed west, going home, but Taja and Val joined another caravan heading east. At night, after they had unrolled their blankets and settled down to sleep, Taja heard the day's discussion continue around her. "It's clear the man's not Callabrion," one of the Shai said. "Scathiel rules still in the heavens."

"Aye," another man said. "I heard that Scathiel did not die an easy death at the sacrifice last year. It was a warning—Callabrion did not ascend."

"They should have killed this man now. If Scathiel rules still then he mocks us, mocks the gods."

"They should have performed the old wedding rites, there on the steps. No one's seen him take Sbona as his bride. Perhaps he hasn't—perhaps that's what keeps Callabrion from returning to the heavens."

"Aye, the old ways are best."

"I hear that he is not unblemished, this king. That he's deformed in some way."

"They should have shown him to us naked, as in the old days."

"They should have killed him, I say. And they will, if the days continue to darken. Mark my words—this ceremony did nothing but postpone that day."

The voices swirled around her. Then the heavy scent of meat and spiced tea thickened her senses. The hill she had seen in dreams rose behind her eyes, steep and sharp, and she slept.

She managed to draw Val a little apart from the main body of the caravan the next day. "Did you hear what they said last night?" she asked, whispering. "They want to kill the king."

Val nodded. "I heard that magic is loosed with the shedding of royal blood."

"I don't think that's true," she said, frowning. She felt the presence of the hill at every step now, and dreamt of it at night; it was like a nagging thought that would not leave her. "I think the power of their wizards comes from their hill, nothing more. But what has happened to Callabrion? The days continue to grow shorter—he did not ascend at the feast."

"I don't know."

"Narrion tried to summon him—I told you that. But he's no poet-mage. I wonder if he'll try again."

"Probably. Nothing can change his course once he decides to do something."

"I hope he doesn't. He knows nothing about the power he unleashed—it would be dangerous for him to meddle in magic."

Some of the Shai joined them then, and she fell silent.

By midday most of the Shai had returned to their homes, to villages and vineyards and pasture. Taja rode easier, feeling freer with every traveler who left them. By the time they stopped for the evening meal only a dozen men and women remained.

The men built up the campfire and sat to eat. They

passed carafes of their hot spiced wine—"king's blood," they called it—over the fire, and laughed and sang while they drank.

In a short while they grew loud, almost bellicose, repeating their arguments for killing the king in fierce voices. Taja thought that the wine had freed their tongue, or perhaps this clan was more garrulous than the others they had traveled with. They seemed different in other ways, too; the men had colorful scarves wound around their hair, and the women wore thick gold chains, and earrings so weighted with gold and jewels, they pulled at their earlobes.

"And what do you think, strangers?" one of the men said, turning to Val. "Is it right to kill the god-king?"

He didn't expect her to answer, Taja saw with relief; she had noticed before that the women never spoke in public. "If the days will grow longer—" Val said carefully.

"If!" the man said scornfully. "You speak like one of the womanish priests, arguing a thing over and over until no one can say what he believes. Let's kill him now. If the days grow longer then we were right, and if they don't—well, they'll chose a new king at Scathiel's feast."

"But if you were wrong it would be sacrilege."

"Sacrilege? Why?"

"To—to kill a king—" Val said.

Taja looked from one man to the other, worried. Val knew nothing but the elaborate debates of the court, the deft wordplay passed from one person to another. But somehow she understood that these people were unused to arguments, that they followed the orders they received from their priests without questions.

"Sacrilege to kill a king?" the Shai said. "Why, when we do it every half-year?"

All around the fire men and women put down their cups and their meat and looked at Val. Their eyes and jewels glittered in the firelight. Taja held her breath.

"I meant that it would be sacrilege to kill a king out of season," Val said. He raised his hand as if to touch his amulet, then quickly lowered it to his side. "Of course this king must be killed at Scathiel's feast."

"This king? What is this king's name, stranger?"

Val laughed. "Well, of course everyone knows—"

"His name," the Shai said.

Val glanced at Taja. Without speaking they got quickly to their feet and began to run. Several of the Shai called out, and Taja heard footsteps behind them. A man grabbed her and she cried out. He put his hand, still greasy with meat, over her mouth.

She kicked and lashed out with her arms as the man dragged her back to the camp. "Who are you, then?" the man who had questioned Val asked. She saw with despair that another of the Shai had captured Val as well; as she watched he took Val's sword and scabbard and studied them by fire-light.

"We're from the north," Val said. "Merchants. We came to see the ceremony, and we won't be treated—"

"From the north," the man repeated flatly. "North Etrara, I guess."

"No! No, we—we're merchants—"

"Bind their arms and legs. The priests will pay us well for spies and witches from Etrara, I think."

"Priests?" another man asked. "But Rugath, we can't go to the priests—"

"Quiet!" Rugath said. "I said they'll pay us well, and they will. Not in coins, but in pardons. For all of us."

They had fallen among outlaws, Taja realized, feeling hopeless. Now she remembered that the men and women had been heavily cloaked and covered with scarves at the beginning of their journey. She had thought the cold bothered them, nothing more. Religious outlaws, she thought, men and women who had disguised themselves to see their god-king. Would Shai never stop surprising them?

One or two of the men began to nod; the shadows cast by the fire glided smoothly over their faces. "Aye, they'll pardon us indeed," someone said.

Wordlessly, the women began to take out coils of rope from their packs and hand them to the men. Two men bound the prisoners. Taja struggled as they tightened the knots. "Quiet," one of them said. "We'll kill you here if you fight us."

"How do you know these folks are from Etrara?" the man who had argued with Rugath asked. "Could it be that they're telling the truth—that they're truly merchants?"

"Merchants!" Rugath said scornfully. "Why would they run if they were merchants?"

"They might have feared we would rob them."

"Look in their purses," Rugath said.

The Shai who guarded Taja and Val fumbled for the prisoners' purses. "Two sovereigns," one of them said, sounding disgusted. "Stamped with a king of Etrara—that fat one who looks like a toad."

"As I thought," Rugath said. "They're witches, witches from Etrara. Come, Cor—when have you known a merchant not to carry dozens of coins and jewels? They take their wealth with them, just as we do."

The company laughed; apparently they found it amusing to compare lawful merchants with a company of outlaws. Cor looked dissatisfied but said nothing.

"I think this man from Etrara is right," Rugath said. "It would be sacrilege to kill the god-king. But what if we substitute another man for the king, as the king himself is the substitute for Callabrion? What if we kill this man instead?"

The men and women laughed again.

"See how well I argue theology?" Rugath said proudly, grinning at the other outlaws. "Would I not make a good priest?"

Eleven

· · · · · · · ·

NARRION AND TAMRA TOOK LODGINGS
at the Dolphin, a small rough-timbered inn by the
Darra River. "It's a strange time to come to Etrara,"
the innkeeper said as they climbed the stairs. "What did you
say your business was?"

"The fish trade," Narrion said. "From Tobol An."

"Fish, well, we could use fish," the innkeeper said. He
opened the door to their room. "The crops aren't growing,
they say. They say we'll all starve this year."

Narrion said nothing. He had not wanted to speak to
anyone except the Society of Fools while he was in Etrara. The
innkeeper said, "Tobol An, now—I've never heard of that.
Where is it exactly?"

"South," Narrion said.

"Ah," the innkeeper said, nodding as if he had been
enlightened. "South."

Days passed with no word from Noddo. Tamra and Narrion could not leave the room; both of them were too well
known to risk being seen on the streets. Narrion grew impatient, pacing the floor, practicing swordplay in the small con-
fined space. They were forced to see the innkeeper, who
brought them their meals, and his daughter, who cleaned the
room, but otherwise they spoke to no one.

After several days the innkeeper grew suspicious. "The fish trade, was it?" he said as he brought them their supper. "I don't see fish merchants thronging to your door."

"Is it your business to question your lodgers?" Narrion asked. The innkeeper had interrupted his sword practice; his hand still gripped the hilt of his sword. The innkeeper backed away and Narrion closed the door behind him.

The next day the innkeeper grew bolder. "Sometimes I'm forced to question my lodgers," he said. He had clearly been thinking about Narrion's question all day. "When I suspect them of doing something unlawful."

"By Scathiel's big toe," Narrion said, exasperated. "We're expecting a message, nothing more."

By good fortune the message arrived the next day. The innkeeper brought it to their room. "I apologize for doubting you," he said, smiling broadly.

Narrion waited until he had gone before breaking Noddo's seal. "I've found Andosto," the note said.

Narrion took the stairs of the inn two at a time and hurried out onto the streets of Etrara. Behind him he could hear Tamra following him.

"Narrion!" Tamra said. He continued on, too impatient to stop. "Narrion!" Tamra called again. "Narrion, wait!"

He turned. He should not have brought her, he thought; she was unused to hardship, to the world outside the court. "What is it?" he asked.

"You walked under a ladder," she said.

"Did I?" He looked around him, saw that she had been correct. He had passed through the connection between the earth and heaven, and in doing so had briefly severed it. Ill fortune, he thought. He had offended the gods at the very beginning of his attempt to raise Callabrion; it seemed the worst possible omen.

He shook his head, trying to banish his evil thoughts. He could not afford to become distracted, not now when he was so close. He turned down the street near the theater and came to Noddo's house.

He knocked. The door opened almost immediately, as if Noddo had been waiting for them. "Come in, come in," Noddo said cheerfully, motioning them into the room.

Andosto sat in one of the high-backed chairs. Narrion, who had known him at court, was unprepared for the sight of him now; he had lost a great deal of weight, and an unhealed scar festered on one hand. "Good fortune, Narrion, Tamra," Andosto said.

Narrion grinned; he liked the fact that Andosto continued to hope for good fortune after he had fallen so low on the ladder. "Good fortune," he said. "Has Noddo explained what I want you to do?"

"You need to get into the palace," Andosto said.

"Can you do it?"

"I think so," Andosto said slowly. "We may have to kill a few of the guards, though, and there will be reprisals if we do. Ten citizens of Etrara killed for every guard."

Narrion shrugged. "We'll have to do the best we can."

"I've made a study of the guards," Andosto said. "I know when their watches change. And I can help you with other things as well."

"Good."

The two men talked a little longer, working out strategy, and then Narrion and Tamra walked back to the inn. He felt confident, his earlier offense against the gods nearly forgotten. The meeting had gone as he'd hoped it would.

Narrion and Andosto had decided to attempt the palace during the dark of the moon, which took place two days after Narrion had met with Andosto. On that dark night Narrion waited three hours after the bells of Etrara tolled midnight, and then walked quietly down the stairs of the inn, hoping to avoid the innkeeper. His caution was rewarded; as he passed the innkeeper's room he heard him snoring loudly within.

He met Andosto at the agreed-upon place on Palace Hill.

Without speaking the two men slipped through the dark to the palace courtyard and came to the slight rise at the fountain of Sbona. They crouched behind the fountain and watched the guards.

"There he is," Andosto said, whispering. He pointed to a guard who was fond of taking a nap as soon as he had finished his first circuit around the palace. This guard and another one beat their swords together and then separated on their rounds.

Narrion and Andosto waited. Stars lit the sky, Sbona's lamps created to help her search for her lost children. They shone brighter than usual in the absence of the moon. The light needs the dark, Narrion thought, just as summer needs winter. He felt more certain than ever that he had chosen the right path.

The two guards returned to the front of the palace and clashed swords again. One of them took up his station before the main door, and the other, the man Andosto had pointed out, moved to the back. They followed him, and were in time to see him stretch out on the lawn in the formal gardens and fold his cloak around him.

They waited until they were certain he had fallen asleep, then walked through the garden to the rear door. The door had been barred from the inside, of course; Narrion smashed a window nearby with the hilt of his sword. The guard stirred at the jangle of glass but did not wake.

They climbed through the window. As Narrion had feared, the Shai had stationed another guard just inside the rear door. The man slashed at Narrion as he came through the window. Narrion twisted nimbly to avoid his sword and then cut him down as he turned.

Ten citizens of Etrara, he thought as they ran down the corridor. Was the death of ten people worth the return of the god to the heavens? He hoped that it was. He hurried on.

They ran to the main staircase, then upstairs to the royal apartments. Another guard stood at the entrance to the rooms. He lunged forward to attack Andosto, and as he did so

Narrion stabbed him in the back. He turned to face Narrion, not yet dead, a look of cold horror on his face. Andosto thrust his sword to the man's heart.

They stood still, waiting to see if anyone had been roused by the noise. When no one came Narrion bent and took the ring of keys at the guard's belt. He opened the door and they stepped inside.

The iron lamps hanging from the ceiling had nearly burned down. In the dim light they saw something wink in the shadows. Someone moved. Andosto turned suddenly, his sword ready. A man stepped from the gloom, his irises glinting silver.

Andosto went forward. "Wait," Narrion said, putting his hand on Andosto's arm.

"Do you know where Riel is?" the man said plaintively.

Gobro's ghost. Narrion began to laugh, not caring that the guards might hear. "I can't find her anywhere," the ghost said.

"Quiet," Andosto said, sounding annoyed. The door to one of the rooms opened and a pale young man stepped out. "Narrion!" the man said.

Sbarra's poet. "Good fortune, Sorth," Narrion said, continuing on toward Talenor's apartment.

"What are you doing in the palace?" Sorth said, hurrying after him. "Did the Shai let you in? Were you captured?"

"No," Narrion said. He went past Gobro's empty rooms, past Arion's and Callia's. One is for Gobro, he thought.

Duchess Sbarra came out of the suite of rooms she had once shared with Talenor. "What is it?" she said. "Narrion?"

"I need to see your husband's library," Narrion said.

"His library? Why?"

"Now, Sbarra. There's no time for questions."

The poet gasped; Narrion guessed that no one had ever treated his patron so rudely. "Follow me," Sbarra said evenly.

She led him and Andosto through her door and down a long corridor. The poet followed after them. Only a few oil lamps burned here. They passed the room that had held so many of Sbarra's nightly gatherings; the duchess pointed to the door beyond that. "Wait here," she said. "I'll get a candle."

Sbarra returned and lit the oil lamps. Narrion followed her inside and nodded in satisfaction. He had never seen Talenor's library. Noddo had been right: books of all colors lined all the walls and reached to the ceiling, many of them treatises on magic. Soft light moved against the polished bindings. The room smelled strongly of leather.

He went to the nearest wall and studied the shelves. There were hundreds of books here, maybe thousands. How in Scathiel's name would he be able to find the one he wanted?

"What are you looking for?" Sbarra asked. "Maybe I can help."

"I need a book of invocations to Callabrion," Narrion said. "The god has not ascended this year, and I hope to persuade him to return to the heavens."

"So it's true," Sbarra said. She was smiling slightly. "You're a religious man, a member of the Society of Fools. Is that why you were always so silent at my gatherings, because you were collecting information for the Society? But you took part in other plots as well, didn't you? Didn't you help Mariel and Callia kill King Gobro?"

"I don't have time for this, Sbarra," Narrion said evenly. "If I'm successful here I'll sit with you over a pot of ale and tell you everything you want to know."

"Why don't you ask Mariel for help? Wasn't she the one who raised you high on the ladder?"

"Mariel and I have had our differences. Can you help me?"

"I suppose so." She went to the shelves and started to look through them.

Narrion watched her, a little surprised. She seemed to know as much about the library as her husband had; she was not Talenor's ornament, his wife and hostess, but a scholar in her own right. He had never known that about her, just as she had not known he belonged to the Society of Fools. All the masks were coming off now, all disguises laid aside as winter and hardship gripped the city.

"Here," Duchess Sbarra said. She took down a small faded book bound in black leather. "I think there's an invocation in this book that might help you."

Narrion took the book. Taja probably has this in her library, he thought. Ironic that we had to travel so many miles to find a copy here. But he knew that Taja would not help him, not after what had happened at the arch of Sleeping Koregath. And even if she would he could not ask her; she had left Tobol An with Val weeks ago.

He leafed through the book. *Keystones and Invocations*, the title said. "It was once in the library of a wizard of Tariel's," Sbarra said.

The poet Sorth looked at the book over Narrion's shoulder. A combination of excitement and awe shone from his face; he had probably never been this close to true wizardry in his life.

"Sorth," Narrion said, the idea coming to him at that moment. He put the book in the purse at his belt. "I'll need you to leave with me. I need someone to recite the invocation."

"I— No," Sorth said. "I'm a poet, not a mage. I can't speak magic."

"Come—don't be afraid," Narrion said.

"I'm not afraid—"

"Good. You'll leave with me then."

"No, I—"

"I think you will. Your patron commands you. Don't you, Lady Sbarra?"

Narrion saw that the duchess was about to refuse; perhaps he should not have been so insulting earlier. But the poet said quickly, with relief, "She's not my patron. I serve Duchess Mariel now."

"Mariel?" Narrion said. He raised an eyebrow.

"We left Etrara without him," Sbarra said. "He was masterless, and Mariel offered to take him into her service."

The poets at court played at being poet-mages, Narrion knew, and liked to emphasize the similarities between their lives and that of the wizards. Sorth had probably complained that without a master he would be a target for all the other court poets. Narrion thought it nothing but affectation; he had never heard of a poet killed by another's verses.

"You sought a master, is that right?" Narrion asked the poet softly.

Sorth seemed to see where Narrion's questions would lead. He shrank back against the bookshelves, looking from Sbarra to Narrion.

"You might be killed if you were masterless," Narrion said. "Poets have the power to kill, is that what you believe? A power like that of the poet-mages. And if you have this power—"

"No," Sorth said. "No, I won't do it."

He seemed terrified. Probably few people understood the dangers of wizardry as well as the poets; they liked to dabble in spells and invocations but they lacked much of the innate power of the true mages. Narrion had never known a kept poet who was not in some way a failed wizard.

"Quiet," Narrion said. "If you have this power, you can surely speak an invocation or two. A few verses."

"Help!" Sorth said loudly. "Guards! Help! Treachery!"

No sun lit the streets of Etrara, but the bells rang out to signify morning. Noddo climbed the steps to Narrion's room and knocked on the door.

"Who is it?" Tamra asked.

"Noddo."

"Oh," she said. "I thought—I thought you might be Narrion. Come in, please."

The door opened and he went inside. "Is Narrion back?" he asked.

"No," Tamra said. She sounded worried.

"Did he say when he would return?"

"No."

"He'll be back. I've never known him to fail—he's always done whatever he set his mind to."

He had meant to reassure her. But she drew a little away from him, and he wondered if he had done just the opposite, if he had reminded her of how little she knew her husband. He and Narrion shared a past of which she knew nothing.

Did she love Narrion, then? Noddo had heard that their marriage was one of convenience, a joining of her family's old wealth with Narrion's newly gained riches. To put her at her ease he said, "Did Narrion ever tell you how he came to join the Society?"

She shook her head.

"You know that some children born in summer are given names that end in 'ion,' " he said. "Like Callabrion. And those born in winter have names ending in 'iel.' All the members of the Society of Fools are supposed to be winter-children, did you know that?"

"But—but then Narrion—"

"Narrion." Noddo smiled a little, enjoying the memory. "He was a boy when he came up to me at the Feast of the Descending God and said he wanted to learn how to dance like a skeleton. I asked him his name, and when he told me I said, as gently as I could, that we did not accept summer-children into the Society. He didn't cry, I remember that. He just turned away, as though he were thinking of something."

"I've seen that," Tamra said.

"He asked me about the Society every year. Somehow he could tell me apart from all the other skeletons, even though he was only a child. And I had to disappoint him every year. He was a summer-child, I said, and we could make no exceptions. I thought he would outgrow his desire."

"But how did he—"

"Years passed. He went to the university. He told me at the feast that year that he was studying very hard, and he smiled that smile he has, as though he knows something you don't. And in the library at the university he discovered a book about the founding of the Society of Fools, and the book said nothing about whether the members had to be winter-children or summer-children. So we let him in. What choice did we have?"

Tamra laughed.

"Aye, it's an amusing story," Noddo said. "But I told it to you for a reason. There's a darkness in his soul that won't go away, something that drew him so powerfully to the Society that we made our first exception in nearly five hundred years. He knew this even as a child, when he asked me if he could join the Society. No matter what his day of birth he belongs to Scathiel, flesh and bones and soul."

"Guards!" Sorth said again.

Andosto moved behind Sorth quickly. He clapped a hand over the poet's mouth; his other arm tightened around Sorth's windpipe. Narrion raised his sword casually; it seemed almost an accident that the sword was pointed at the poet's stomach.

"What—what will you do with him?" Sbarra said. "It'll mean your death if you kill a poet, you know that."

"Quiet," Narrion said roughly, listening for the guards Sorth had called. No one came. "Death if you kill a poet," he said scornfully. "That's another story they tell, to make themselves as important as the wizards. Do you truly think the other court poets will band together and write me out of existence? Kill me with their dreadful meter? Slay me with bad similes?"

No one spoke.

"Mariel might be upset for a while," Narrion said. "Her honor is at stake—she's his patron, after all. But Mariel's lost any power she might once have had—I have nothing to fear from her."

"Let him go," Sbarra said.

Narrion said nothing. Sorth squirmed in Andosto's grasp. "Promise him you won't take him with you," Sbarra said. "He'll be silent—he wants no more than to be left alone."

Andosto let go of his prisoner. "Don't—" Narrion said. Sorth raised his voice over Narrion's. "Help!" he said. "Murder!"

Narrion thrust his sword forward. Sorth sagged against Andosto, who pushed him away. The poet fell to the floor. Blood welled from his mouth; it looked golden in the light from the lamps.

Now they could all hear the sound of footsteps hurrying up the stairs. Narrion hurried away from the library and ran quickly down the corridor, then out into the main hallway. He had once seen a servants' staircase but could not now remember where it was. Andosto followed him.

They came to the end of the royal apartments. There had been a door here, he was certain of it. He pulled aside one of the hanging tapestries and saw only a wall, pushed against another and felt something give way on the other side. He moved the tapestry aside thankfully. A door stood behind it, half-open.

They hurried down the stairwell. It was dark here; no lamps had been spared for this part of the palace. Despite the gloom he took the stairs two and three at a time, going forward mainly on instinct. Behind him he heard Andosto blunder into a wall and continue on. He opened the door at the foot of the stairs, felt a cold wind on his face.

Once outside the palace they ran through a darkness barely lighter than that of the stairwell. Despite that, he knew somehow that it was morning. The watch would change soon, and the dead guards would be discovered.

He ran faster, turning once to look back at the palace. The noise they had made had roused the sleeping guard, he saw; the guard stood stupidly as the others came out of the palace. That would stop them for a minute, Narrion thought, and a minute might be all they needed to get free.

As they ran the darkness lightened a little, becoming a dirty gray. Narrion led Andosto through crooked roads and back alleys, the hidden streets he knew that appeared on no map. The book hit his leg as he ran, a welcome weight.

Finally they reached the Darra River and the inn at the sign of the Dolphin. He hurried up the stairs, ignoring the innkeeper's shouts, and opened the door. Andosto ran after him.

Tamra and Noddo turned toward him. "Come quickly," he said. "We have to leave."

"Leave?" Tamra said. "Why?"

Narrion looked at Noddo. "Can we go to your house?"

"I—I suppose so," Noddo said. "But—"

"We have to hurry," Narrion said. "I've killed two people—three, but the Shai won't count a court poet. And the innkeeper saw me come in this morning. Do you think that when the Shai start asking questions he'll pretend he saw nothing? Can we trust him to keep silent, especially when the Shai will offer a reward?"

Tamra began to collect a few things. "There's no time for that," Narrion said.

They went down the stairs. "We'll go on to Noddo's," Narrion said to Tamra. "Settle the bill with the innkeeper and meet us there." He hurried out into the streets without waiting for an answer.

Noddo and Andosto followed him. Somewhere a guard called, and another answered. They ran quickly past the theater and turned down the crooked way that led to Noddo's house.

Once inside Narrion took out the book he had gotten. "Sbarra gave me this," he said, showing it to Noddo. He opened it; there on the first page was an invocation to the god Callabrion. It seemed a good omen. "Great king," he said. "Our sovereign and ruler—"

"Are you going to begin now?" Noddo said.

"Of course," Narrion said. "Why not?"

"Because—because you know nothing of magic. Study the book first, and decide which verses you'll need. Don't be so impatient."

"Noddo," Narrion said, as carefully as he could. The excitement that gripped him was strong, too strong to allow him to stop now. "The Shai might have seen which street we took. If they did they'll question your neighbors, and it will be only a matter of time before they are led to us. We might have only a few hours. Forgive me, my teacher, but I think that in this matter we cannot afford patience."

"Then we'll go somewhere else—" Noddo said.

Narrion ignored him. He began the invocation to Callabrion again. As he spoke he felt certainty rise within him; this time he would succeed, this time the summer god would yield to his will. And he would not need Sorth, that pale, puling imitation of a wizard, to help him.

The currents of magic began to move around him. Understanding was nearly within his grasp; soon he would be able to control the magic, to shape it to his purpose. He paged quickly through the book, looking for a poem with an appropriate keystone.

The correct verse eluded him. He sensed the magic begin to slip away; the power around him grew stronger, wilder. He turned the pages rapidly. Noddo called out to him but he could not hear what he said over the gusts of magic.

He glanced down a page, saw a poem with its keystone— "fire"—printed in red. What better word to use to summon Callabrion? He read the verse quickly, hoping to finish before he lost control of the spell completely.

The room around him, chilly like all the rooms in Etrara, began to grow warm. He turned the page and continued to recite, certain now that he had chosen the correct verse. As he neared the end of the poem he saw, too late, that the second keystone was the word "ember."

The room grew warmer. The heat was pleasant, lulling him nearly to sleep. It would be dangerous to stop the spell in the middle, he knew, and so he read on, reciting the words without really seeing them, until he came to the end.

His eyelids closed. At that moment he understood the extent of his folly, saw clearly that he had spoken a sleeping-spell. Soon he would sleep, perhaps forever. He struggled against the spell but the very words he had spoken worked against him, calmed him, smoothed the currents of his fear.

He opened his eyes. He tried to turn the page, to find a counterspell. His hand grew heavy; he could barely lift it.

Someone whispered something. Noddo? He tried to raise his head. No, Noddo was asleep.

The whisper came again. He shook his head, trying to come awake. The voice sounded familiar; he thought that he had once known and trusted this person. He was in the presence of a strong poet-mage. Who could it be? He listened intently.

The mage spoke louder. Narrion heard the words of a poem and struggled to repeat them, understanding that they were the counterspell he had sought. As he recited the verses he saw with admiration how the poet-mage was constructing the poem, choosing keystones and alliteration and meter almost effortlessly.

The warmth left the room. Andosto woke, gasping. "Narrion!" Noddo said, urgently. "Narrion, stop!"

But Narrion could not stop. The voice continued, giving him the verses he needed to summon Callabrion. He spoke them with joy, seeing with the poet-mage where they would lead, almost able to anticipate the rhymes. The two keystones joined brilliantly. The poet spoke a final invocation and then was gone.

A fourth man stood within the room.

The man wore patched breeches and a faded tunic; his hair was white and streaked with dirt. "Who—" Narrion said.

The man said nothing. He stood blinking in the center of the room as if he were witless.

"I know you," Narrion said finally. "I've seen you in Sbarra's rooms, at her gatherings. But you— Who are you?"

"Who?" the man asked, a mournful echo.

"What is your name?"

"My name?"

"I summoned the god Callabrion," Narrion said, feeling

the exaltation of the last few moments fade. Surely this man could not be Callabrion; Narrion saw no trace of the immanence of the gods, the radiant light he had heard others speak of.

"Callabrion," the man said slowly. Narrion sighed impatiently. His first guess had been correct; the man had lost his wits. "Callabrion. I could be . . . Yes. Yes, I think I might be Callabrion."

Narrion looked at the others in the room. Andosto frowned; Narrion remembered that he was rumored to be Callabrion's grandson.

"Callabrion—yes, that's who I am." Before Narrion could stop him he sat on a chair and took off one of his boots. The big toe on his right foot was missing.

Narrion forced himself to say nothing. He felt tricked; he thought that there might be dozens of men in Etrara who had lost a toe. And yet he remembered the story, how Sbona had searched over the earth for the remnants of her murdered children, how when she had gathered them together she had seen that Callabrion had lost his right toe and Scathiel his left. He shivered despite himself. Could the man's claim possibly be true?

The man seemed to see Andosto for the first time. He stood hesitantly, still holding his boot. "My son?" he asked. His voice was that of an old man, trembling, querulous.

Andosto nodded.

The man who claimed to be Callabrion went toward Andosto and embraced him. Andosto held him awkwardly. Now Narrion thought he could see light emanating from the man, but it was thin, uncertain. They released each other; Callabrion returned to the chair and sat slowly.

Narrion shivered again. If this man was truly Callabrion then he was in the presence of something ancient, holy. He had not expected the feeling of deep awe that rose from somewhere within him. This man was Sbona's child, Scathiel's brother. The god of summer.

"Why—why didn't you return to the heavens this year?" Narrion asked.

"The heavens," Callabrion said. He hesitated. "Yes, I was supposed to ascend to the heavens."

"Why didn't you go?" Narrion's voice was almost gentle. "Your bride Sbona waits for you."

"I—I don't know. I fell in love."

"In love? With who?"

Callabrion looked around him, as if hoping to find the answer with him in the room. "I don't know," he said again. "With—with the earth."

"With—"

"Yes." Callabrion stood; he spoke more forcefully now. The light that shone from him grew stronger. He seemed to become younger before their eyes; his thick white hair radiated out from his face like the rays of the sun. "With sun and stone, wood and water. She created well, my mother."

"But you—you've lived with us on earth before. Every year, for thousands of years."

Callabrion nodded. "And I never saw it before. Never truly saw it, until now. The earth holds more beauty than heaven does."

"You must return to the heavens, my lord. You must wed Sbona, or the sun will fail. The earth you love so much will die."

"No," Callabrion said. His voice was deep, commanding. The light of his face was nearly blinding now; Narrion was forced to look away. "No, I will not."

No one spoke. What could they say to him, to this god? His eyes shone like suns; his hair was like a crown of white gold. His legs were as strong and powerful as the trunks of trees.

The door opened, and Tamra stepped inside. She stopped a moment, her eyes blinking in the blazing light. She looked from Narrion to Callabrion. Then, as her husband and the others watched, she bent to the god Callabrion in a deep curtsy. "My liege," she said.

Twelve

· · · · · · ·

THE DAY AFTER THE OUTLAWS HAD CAP-
tured Taja and Val they changed direction, heading
west toward the city Taja had seen. Taja thought that
Rugath probably hoped to give them to the priests there. And
what would happen to them then? They might be sacrificed,
as Rugath had said; surely people who killed their kings would
not balk at murdering two strangers.

The closer they came to the city the quieter the men
became, as if to match the seriousness of their errand. As they
approached the city both men and women stopped and muffled themselves in layers of cloaks and scarves and head-
dresses. Taja dismounted awkwardly; the Shai had left her
hands bound.

One of the women slipped a bulky red and gold cloak
over Taja's shoulders. She nearly shrugged it off, thinking that
she and Val might be able to attract the attention of some
other clan traveling east. But any other clan would give them
to the priests as well; they were the enemy, from Etrara. She
kept the cloak on. It smelled of sweat and strange spices.

They met few people traveling toward the huge city; Taja
thought that most folks had returned to their homes after the
ceremony. The clan rode in silence until they came to the
dead vineyards. "Perhaps it's witchcraft that's blasted these

vines," Rugath said. "We've conquered Etrara, but they can command the very forces of nature. They hope to kill our crops in the ground, to starve us out of Etrara."

"Is that true?" Cor asked quietly. Taja had not even noticed him come up and join them. "Are you witches?"

"No, of course not," Taja said. "We're merchants—I—"

"Aye, we're witches," Val said, speaking over her. "We've spent the night on Wizard's Hill."

Cor paled. "Have you indeed?" he said, nearly whispering.

"Aye," Val said. "Do you know what happens to those who kill a poet-mage? First their flesh rots off their bones. Then their bones dissolve—"

Cor made a noise deep in his throat and urged his horse on ahead. Val laughed softly.

"Do you think that was wise?" Taja asked quietly.

"They might not kill us if they fear us," Val said.

"Well, perhaps. But perhaps they'll kill us sooner."

They reached the city two days later. The twisted streets were deserted; their horses' hooves sounded loud against the cobblestones.

A man rode out from one of the alleyways. He wore a golden helmet and breastplate; Taja noticed that Val started at the sight of him. A soldier, she thought, or a man of the watch. "Hold!" he said.

"We bring two prisoners to the temple," Rugath said. "Witches from Etrara."

"Etrara?" the soldier said doubtfully. He looked at Taja and Val, both weighted down with layers of Shai clothing. "I'll have to come with you."

Rugath seemed about to argue. Then he shrugged. "As you wish, my lord," he said.

Rugath said nothing more as they rode to the temple. Several young men dressed in blue stood at the foot of the steps; they clashed their swords together as the Shai soldier approached them.

As Taja saw them she realized she knew the details of

their lives as surely as if they had told her. These were the acolytes of Sbona; the next god-king would be chosen from among their ranks. They felt excited at the prospect, eager for the honor and the chance to live in luxury for half a year. But at the same time she sensed their uneasiness, their feeling that no honor was worth death six months later.

The acolytes and soldier spoke together for a few minutes, and then the soldier said something to the outlaws that Taja did not catch. The Shai dismounted, and after a moment she and Val did the same. A few of the acolytes came forward to take their horses. Taja gave hers up reluctantly; it would be difficult to escape without it.

They climbed the steps to the temple. Two of the acolytes had come with them, and these spoke to others just inside the door. Now Taja could see that a great hallway ran down the length of the temple, lit only by iron lamps on twisted chains.

One of the acolytes said something to Rugath. "Never!" Rugath said. Taja had never heard him speak so loudly; his voice echoed off the marble walls of the temple. "By Scathiel's big toe I swear—"

"If you do not give up your weapons you will not be allowed into the temple," the acolyte said. "Only the god-king's servants can carry weapons in a holy place." He and the others stood before the outlaws, their hands on the hilts of their swords.

Rugath shrugged, apparently resigned. He took a sword from a scabbard at his side and a knife from his boot, and the other outlaws followed his lead. Taja watched, surprised and a little alarmed, as the pile of weapons in the hallway grew. Val's sword was thrown down; the outlaw who had taken it when they were captured had evidently kept it. She had had no idea that they were so well armed.

When they had finished, the acolytes motioned them down the corridor. Identical rooms opened off on either side of them. The rooms on the right were brightly lit, and draped with the gold and green banners of Callabrion. People bustled in and out, coming out to speak with the acolytes and even with Rugath and the other outlaws.

Taja caught only a quick glimpse of the rooms on the left. They were dusty, the pale light coming through windows obscured by dirt. Hangings and tapestries in blue and silver, Scathiel's colors, covered the walls; gray spiderwebs dimmed their luster.

An acolyte motioned them forward into a room on the right. They had come to the throne room, Taja saw; a great chair fashioned of gold and emeralds stood before them. She turned and saw an identical room across the hall, and a tarnished throne of silver and sapphires, before her way was blocked by the crowd.

A handsome young man sat on the golden throne. Taja was surprised at the expression of slack indolence on his face; he looked as if he might be drugged. Priests in white stood ranged on a platform behind him. She looked for the old woman, the goddess-queen, but could not see her anywhere.

Soldier and acolyte and outlaw bowed their heads toward the king, and after a moment Taja and Val did the same. He gave no indication that he saw any of them.

"Are these the prisoners?" one of the priests asked, indicating Taja and Val. Suddenly Taja understood that this man was the true ruler of Shai, that the god-king and the goddess-queen had no power, no tasks except those they were assigned at the festivals. The priests here were nothing like the astronomer-priests in Etrara, whose sole task was to study the motion of the sun and stars.

"Aye, my lord," Rugath said.

Two priests stepped down from the platform to study them. One pushed back the hood of Val's cloak, and Taja remembered her earlier fear. What would the Shai do if they discovered Val's identity? How would they treat the true king of Etrara?

"This is the first time in memory that the Tathlag have entered the god-king's temple," the ruling priest said. "Tell us why we should let you go free."

A few of the outlaws looked at each other, a complex glance that Taja did not completely understand. She wondered if it meant that some of the outlaws doubted their chief, that Rugath's hold on the clan was uncertain. The thought cheered her a little; she and Val might be able to take advantage of a division in the Tathlag clan.

"We bring you these captives to demonstrate our loyalty to Shai, and to the god-king," Rugath said. "If we were nothing but thieves and clanless men, as you and others have claimed, we would have kept these witches for ourselves."

"Witches?" the priest asked. A few of the men near Taja and Val stepped back uneasily.

"Aye, my lord," Rugath said. "So they told us. I thought they might be sacrificed in place of the king, so that—"

"Quiet," the priest said. "The Tathlag clan stands very low on the ladder—certainly not high enough to tell the god-king what to do. We will take these prisoners, and then decide what to do with them. And we will take you as well."

Acolytes moved forward to seize Taja and Val. Others took Rugath and Cor and the men surrounding them. "But—" Rugath said. "But my lord—"

"Quiet."

At that moment Taja saw that her insight had been correct, that men in the clan doubted Rugath's ability to lead, and for very good reason. Rugath had enough charm and bluster and cunning to guide a small tribe of outlaws, but he was no match for the subtleties of the god-king's court. He had fully expected to walk into the temple and receive his pardon.

"Don't—" Cor said, holding his hand out to Taja and Val. The acolytes forced it down roughly.

"Don't?" the priest asked.

"Don't kill them. It'll mean your death to kill a witch, and ours too. We brought them to you—the witch's curse will light on us all."

A few of the acolytes looked uneasy. "Ah," the priest said. "But are they witches? We have only your word for that."

"They told us so," Cor said. "They said they've been to Wizard's Hill."

One of the acolytes turned pale, exactly as Cor had. But the priest laughed. "Wizard's Hill!" he said. "How did a man and woman from Etrara manage to reach Wizard's Hill?"

Rugath spoke a few words. In the space of a blink all the outlaws, even the women, had taken out swords, drawing them from cloaks and boots and hidden pockets of clothing. They had given up only a fraction of their weapons in the hall, Taja saw.

Rugath held his sword toward the acolytes, keeping them at bay, and at the same time motioned the outlaws into the hall. They moved warily, used to fighting. The servants of the god-king stood uncertainly for a moment and then came after them, drawing their weapons.

In the confusion Taja ran for Scathiel's throne room across the hall. One of the outlaws followed her and broke a window with the hilt of his sword. Cold wind whistled through the room, blowing up dust and cobwebs. People ran for the window.

Rugath and a few others hurried after them into the throne room. Blood flowed down one of his arms, and he was breathing heavily. Taja saw him engage one of the acolytes, and then the press of people crowding her against the window was too great and she had to turn.

The man in front of her clambered through the window to safety. She held out her bound hands and jerked the rope against the broken glass. The rope frayed but did not break. Someone fell against her and swore angrily. She tried again; this time she managed to cut the rope and climb to the window. As she turned to drop to the ground she saw Rugath fall to the acolyte's sword.

The man who had pushed her followed her out the window. A woman came after him, holding her heavy skirts as she fell to the ground. Then, to Taja's vast relief, she saw Val leap from the window and run toward her.

"Rugath's dead," he said. "Come—we've got to hurry."

A few of the outlaws moved toward them. "Let them go," Cor said.

"Let them . . ." said one of the outlaws.

"Aye. Rugath's dead. I'm the leader now, and I say to let them go. It'll mean our death if we kill them, or allow them to be killed."

The outlaws hesitated. "Come!" Val said again. He began to run, and she followed him.

They hurried down the strange crooked streets of the city. No one came after them, and she thought that the acolytes must have been stopped by what remained of Rugath's band. It was strange to think of Rugath dead; he had been so filled with life, so exuberant. She would not have expected a man of the Shai, a people used to obedience and conformity, to do what he had done, to confront the priests in their own temple.

After a while she and Val slowed. She saw that he had cut his bonds on the window as well, and the sight of them made her think that they should find a knife to finish the job; a clanless man and woman wandering through Shai tied with bonds of rope would surely attract some attention. And they had to get rid of their heavy cloaks as well; they could not afford to be mistaken for outlaws.

But they saw no one on the streets, and Taja began to think that they might keep the cloaks after all. The bulky fabric covered their darker features and made them less conspicuous.

"I'm almost sorry he's dead," Val said, echoing her thoughts about Rugath. "He seemed more like a man from Etrara than a clan chief. A courtier, or even a king."

"Aye," she said. "He was like a man in a tragedy. He had too much ambition for a man of the Shai—it was almost inevitable that he died."

She led the way through the twisted maze of the city, stopping when the streets branched out into two or more directions. Yet every time they stopped she was able to choose a street and continue on.

After they left the city the rough spire of Wizard's Hill

appeared in her mind for the first time since they had been captured. It called to her, drawing her toward it. She hurried on, anxious to reach their destination.

A day later Taja saw a more direct way to the hill, and she turned south onto a dirt track that led off the main road. Val followed. They had said little all day; both were hungry and worried about pursuit.

They passed fields and farmhouses. Dogs barked at them from the safety of their houses, and when she and Val came to the barns and storehouses she saw that they were locked. She had heard of similar things happening in the provinces around Etrara; farmers wanted to protect what little food they had as the crops began to fail. She nearly groaned aloud with hunger. And something else had started to worry her: the Shai had taken Val's sword. How could he guard her while she spent the night on Wizard's Hill?

When night fell they stopped at an open field and spread their cloaks on the ground. There was little warmth in Val's arms; he held her as she lay on her back, shivering and staring at the thin shell of the moon. The next night would be dark, moonless. Only once did she think of turning back, but she put the thought away from her as something impossible, as if a fish had thought of walking on dry land.

"Taja?" Val said. "Are you awake?"

She turned to face him. "Yes."

"I thought of something that might help you. I met a poet-mage during the war, Anthiel, and he told me something about the ways of magicians. He used solid words as his key-stones, he said—tree and rock, table and door."

"Solid words," Taja said. The advice meant little to her; she had not thought of the night she would have to endure on Wizard's Hill. All her strength had gone toward getting there. She turned over and drifted off to sleep.

She saw blackness broken by a thousand stars when she woke; the sky reminded her of a courtier's jeweled cloak she had seen the night she had ridden to Etrara to find Val.

Despite the darkness she knew that morning had come. She roused Val and they set off.

The weak sun rose some hours later, barely lightening the world around them. As they walked she forgot everything but the hill that loomed before her in her mind. Once Val said something and she started, remembering with surprise that she was not alone. "What?" she said impatiently.

"There are orange trees here," he said.

She could not imagine what he wanted. But he turned off the path and picked a few of the thin-skinned, wizened oranges and gave her one. "Eat it," he said, peeling one and taking a bite. "Gods, it tastes horrible."

As she ate she realized how hungry she was. But a few steps later she stopped, all thoughts of the orange in her hand forgotten. They had topped a rise and she saw, off in the distance, the silhouette of Wizard's Hill. It looked exactly as she had seen it in her dreams.

She hurried on, not turning back to see if Val followed. The land around the hill was featureless, with no houses or pasture or cropland to break the flat expanse. After she had gone some distance she realized that the bleakness of the land made the hill look closer than it really was; they would not reach it until nightfall.

The hill grew larger as they walked. Its pointed top seemed to reach to the heavens, to the court of Sbona. One side was jagged, as if something had broken off from it long ago; the other was smooth and looked impossible to climb.

The pale sun had set by the time they reached the hill. She could no longer see the top; black had merged imperceptibly with black.

"Look," Val said.

Strange shapes of stone and metal crouched at the base of the hill. The ruins looked nothing like the arch of Sleeping Koregath, but she thought they shared some kinship with it; they had been built by the same people, perhaps, or ensorcelled by them. Would the ruins come alive sometime in the night? She shook her head; her task would be difficult enough without such child's fancies.

She began to climb. "Wait," Val said. "This path doesn't lead all the way up. Look—it's blocked by that boulder there."

She stopped, impatient at the delay. Had they come this far only to be turned back by the hill itself? But Val had gone around an outcropping of rock and called back to her. "Over here," he said.

She didn't wait to hear more, but pushed in front of him and began to climb.

For a while she could hear Val behind her, but soon she thought of nothing but the hill. She felt that everything she had ever done, her strange lonely childhood by the sea, her work as the librarian of Tobol An, her meeting with Val, all of it had been nothing compared to her ascent of Wizard's Hill. Her life before this could be summed up in ten lines of verse and spoken by a Prologue in a play; here, on this hill in front of her, her true life would begin.

She pulled herself up over several large boulders. The path leveled out and she hurried on.

"Taja!" Val called behind her. "Taja—where are you?"

She had made it to the top, she saw; there was a small plot of level ground ahead of her, with nothing on it but a white stone shining palely in the darkness. She walked toward the stone and sat, knowing as she did so that countless men and women had done the same before her.

"Taja—the hill won't let me join you. I'll wait for you here, and guard you. May all the gods protect you and defend you. May I see you whole and well tomorrow morning. Good fortune!"

Val stood near the crest of the hill. Strange forms had approached him as he climbed, blocking his way to the top: soldiers and trees and great cats, apparitions like the ones he had encountered in the Teeth of Tura.

Taja had appeared not to see them. Well, he thought, the

mountain existed for her and for people like her, wizards, poet-mages.

There were more shapes here, metal and stone like the ones they had passed at the mountain's foot. He went closer. These forms were not as ruined as the ones he had seen earlier; perhaps the power of the mountain had preserved them. He could see statues nearly twice his height, smoothed by generations of wind and rain; looking up he saw that what was left of their faces still showed an unearthly beauty and wisdom.

He would spend the night here, then, guarding her and praying to Callabrion. And if she descended whole in the morning she would be a poet-mage; she would help him take the throne of Etrara. He glanced up once but the dark bulk of the mountain kept its secrets; he could not see Taja any-where.

What if she failed? How would he face Pebr if he brought her dead body back to Tobol An? Worse, what if she went mad, if she spent the rest of her life staring sightlessly from the windows of Pebr's cottage?

He shivered. He had met sorcerers before, Penriel and Anthiel, but never one who had gone to Wizard's Hill. What would happen to her? Had she understood what she was doing when she agreed to help him? What had he unleashed in his desire to be king?

Dead, or mad, or a poet, she thought. Almost as if the thought had conjured up whatever force was at work on the mountain the sky above her began to slide sickeningly, to change places with the earth below. The stars wheeled beneath her. A shape appeared from the plains overhead, a great bird of prey. The bird flew toward her, and as it came closer she saw that it carried a warrior on its back, his sword aimed unerringly toward her heart.

She drew a deep breath. It had begun, then. She spoke an invocation to the gods and began to construct a spell to turn the apparition aside. Halfway through her second verse she saw how the poem should end, how the two keystones came together in a phrase that strengthened both of them. She spoke the words triumphantly. The bird gave a loud cry and disappeared.

A ship came toward her out of the strangely twisted sky, its hull and mast shining like pearl. She saw that each challenge would require a different spell, that her invention must not be allowed to flag once during the night. She recited a brief prayer to the goddess Sbona, mother of light, and found to her surprise that the first word of the prayer—"mother"— could be used as a keystone. Solid words, just as Val had advised. She spoke the rest of the spell confidently. The apparition wavered, frayed into gusts of light, and was gone.

Nothing moved in the sky for a long time. But someone came toward her over the crest of the hill, a soldier wearing a tattered cloak and carrying an old rust-eaten sword. His eyes glittered silver in the darkness. He was a ghost, she realized, one of the many who had spent the night on the mountain before her.

Dozens of ghosts crowded around her now, clamoring for her attention. A man held his arms out to her beseechingly; she could see the places where he had slashed his wrists with his sword. A woman with a glittering crown came after him, the legendary Queen Ellara I, the beloved of Callabrion. She hadn't realized that Ellara the Good had been both ruler and poet-mage. And there was Cosro, a short round man who had been capable of writing both piercing satires and sonnets of surpassing beauty.

Cosro smiled at her. She remembered the stories told about him, that he was unable to lie, and she wondered what that smile might portend. It seemed knowing, almost unpleasant.

She forced herself to look back toward the sky. Another sending came toward her, a great forest of moving trees. She began an invocation, thinking that the challenges were simpler than she had anticipated. But then why had Cosro smiled?

One of the ghosts began to whisper to her. She shook her head, trying to concentrate on the sending before her. The muttering of the ghosts became louder. She hurried through the remaining verses of the spell, hoping to finish before the sighing voices of the ghosts forced out all other thought.

Pictures formed before her, blocking out the sight of the trees. She shook her head but the pictures remained. She was in Soria, watching a thin, unhealthy-looking woman come toward her from an alleyway. She remembered seeing the woman when she was a child, remembered asking Pebr who she was. Pebr had hurried her into a shop; he had pretended to have business there.

Now she realized that the woman had been a prostitute. But why had she been shown this picture? The voices of the ghosts grew louder, a susurrus rushing past her like a brook in full flood. She was helpless against this magic; it had none of the formal logic of meter, alliteration, rhyme. A whisper came out of the darkness, a mocking echo of the invocation she had used earlier. "Mother of light."

Was this woman her mother? No, she thought. Revulsion twisted within her so strongly that she almost screamed aloud. Another ghostly voice whispered: "Aye, your mother . . ." She shook her head again, but the insinuations continued.

The pictures wavered for a moment and she saw that the apparition of the forest had moved closer. She had forgotten most of her spell, could not even remember the meter she had chosen. Panicked, she spoke something, anything. The trees gusted as if blown by a wind and then returned, as solid as before. She reached for her keystones, joined them in a final phrase. The trees frayed outward again, grew transparent, and then disappeared.

As soon as they had gone the picture of the woman returned. Could the ghosts be right? She did not remember her parents. Pebr had said they were fisher-folk, but Pebr might have lied. At that thought she heard Cosro whisper, "Aye, Pebr lied."

Cosro. Cosro, who always told the truth. She closed her

eyes, barely caring what apparition might be sent against her. Despair overwhelmed her. She rested her head on her arms, wanting only for the night to be over. She understood then why the ghost she had seen had killed himself.

"God's child," one of the ghosts whispered mockingly, and the others laughed. "Was your father Callabrion or Scathiel?"

"You are like your mother," someone else said. "Think of your feelings for Val. You want him, don't you? You, the daughter of a woman as common as dirt, a woman at the very base of the ladder. You even believed his protestations of love for you. You must have known he didn't mean it—courtiers flatter as easily as breathing."

"It's ludicrous, isn't it?" another of the ghosts whispered. "To think that the king will even notice you after he claims his birthright, that he would ever think of you as other than lowborn."

She looked up. The ghosts massed before her stepped back a little, and she saw with surprise that they feared her. At that moment she felt her power grow within her, knew with certainty that she was the strongest poet-mage to sit on Wizard's Hill since Cosro. Hadn't she triumphed over every apparition sent against her?

She faced them all defiantly. It didn't matter who her mother had been. She would be stronger than the ghosts before her, strong enough not to give in to despair.

Another form appeared in front of her. No glow of silver came from the eyes; this person was not a ghost. Val? she thought. How had Val braved the terrors of the night to come to her? But the person before her was smaller than Val, and bent over like someone of great age. "Very good, my child."

"Mathary?" Taja said, astonished. "Why— How did—"

"You have survived your night on Wizard's Hill," Mathary said. The ghosts hurried away before her, dispersing into the night air. "By our customs another poet-mage must come to welcome you among us."

"Poet—but then—are you a poet-mage?"

"Aye, my child."

My child. Taja gasped, hardly daring to hope. "You're—you're my mother," she said.

"Aye."

Pebr had lied, Taja thought. Pebr had lied and Cosro had told the truth. She wanted to ask a thousand questions, but at the same time she thought that all her questions had been answered with one word. She understood who she was now; that seemed all she needed to know.

But Mathary was speaking. "I was one of Tariel's wizards. My husband was as well, your father. Godemar, Callia's mother, wanted her daughter to succeed to the throne, but she knew that she would have to defeat us all before she could kill Tariel. We were prepared for magic, but not for ordinary poison. I was fortunate—I was not at the banquet where the wizards died."

"But where—where were you?" Taja said, whispering.

"You were sick that day—I stayed home to nurse you. You saved my life, my child."

"And then you came to Tobol An."

"Aye. After the poisoning Lady Godemar and her wizards turned their attention to me. Her wizards were strong—Penriel's father was one of them. My husband was dead, by Godemar's hand, and I could not think what to do, where to go. Then I remembered my husband's brother Pebr, and I managed to escape to Tobol An. Pebr offered to raise you—you would be in great danger if Godemar discovered where I was." Mathary shivered a little, remembering something. "So Pebr took you away from me. I didn't know he would turn you against me, against all magic. His brother had died, you see, and he wanted to keep you safe. . . ."

"All these years—" Taja said, breathing the words. It seemed incredible that such a secret had been kept from her. "All these years you pretended to—to be a little foolish, a harmless old woman—"

The other woman shook her head. "It may not be pretense, after so much time. When they came after me I was badly injured. I had to give up a good deal of my power just to survive."

"And my father—"

"He was a good wizard, and a just one. Our heritage was strong within you—I hoped that despite Pebr you would one day find your way to Wizard's Hill. You did well, my child."

Mathary was crying, Taja saw, and that seemed the strangest of all the strange things she had seen that night. Why should she cry? Taja had learned the truth and come into her power at the same time; from this night forward there would be no more lies. Mathary's long time of waiting was over.

She reached out to the other woman uncertainly. My mother, she thought. The words seemed strange, foreign; she had never used them before.

Mathary came forward and held her in a long embrace. Then she stepped back and wiped her eyes. "A foolish old woman," she said. "Come—Val is waiting for you."

The wind whistled loudly past Val as he sat among the old ruins. Several times he thought he could hear shouts from the summit of the mountain, someone reciting a string of strange words, and once a silver light flared out and shook from horizon to horizon.

He forced himself to stay where he was; he could do Taja no good if he went scurrying toward her like a rabbit. But it galled him to do nothing; he wanted to fight an enemy he knew, someone of flesh and blood, not insubstantial things made of sorcery. He spoke the same mindless prayer to Callabrion he had been repeating all night, and felt again for the amulet beneath his tunic.

A light moved on the plain before him. He stared at it, trying to bring it into focus. The plain was dark; the only light came from the stars. Had he truly seen it, or had he conjured it up out of boredom and fear? No, there it was again, closer this time.

He stood, reaching out blindly in the dark. His hand fell

on an iron bar and he picked it up. It would do against a lone traveler, a single bandit or outlaw, but what if he faced a clan the size of Rugath's? Or what if others had seen the shining light and had come to investigate?

The light moved closer. It resolved itself into a string of lights, torches. The torches turned and headed toward the base of the mountain, then disappeared as the men began to climb.

Val stood, uncertain. Moments later the torches appeared again, bright enough now so that he could see the men carrying them, acolytes wearing blue and priests dressed in white. They came closer, stood before him.

"You said you'd been to Wizard's Hill," a priest said. Val thought he might be the same man who had spoken to them at the temple. "An absurd claim, of course—only men and women of Shai can spend the night on that hill and survive. But we thought that perhaps you had given away your intentions, that perhaps you were going to Wizard's Hill. And so we followed you."

Val said nothing.

"Take him," the priest said. "And there was another, a woman—"

The acolytes came forward. Val raised the iron bar. At that moment he saw something move at the edge of his vision. The acolytes stopped, hesitant.

Val turned quickly. Taja stood there. A corona of light surrounded her, and there was a distance in her eyes that he had never seen before. For a moment he thought he saw someone behind her, but then the light faded and the figure was gone.

"Drop your weapons," Taja said. The acolytes' swords clattered to the ground. "Go back to your temple. You have never seen us. You do not even know that we are here, in Shai."

"We have never seen you," the priest said. He turned and led the men away from the mountain.

Val looked at Taja. She seemed a figure out of legend,

wise and stern and unapproachable. A queen made of light.
He did not know how he should think of her. Was she still the
daughter of fisher-folk that he had hoped to dazzle with fine
words and splendid poetry? Or did she stand high above him
on the ladder, as far above him as a king to a peasant girl?

"Come," she said to Val.

"Who was— Was there someone with you?"

"Aye. My mother."

She said nothing more. The mystery of her initiation
surrounded her; he thought that she might still be half walking on strange paths he could not imagine. What had happened to her, there on the mountain? Hadn't she told him
once that her mother was dead?

He bent to take one of the swords dropped by the acolytes
and followed her. She led him along the featureless plain,
then turned and continued along a dirt road leading north.
He would have missed the path in the dark; he wondered how
she had found it.

The sun rose, revealing a gray and featureless world
before them. She stopped and looked at him; she had the
disinterested gaze of a cat, or a god. She said a few words and
the bonds of rope at their wrists dropped to the ground. And
something happened to his cloak as well; the bright gaudy
colors of the outlaws swirled and then changed to somber gray
and black.

A short while later they came to a locked storehouse. She
spoke something and the lock broke open and fell to the
ground. He hurried forward and opened the door, remembering suddenly how hungry he was. Shelves of nuts and dried
apples and cured meat stood before them.

To his surprise she sat on the dirt floor and began to eat.
But she would probably be able to tell if they were threatened,
he thought, and he joined her. The food tasted wonderful
after days of hunger.

Suddenly she stopped and looked up. "What?" he said,
alarmed. "What is it?"

"I don't—"

"Is someone coming?"

"Something . . ." she said. "I think— Yes. It's Narrion."

"Narrion?" he said, astonished.

"He's trying to summon Callabrion."

"How do you know?"

She raised her hand for quiet and began to speak. He listened, amazed, as she spoke what seemed to be a counter-spell for magic that had somehow spiraled out of control. Then she began a poem of such complexity that he soon lost the thread of it, and only realized how brilliantly it had been constructed when she finally joined the two keystones together. She recited a final invocation and then fell silent.

"What did you do?" he asked.

"I called up Callabrion for him," she said. To his surprise he saw that she was smiling; she had started to come back from wherever she had been. "And what will he do now, I wonder? No one sees a god face-to-face without being changed in some way. I wonder if he considered that."

Thirteen

· · · · · · ·

NARRION FOLLOWED CALLABRION TO the Street of Stones and turned with him toward the Darra River. The Street of Stones was too wide, too public, for Narrion's liking; it was one of the main thoroughfares of Etrara. But Callabrion had insisted on going out into the city, and Narrion could not let him wander through the streets alone. He sighed. Whatever he had expected when he had summoned the god it hadn't included acting as nursemaid.

Three Shai guards came toward them. Narrion pulled up the hood of his cloak and pretended to shiver with cold. The guards continued on.

Narrion threw back his hood and shook out his long hair. It was warm work following Callabrion; the god seemed made of fire. He could not remember when he had last been so hot.

They came to the bank of the river. Callabrion stopped and stared down into the clear depths. Small waves beat against the shore.

"Where would you like to go, my lord?" Narrion asked. He wanted to take Callabrion to the observatory; he would enjoy seeing the faces of those cowardly priests when they realized just who it was who visited them. That would be a jest worthy of the Shadow King, the Lord of Misrule himself. But the Shai guarded the observatory, letting no one in or out.

"Where? Here. The river."

"The river, my lord?"

"Yes." Callabrion looked at Narrion. His strange eyes, the golden green of the sun on leaves, shone with delight. "The changing colors, and the sounds it makes against the shore . . . Look—it moves quicker there, where it is forced between the pilings of the Darra Bridge. Do you see it?"

"You must forget the earth, my lord. The earth will be here when you next return."

Callabrion said nothing.

"You must ascend to heaven," Narrion said. "There is a balance in all things—summer must follow winter."

"You killed a kinsman of mine, did you not?"

Narrion looked up quickly. Callabrion's deep, even voice had not changed; he might still be discussing the river. "I— What do you mean?"

"You killed King Gobro, a son of Sbona."

"I did not kill him, my lord. Callia and Mariel asked me to find poison, nothing more." He had made the same excuse to Val, he remembered, but what had seemed reasonable in the palace of Etrara now sounded hollow, contrived.

"Did you think of what might happen if Callia ruled? Her poor judgment, her disastrous war? You speak of balance, but there is no balance in your own actions. You have bound yourself too closely to Scathiel, the god of death."

"I—"

"Was it worth it to kill Gobro? What good is your high position now?"

"I— Nothing," Narrion said bitterly. He looked down at the river. "It is worth nothing at all."

"We should go," Callabrion said gently. "The others will be worried."

They walked back to Noddo's house, saying nothing. Once there Narrion took out the key Noddo had given him and opened the door. Tamra looked up; she held conjuring sticks in her hand.

Noddo hurried toward them. "Did he say anything about returning to the heavens?" he asked quietly.

Narrion shook his head. "We'll have to think of something," Noddo said. "The days grow shorter—"

"Close the door," Tamra said. "It's cold as Scathiel's heart out there. Come inside and wager with me." Narrion closed the door and locked it carefully behind him.

Callabrion moved to the small table and took the sticks from Tamra's hand. He threw one down. His image gazed back up at him from the conjuring stick, the green and gold face of the summer god. "Summer," he said, and laughed.

The door opened again, letting in a gust of cold air. Narrion turned quickly, one hand on the hilt of his sword; he would have sworn by all the gods that he had locked the door.

At first he did not recognize the two people who came into the room. They wore bulky gray and black cloaks that nearly hid their features. But as he watched the colors shifted, swirling to become the barbarous hues of the Shai: red and gold, purple and black.

The man shook back his hood and looked around him. There was a purposeful expression on his face that Narrion had never seen before. But it was the woman who caught and held his attention; she seemed to command a power as unmistakable as Callabrion's.

"Good fortune," the man said.

"Val?" Tamra said.

"Val, yes. And Taja, who has spent the night on Wizard's Hill, and is now a poet-mage."

"You—you were the mage I heard," Narrion said to Taja. "The wizard who helped me summon Callabrion."

Taja nodded. "Yes. You must not meddle in magic again, Narrion—it is too subtle for your understanding." She turned to Callabrion and bent in a slight curtsy. "My lord," she said, and then looked back at Narrion. "You have your wish— you've summoned a god. What do you intend to do with him?"

"I thought to ask him to return to the heavens," Narrion

said. "The days grow dim and cold, the crops begin to fail throughout Etrara. . . . Perhaps you could help me."

Taja shrugged. "Over the gods I have no power," she said. "We've come to free Etrara from the Shai."

Andosto looked up sharply at that. "To free—" he said. His face bore a strange expression, a mixture of exaltation and purpose.

Before they could respond the god Callabrion spoke. "I know you," he said, his green eyes lighting on Val.

"Yes, my lord," Val said. "You argued in defense of love at one of Lady Sbarra's gatherings. And I agreed with you."

"Yes. I remember that. But I think that I've always known you, that you are a kinsman of mine. A child of Sbona. A son of Sbona, yes, and the rightful king of Etrara."

"King—" Narrion said. He looked at the man he had thought was his cousin, astonished beyond words.

"King, yes," Val said. "The son of King Tariel III and Queen Marea. There are records in the library at Tobol An, if any doubt me." He looked at each of them in turn. No one spoke. "I've come to claim my birthright."

King Valemar, Narrion thought. His legs seemed unable to hold him; he sat down at the table next to Tamra. How had he miscalculated so badly?

But the day was to hold one final surprise. Andosto drew his sword from its scabbard and sank to his knees. "My king," he said. "Will you accept my sword?"

"I will," Val said. "I would be pleased to command a man who fought so bravely against the Shai. Rise, my friend."

Andosto stood slowly. "What do you intend to do?"

"I have some ideas," Val said. He looked around him. "And in this room I see a god, a king, a poet-mage, a warrior and two Fools. Surely together we can make some plan that will stand against the Shai."

Val looked around the table. For just a moment he wondered how he was to lead this band of people; he did not have a fraction of their experience. Then he put his doubts aside and concentrated on the task before him; he would have to learn a great deal in a very short time if he was to be a king.

"I think we should begin with small raids on the palace," Andosto said. "Skirmishes with the watch."

Val made a note on a piece of paper in front of him, and nodded at Andosto to continue. "I've done it before," Andosto said. "It's a way to gain support among the people. More and more of them will come to join us."

"They say the Shai execute ten people for every man of theirs killed," Taja said.

"We'll never free ourselves without bloodshed," Andosto said.

"Is that true?" Taja said. "We could use sorcery."

"The Shai have a poet-mage," Andosto said.

"Kotheg," Val said thoughtfully. "I saw him in the mountains."

"They might have more than one," Narrion said. "You said yourself that Wizard's Hill is in Shai."

"Even with one wizard, a battle of sorcery is always dangerous," Noddo said. "We might lose more soldiers than with Andosto's skirmishes."

"And we might not," Taja said forcefully. "Why not let me try it?"

"You might be killed," Andosto said.

"So might you—"

"Quiet," Val said. Everyone turned to him, expectant. "We'll try Andosto's plan at first," he said. "We're not strong enough for anything else right now—we need to win more followers among the people. And we need to learn more about the Shai, to discover how strong they are and if Kotheg is with them. Then we'll fight them with magic. Will you be ready, Taja?"

"Of course, my lord."

"Good," Val said. "I'll lead a raid tonight."

"My lord," Andosto said. "You must not risk your life on a raid. I have friends who feel as I do about the Shai—I'll go."

"A king must protect his people."

"You protect them best by keeping yourself safe."

Val said nothing. Noddo had taught him the dreadful counting rhyme the Shai sang, and he had heard it once himself on the streets: "One is for Gobro . . ." Four was for Callia, he remembered; would five be for Valemar?

He sat back, defeated. "Very well," he said. "May all the gods go with you, Andosto."

That night Andosto went out into the streets of Etrara and called upon his friends, the men who had gone with him on his other skirmishes against the Shai. They were reluctant to fight, unwilling to call death down on themselves and their neighbors. But he told them about the new king, and as he spoke he watched them grow eager, excited at the news.

When he had collected his men they headed east down the Street of Roses. They passed under the triumphal arch the traitor Talenor had built; a few of them spat on it as they went. Then they reached the gate that opened east, to Shai: the Gate of Roses. They concealed themselves near the wall inside the city.

Wheels and horses' hooves sounded in the distance, and Andosto looked out carefully through the gate. A convoy was headed toward them, one of the caravans that came nightly from Shai, bringing the food that was becoming rarer and rarer as the days declined and the crops rotted in the ground. Andosto saw two men in bulky robes riding horses at the head, and then half a dozen carts and wagons. He frowned. They had added guards to their convoys since his last raids; the two men in front could not be anything else.

One of his men stepped out of hiding and stood in the road, blocking the convoy. The guards were forced to pull up on their reins, and the rest of the convoy came to a halt. "Have you seen my wife?" the man said. "I can't find her anywhere."

"A ghost," one of the guards said to the other. "Don't be frightened."

"I'm not frightened," the other guard said, but Andosto heard the shiver of fear in the man's voice. Taja had said that all the ghosts in Shai were bound in some way to Wizard's Hill, and he believed it; no country where ghosts were common would kill their kings as recklessly as the Shai did.

"She told me she would meet me here, at the Gate of Roses," Andosto's man said, sounding plaintive. "Have you seen her?"

"Move aside," the first guard said. He touched his reins and the horse danced a little, unable or unwilling to move on.

"What's happening here?" someone from the convoy asked.

"There's a ghost in the road," the second guard said.

"A ghost?"

The sound of muffled conversation came from the convoy, and then Andosto heard the creaking of wheels as men climbed down off their carts and wagons. Probably they had been raised on stories of the ghosts of Etrara, just as he had been told the people of Shai drank their king's blood. They crowded forward, fearful and eager.

Andosto moved back toward the carts. His men followed. One man had remained to guard the convoy; he had risen in his seat and was craning his neck to peer past the crowd. Andosto's men came up behind him and pulled him down, binding his hands and mouth. It was done so silently and skillfully that no one from the convoy turned to look.

Andosto signaled to his men to wait. He climbed up to the bench behind the driver and looked out at the Shai, watching as they moved farther and farther down the Street of Roses. If all went according to plan the man who acted the ghost would lead them as far from the convoy as he could, speaking of enchantments and the strange knowledge acquired after death.

Andosto motioned to his men again. A few of them climbed onto the carts and quickly tossed down wooden boxes and clay jars to the men waiting below. Others hurried to store the provisions in an abandoned well; the cover would be dragged back over the well at the raid's end and the provisions retrieved later.

A man rolled a cask of what smelled like wine to the edge of the cart. It slipped and hit another cask. The man cursed softly.

One of the men from Shai turned, called out. Andosto and the others jumped from the cart and ran down one of the narrow alleys inside the city wall. He heard running footsteps, too many of them to be his men; the Shai were following them. At a junction of three streets he and his men split up. Someone cried out; someone else screamed.

He hurried on toward the agreed-upon meeting place. The sounds of pursuit were far behind now.

The next morning Val sat at the table and studied the crude map of Etrara he had drawn. The lines of the map—the city walls and gates, Palace Hill, Darra River—began to blur and he forced himself to pay attention. Andosto had left the night before and hadn't come back.

A noise from outside roused him. He went to the window and then dropped back as he saw several Shai soldiers leading a group of citizens of Etrara. A herald for the Shai began to call out in a loud voice, but Val understood what had happened long before he heard the man's explanation. Andosto's raid had been successful: these unfortunate men and women would be killed in retaliation.

Val sat back at the table and put his head in his hands. He had hoped he would not have to face this when he had asked the others to fight the Shai. How could he deal with a people who had no honor? And they had called him decadent!

Had he been wrong to order the raids? Had people died because of his mistakes?

Someone sat next to him. Val raised his head and saw Narrion. What did the other man want? "This is what happens in war," Narrion said.

"Not in any war I was ever in," Val said. "This is— It's dishonest, and cowardly. . . ."

Narrion shrugged. "All wars are the same. One side has

something, and the other side tries to take it from them by force."

"But some causes are more honorable than others. We're trying to free what is ours, not take something from the Shai."

"Oh, the reasons for war differ. But the result is always the same—pain and sorrow, confusion and death. War belongs to Scathiel, whatever the others might say."

"And you believe that this is a good thing? You and the Society of Fools?"

"We say that it exists. That's all."

"But how can I—" Someone screamed in the street. Val stood, as if driven from his seat by the scream, and began to pace the small room. "How can I stand by and let this—this horror continue?"

Narrion turned to watch him. "I don't know," he said. "The followers of Scathiel only ask questions—we're not used to answering them."

"And who provides the answers? Callabrion?" He looked over to where Callabrion sat with Tamra, their heads bent over a game of chess. He lowered his voice. "It's been a long time since Callabrion answered anything."

"Sometimes it's just enough to ask the question," Narrion said.

Andosto unlocked the door and came in. Val turned quickly. "What happened?" he asked.

"You saw the Shai," Andosto said, motioning toward the street outside the room. "We took some provisions for Etrara, but we had to kill a guard."

Val nodded. He took a deep breath, forced himself to put his doubts aside. "How many soldiers were there?" he asked. "Did you see Kotheg? Come—sit here and tell me all about it."

The skirmishes continued. So did the retaliations, ten citizens dead for every Shai killed. Twice Val thought to give the order to stop the raids; he thought that nothing could be worth so many deaths, not even the freedom of Etrara.

But the amount of information Andosto and Narrion brought back with them grew: soldiers and troop movements and times of the watch. And more and more people joined them each night; excitement ran through the city like a river.

A week after they had begun the raids Narrion and Andosto went out and did not return. Val spent the morning pacing the room impatiently. "Sit, Val," Noddo said. "Your worry won't help them."

Val glanced around him. Noddo sat with Val's map of Etrara in his lap; Tamra and Callabrion were studying the chessboard on the table. The god could not toss the conjuring sticks without casting his own face, the face of the summer god; he had quickly abandoned the sticks and played game after game of chess with Tamra instead. He had resisted every attempt to draw him out; he would not talk about his place in the heavens at all.

Val wondered if Narrion had been wrong about Callabrion. Perhaps he did not return to Sbona's court because he had forgotten his life there. Perhaps he had wrapped himself so completely in the beauty of the world, had lost himself so fully in his mother's earth, that he did not remember the way back to her. If that was true then all Narrion's arguments would not change things; the god needed something more.

Val shook his head. Now was not the time to worry about Narrion's schemes. "My worry won't help them, no," he said. "But I might rescue them."

"And get yourself killed as well?"

"It's time to do something," Val said. "The others are risking their lives while I sit here in safety. And I'll have Taja with me, a poet-mage."

"What about Kotheg?" Noddo asked. "Is he in Etrara? Does Taja know enough to stand against him?"

"I don't know," Taja said. "But I won't learn more by staying here."

"Let's go," Val said. He opened the door and looked out. A gust of icy wind blew past him down the deserted street.

He shivered and pulled his cloak closer around him. As

he glanced down he saw the shimmering colors of the cloak fade back toward somber black and gray; Taja was renewing her spell.

"Wait," Noddo said. "Take me with you."

Val shrugged. He didn't think the older man could help in any way, but he could not prevent him from coming along. He turned to look at him. If I could have anyone in this room, he thought, I'd take Callabrion. Who could stand against us if we had a god on our side?

But Callabrion was still playing chess with Tamra. His hand, nearly as big as a dinner plate, moved out over the board; it hovered over a knight, then lifted his astronomer-priest. He did not glance up as they set out.

"Do you know where they are?" he asked Taja.

She nodded. "I think I can find them for you," she said.

The streets were silent. Darkness lay upon them like thick soot. Lamps and candles shone from the houses as they walked by, but the light seemed unable to penetrate the gloom.

"The Shai issued an edict," Noddo said. His voice sounded muffled in the layers of shadows. "Ever since the days started getting darker like this. Every house has to keep a light burning."

They came to the Street of Stones and headed toward Palace Hill. Almost immediately Taja stopped. Val followed her gaze. Andosto hung in an iron cage above them.

"Andosto!" Val said, not daring to speak above a whisper.

The man in the cage above them stirred. For a dreadful moment Val thought that they had made a mistake, that this person could not possibly be Andosto. He looked weary, defeated. "I am called Borno," the caged man said. "I know no one named Andosto. Do you have any food?"

"Sorcery," Taja said. She was whispering as well. "I've never seen anything like this. They've made him forget who he is."

"Andosto," Val said again. "Wait for us—we'll find a way to get you down."

"My name is Borno," Andosto said. "Go away—please go away. If I'm seen with rebels I'll be killed—they told me so."

Val looked up and down the street, remembering the information Andosto and Narrion had brought him. The watch might come upon them at any moment. Then he looked back at the cage. He could not believe that anyone could be so changed; they had taken not only Andosto's name but his sense of who he was. "Can you do something?" he asked Taja.

"I'll try," she said. She began the words of an invocation, chose a keystone.

"My lord," Noddo said. His voice was urgent.

A troop of men came toward them down the street; in the gloom Val could not see how many there were. Their swords caught the light from the houses and shone silver in the darkness. Taja finished her verse quickly, quieting the currents of magic she had raised. They stared at the men as they came, uncertain whether to flee or fight.

The man in front went down on his knees and offered Val the hilt of his sword. "My king," the man said.

"Rise," Val said.

"My name is Oldo, my lord," the man said, getting to his feet. "We've heard about you from Andosto."

The word "king" was a kind of keystone, Val thought. It changed things as if by magic; it bound together people who would not normally have anything to do with each other. This man will follow any command I choose to give him, Val thought, and follow it without question. For the first time he felt shaken with the extent of his power. Suddenly he understood Gobro's lovers, Callia's cruelty.

"They've ensorcelled him," Oldo said, indicating Andosto. "We hid and watched their poet-mage. A man named Kotheg, with a face like a stone."

"Kotheg," Val said.

"He was mad," Oldo said. "He mumbled his verses, and then screamed them aloud. In the village where I grew up they say that all poet-mages are mad."

Val looked around him into the gloom. "The watch will come soon," he said. "We have no time for spells. Do you know where Narrion is?"

"Narrion?" Oldo said. "I don't know."

"Go away!" Andosto said loudly. He began to rock the cage back and forth in his terror. "I told you—I won't have anything to do with you. I'm not a rebel."

"Narrion's near the palace, my lord," Taja said.

"Is he caged? Ensorcelled?" Val asked.

She frowned. "I don't think so."

"Good," Val said. He turned to Oldo and his men. "Come with me."

Oldo nodded. He gave orders to the troops standing before him, and they went up the Street of Stones toward the palace.

Val kept an eye on the cages above him as they walked, in case Taja had been wrong. But he did not find Narrion, though he saw a few people he recognized from court. The courtiers all turned away as the troops passed, clearly hoping that Val had not seen them in such reduced circumstances.

At last they came to the courtyard of the palace. Wind ruffled the water in the fountain of Sbona. Val stood for a moment, trying to decide what to do next.

Someone called out in the gloom; someone answered. In less than a heartbeat the palace guard had assembled before them, their swords raised for battle.

Once again Val was not allowed to fight; Oldo and the other rebels kept him away from any danger. Instead the troops looked toward him for guidance, for strategy. He stood at the edge of the palace courtyard and wondered, not for the first time, what he had wrought. The lives of these men were in his hands.

More guards came from the palace. He could barely see the clashing figures in the darkness. If the information Narrion and Andosto had brought him was correct then the palace was unprotected now; all the guards had come out to meet his men. He raised his arm and motioned Oldo and the others toward the outer door.

"Good," someone said near him. "Exactly what I would have done."

Val turned quickly. Narrion stood there, his slight smile barely visible in the dim light.

"Narrion!" Val said. "Where have you been?"

"Escaping the watch."

Val looked back toward the battle. The sound of sword on sword came to him clearly through the darkness. In the gloom he could not be sure, but he thought that no more guards issued from the palace.

More people were coming up the Street of Stones toward the palace. Some of them carried ancient swords; others had no weapon but a kitchen knife. "King Valemar!" someone called, and for a brief, crazy moment Val wondered who it was the man meant.

"Salute them," Narrion said, his tone amused.

Val gave what he hoped was a royal salute. A few men cheered. More and more joined in, their voices ringing out in the empty street; Val heard his name echo from the stone and marble around him. Now he could see a crowd of men, a darker river flowing through the streets of the soot-black city. Some wore the homespun cotton of the lower rungs; they had come all the way from across the river.

He began to laugh, covered it by motioning the men forward. But it looked as if the battle was breaking up, the guards falling back. Some of them lay dead or wounded; others had fled. Could it be that easy? Would they overrun the palace now, take control of the city?

"Behind you," Narrion said.

Val turned quickly. Shai soldiers had come up the Street of Stones, dispersing the men of Etrara as they went. Some of them rode horses; all wore the golden helmets and armor Val remembered.

The men in the courtyard turned to face the soldiers. The Shai pushed their way though the men in the streets. They were hemmed in now, fighting on either side of them. For a brief moment Val wondered if his people could overwhelm the Shai, if both sides would be able to join forces.

Then the battle swirled around them, became confused. He could not see distinct armies anymore, only individuals fighting one another. A soldier on a horse moved forward to cut down one of the rebels. Another of Oldo's men hurried forward but he was too late; he was trampled by the horse as the sword killed the first man.

Val heard horses screaming, and the clash of swords. Someone was calling out orders in the barbaric accent of the Shai.

Through it all the Shai pushed forward, toward the palace. Finally they cleared a path through the fighting and gained the door to the porter's room. They filed through the door and hurriedly pushed it shut behind them.

Early night fell; inky blackness surrounded the men on the streets and in the courtyard. They looked at each other as if waking from a dream. The silence seemed tangible after the noise and confusion of battle.

"What happens now?" Narrion said.

"Now it becomes a battle of magic," Val said. "We'll make camp here, and Taja will fight in the morning. If, that is, there is a morning."

Fourteen

· · · · · · · ·

V AL'S WORDS PROVED PROPHETIC: NO dawn lit the streets of Etrara the next day. A thin rind of frost lay over the water of Sbona's fountain. Val stood, shivering, and wrapped his cloak closer around him.

Pale, weak light grew up around them, almost as if seeping from the stones. All around him men were waking and peering at each other in the dim light, expressions of disbelief and amazement on their faces. Val could almost guess their thoughts; each wondered if he had truly fought with the Shai the day before.

In another minute, Val thought, they would disappear, melt back toward the shops and houses of Etrara, become once more the obedient citizens of an occupied country.

Then one man turned toward him, and another. Silence spread out in waves from where he stood. Slowly, all the men around him went to their knees.

He should speak to them, he knew. But what could he say? He did not even know what to call them; he had never spoken to so many of the lower rungs before.

"My friends," he said. Suddenly it was easy to continue. He told the men of his love for Etrara, the seven-gated city, once proud but now fallen to the Shai. He spoke of his hope to see Etrara free again, and he saw the long rows of men nod.

Callia could have done this long ago, he thought. If she hadn't treated her subjects so cruelly, if she hadn't fled to the countryside, she could have been one of the heroes of Etrara. Triumphal arches would have been built in her name; generations yet unborn would have written songs to her.

As Val watched, a group of men at the edge of the crowd broke away and began to hurry down Palace Hill. He thought he saw Oldo and the rest of Andosto's rebels among them. The sight unnerved him. They had decided not to fight for him.

Would the others follow them? What could he have said that would have kept them here? He paused in his speech and looked out over the crowd. No one else moved.

He finished speaking. The men cheered, their voices loud enough to be heard by the Shai. As if in answer he heard trumpets sound from the palace. The porter's door was flung open, and the Shai marched out into the courtyard to do battle.

But Val could not spare the time to watch them. Someone moved in the window of a high turret in the palace. Val recognized the face; he had come to know it well in his sojourn in Shai. "Kotheg," he said. The name felt like a curse in his mouth.

He looked around for Taja, saw her make her way toward the rise by Sbona's fountain. Her face was impassive; her eyes seemed to see to a place beyond the battlefield.

Kotheg said a few words. At first Val could not hear the wizard over the clamor of battle in front of him. His voice grew louder, stronger, until he was almost screaming. Was he mad, as Oldo had said? Was it true that all poet-mages were mad?

Kotheg chose solid words for his keystones, as Anthiel had recommended, "stone" and "sword." He wove the two together in a sentence so intricate Val did not see how he could possibly finish it, but the poet-mage reached the end of his verse easily, with a phrase that seemed inevitable. Val gasped in wonder at his cleverness.

A great chorus of bells pealed out over the courtyard. Soldiers on both sides dropped their weapons and put their hands to their ears, cringing away from the sound. Val felt panic in the pit of his stomach; he wanted to flee the battle- field and never return.

Some soldiers around him did run, their hands still clasped over their ears. The men of Shai fled too. Kotheg must be confident indeed, Val thought, if he thinks he can win this battle without soldiers.

Something gleamed in the air above him. Val looked up and saw a vast thicket of swords, all poised to plunge down- ward to the men below.

Taja spoke. He had nearly forgotten her; the panic Ko- theg's spell had raised had driven every other thought from his mind. To his surprise she took Kotheg's keystones— "stone" and "sword"—and began to weave them into her own verses. He had never heard of anyone doing such a thing.

But as he listened he understood that she was turning the words against the other poet-mage, subtly shaping her verses so that she made the keystones her own. The swords became a dazzling silver rain and dropped harmlessly to earth. Some men lifted their faces toward the rain and laughed with de- light.

Taja continued to recite her verses, introducing a third and then a fourth keystone, juggling all four in intricate pat- terns. The maddening noise of the bells diminished. Mist began to rise from the marble paving stones in the courtyard.

Kotheg spoke over her. For a moment Val wondered if he would use Taja's cleverness against her and take over her keystones as well, but he introduced new words instead. Val thought that he might be less able to shift his strategy when he had to; he was older and therefore less resilient. But he would also be more experienced; Val could easily imagine him poring over old books for their lists of keystones.

But Taja had had access to the old books as well, Val thought, remembering the books of the wizards she had shown him, and the long lists of what he knew now were

keystones. He watched with fascination as Taja took up Kotheg's challenge. They cast their spells and counterspells
across the courtyard, braided verses in which keystones sparkled like jewels. She understands him, Val thought, and he
her; no two people on Sbona's earth are so well matched.

The noise of the bells subsided, calmed by Taja's verses.
Kotheg spoke a few words and the mists Taja had called up
disappeared. A last bell tolled out over the courtyard, but the
unnatural fear it had caused was gone. Soldiers hurried to the
battlefield.

The soldiers were too eager, Val saw; they were excited at
the opportunity to return to the battle. They flung themselves
against the Shai without caution. "Wait!" Val called.

"What a mess of things you must have made in Shai," a
voice said near him.

This time Val didn't need to turn to know who stood
there. "Everyone made a mess of things in Shai," he said.

"You should have waited for me here."

"There was no time," Val said, finally looking at the man
next to him. Narrion yawned and brushed his hair from his
eyes. "How in Callabrion's name did you sleep through that
unearthly noise?"

"I'm awake now. Hold some of the men back—the Shai
might have more soldiers to send against us."

"I know," Val said.

But there were no men to hold back; everyone had joined
the fighting in the courtyard. Val shouted into the confusion.

No one seemed to have heard him. He shouted again.
The trumpet sounded, and more men issued from the palace.

The first rush of enthusiasm had carried the men of
Etrara far into the courtyard. But as more and more soldiers
came toward them they began to look around in horror, as if
realizing only then where they were. A few turned, trying to
retreat, but they were quickly surrounded. Others stood as if
enchanted, rooted by panic and terror.

Kotheg spoke into the confusion. Taja shouted over him.
Val looked at her quickly; every muscle in her body seemed

strained in her attempt to hold Kotheg back. Val had not thought wizardry was such terrible work.

Men wearing the clothing of Etrara rose up from the battlefield. The Shai soldiers closed with them, only to stand back, amazed and fearful, when their swords met with nothing but air. More soldiers formed; the courtyard filled with people.

Kotheg spoke quickly. His loud, rough voice seemed to be reciting lists of curses. The phantom soldiers grew transparent. The Shai soldiers pressed forward, heartened by their mage's skill. Taja spoke louder, her eyes closed in concentration, but the soldiers she had called up continued to fade.

In the gloom the Shai soldiers in armor seemed to shine with their own light. A wave of gold swept the courtyard, pressing forward toward the fountain of Sbona. As he watched Val saw one Shai soldier after another overwhelm his opponent. The Shai began to close ranks, marching steadily toward him and Narrion.

Narrion grabbed his arm. "We have to get to safety," he said. "Quickly."

"No. Wait." Val shrugged Narrion away and put his hand on the hilt of his sword. But how much help he could possibly be against the might of the Shai? He looked again at Taja. Her eyes were closed; she seemed almost defeated.

"Awake!" Oldo called as he and his men hurried down the Street of Stones. "Awake! The city has risen against the Shai. Awake and come join us!"

The men pounded on doors and shuttered windows with the hilts of their swords. "Come join us!" they called, their voices exultant. The men of the watch had all gone to the courtyard; this time no one would cage them for speaking their minds.

Up and down the street men and women were stepping outside, carrying the lamps required by Shai law. In almost every doorway the same drama was repeated as men hastily grabbed old swords and armor and hurried out to follow Oldo and his men. Others ran down the twisted streets and narrow alleys of Etrara, shouting breathlessly to Oldo, "I'll get my cousin!" "My father will want to join us!"

But Oldo did not turn back to the courtyard. He continued down the Street of Stones until he came to the cage he remembered. He motioned to a man carrying a lamp, and as the man stepped forward he managed to make out Andosto in the dim light.

"No," Andosto said. "Go away—the watch will come."

"The watch is busy elsewhere, my lord," Oldo said. He lifted a ladder away from one of the houses and set it against the cage support, then said a brief prayer to the Ascending God and climbed to the top.

"A saw!" he called down to the men waiting below, and one of them ran back to his house to fetch it.

The man returned with the saw and handed it to him. He put it between the bars of the cage and began to work to break the lock. "No," Andosto said, almost incoherent with terror now. "Oh no. Please."

A crowd gathered at the base of the cage to watch. Some of them called encouragement; others looked around uneasily for the watch.

The lock broke. Oldo opened the door and helped Andosto down the ladder. The other man went slowly, hesitantly, picking his way past the ribbons and bells twined in the rungs as decoration. "Don't worry," Oldo said gently. "You're free now."

When he reached the lowest rung of the ladder Andosto became frightened again. "The watch," he said, turning as if to climb the ladder. "They told me they would bring the watch."

The crowd stirred uneasily, clearly wondering why Oldo had gone to such trouble for this coward. A young woman pressed forward. A tall, broad-shouldered man came with her. As the man approached Oldo saw the lines in his face, the white-gold hair that rayed out from his head; he was older than he seemed.

"Move aside, grandfather," Oldo said, not disrespectfully. He turned to Andosto. "Come, my lord."

"He's—that man is my grandson," the old man said.

"Your grandson," Oldo said, surprised. "Well, then, tell him who he is and what he has to do. He thinks he's a man called Borno."

The man touched Andosto lightly on the face. "My son," he said. "You are my child Andosto, the grandson of my beloved Torath. Do you remember?"

Andosto shook his head.

The man touched Andosto again. Andosto's eyes seemed to clear, and he looked closely at the man standing before him. "Aye," he said. "My grandfather. Callabrion."

Oldo stared at the two men. He had heard the rumors, of course; some said that Andosto was the grandson of the god Callabrion. He had never believed it, thinking that people had invented the story to explain away their own cowardice. "I could be as brave in battle," they seemed to be saying, "if I were descended from a god."

Could it be true? Could his commander be the child of Callabrion? A light seemed to shine from Andosto, the immanence of the gods. Oldo felt shaken with wonder.

But he knew that they could not stand here forever. He was a practical man, unused to these holy matters. "We must hurry, my lord," he said to Andosto.

"Aye," Andosto said. He signaled to his men, and they turned to go up the Street of Stones. The men Oldo had gathered followed them.

A son of Callabrion, Oldo thought, a child of summer. Well, it would give them an advantage in battle, if nothing else.

Something moved up the Street of Stones. Narrion turned quickly, unwilling to take his eyes off the battle in the courtyard.

A group of men marched toward them, more Shai soldiers, probably. It was over, then. Beside him he saw Val draw his sword.

"Don't be a fool," Narrion said urgently.

The men came closer. In the darkness it was hard to make out their features, but as they approached Narrion saw that these could not possibly be soldiers from Shai. Some wore silken tunics, fur collars, and the great chains of their houses. Their hands seemed weighted with their land-rings, and they carried swords with lineages as great as their own, from battles so ancient they had become legends. Others wore faded and patched homespun, and held scythes and pitchforks: farmers, from the land outside the city walls. And someone had freed the people in cages, now that the watch was occupied with the fighting; Narrion saw noblemen he had last seen caged.

At the end of the procession came Oldo and his men. Val laughed, a strange sound in the gloom. "I thought they'd run away," he said. "I thought they'd had enough of fighting."

He turned to Narrion. "I won't forget that you called me a fool," he said. "If we win this battle I expect to be made a member of the Society."

Narrion said nothing. He had miscalculated again, had thought the battle over. Callabrion's optimism had triumphed over Scathiel's pessimism.

He looked at the man he had thought he knew so well, the innocent courtier he had used to further his own ambitions. Val had turned; his hands were stretched out to Oldo's men in welcome. His cloak was thrown back, and his eyes held strength and wisdom. He seemed a king out of legend, a son of Sbona.

Callabrion was right, Narrion thought. He had bound himself too closely to Scathiel, the god of darkness and pain and death. He had been about to run from the battle, to leave the fighting to others. He had killed Damath, and caused King Gobro's death. Even his attempt to return Callabrion to the heavens was motivated by greed and selfishness: if Scathiel ruled forever the earth would die, and he, Narrion, would not be able to enjoy his new-gotten wealth and power.

And here beside him stood a man who seemed bound to Callabrion, a king of light. He had disrupted Val's life to pursue his own ends, and yet Val seemed not to have been touched by his machinations; instead he had risen high on the ladder. They were two sides of the same conjuring stick: life and death, light and shadow.

What would happen to him if Val won out against the Shai? Would he continue to hold his high position, or would Val take revenge for the time he had spent in exile in Tobol An? Should he change his life? Should he swear fealty to Callabrion, the god of summer? Narrion laughed harshly, and turned his attention back to the battlefield.

Val watched as the men came up the street. A broad-shouldered man strode at the front of the procession; he turned aside and came toward them. "Andosto," Val said when he reached them.

"My liege," Andosto said. "I have knelt to you once and received your favor, and I have failed you. I know I am not worthy to ask your pardon—I can only say that I will not fail a second time. You have my sword, and it is yours to claim whenever you have need of it."

"I thank you," Val said. Was this the same man who had trembled in fear in his cage?

Andosto rubbed his hand over his eyes. "I was someone else for a time, my liege," he said, as if seeing Val's doubts. "They made me a coward called Borno."

"How did you overcome their sorcery?"

"I remembered who I was," Andosto said.

Val watched in amazement as the other man went toward the courtyard. I remembered who I was, he had said, as if it could be that simple. Val had not been ensorcelled as Andosto had been, but he thought that he might never come to know himself that completely. Courtier, poet, soldier, actor: in the past year he had played more roles than he could count. And now he acted the part of a king, and the people around him had taken up their parts and become his courtiers and soldiers. But there was more to being a king than he had guessed. What would happen when the play ended?

He looked out over the battlefield. In the dim light he could make out the figure of Andosto at the head of a group of soldiers, pressing toward the palace. The tide of battle began to shift as Andosto encouraged the men. All of them had heard of his exploits in the war against the Shai; some had even fought under his command. With his leadership, and with the reinforcements that had come from all over Etrara, the men began to fight with a new heart.

"Look!" Val said. "The Shai are retreating toward the palace."

"The day is not yet over," Narrion said. "I'm certain someone has gone for more men. The Shai have soldiers in most of the outlying provinces."

The darkness around him began to deepen: soot gray, charcoal gray, nearly black. Val strained to see the men in the courtyard but the air before him became black as pitch. Early night had fallen; he could barely make out Narrion in the gloom.

He heard the sound of sword clashing against sword, and then silence came from the courtyard. Men put away their swords; the citizens of Etrara began to make camp, and the Shai soldiers hastened toward the palace. Could it be night already? He had heard the bells of midafternoon a few minutes ago.

He looked up toward the heavens, searching for the constellations he knew: the Ladder, the Keys, the Palace of Sbona. But he saw nothing he recognized; unfamiliar stars arched across the sky. He shivered.

Campfires bloomed in three or four places across the courtyard, their light shining red-gold in the black night. "Come—let's get warm," Narrion said, leading the way toward one of them.

It was far too early to sleep. On their way across the courtyard Val and Narrion passed men wagering with conjuring sticks or telling stories or singing bits of old ballads. They sat at a fire and listened to a storyteller repeat the old tale of the battle of Arbono. And what stories are the Shai telling each other this night? Val thought. Tales of their own heroism, probably, accounts of battles won and enemies overcome.

Someone looked at Val, looked again as if to make certain that the flickering light had not played tricks on him. "My liege," he said, startled.

Others looked as well. "King Valemar!" someone else said. All around the fire men stirred, turned toward him, whispered to their neighbors. The storyteller stopped in the middle of a sentence.

"My liege," one of the men said shyly. "May I ask you a question?"

Val nodded. "Certainly."

"We have heard rumors—folks say that when you have gained the throne you will return Callabrion to his rightful place in the heavens. Can that be true?"

Val hesitated. What could he promise this man? A twig in the fire snapped, sending up golden sparks. The man beside him stirred impatiently. Val nodded again. "I will try," he said.

"You must, my lord," the man said, serious now. "The land cannot survive much more of this cold and darkness."

Val looked around the circle at the men. Their eyes shone in the firelight; their faces were grave. What had he done? He had given them his word, the word of a king. They would hold him to it, he knew. They looked capable of anything, capable even of killing him like one of the Shai kings if he could not restore summer to Etrara.

Then one of them moved, breaking the spell. "May I continue with the tale, my liege?" the storyteller asked.

"Of course," Val said.

The storyteller took up where he had left off. As Val listened he realized that the other man was altering the tale, though it was done so subtly that most of his audience had probably not even noticed. The hero of the story became not

Brion, the warrior who defeated the Shai after the country had been torn by civil war, but Tarea, the daughter of King Galin who had ascended to the throne when she was just ten years old. And whenever the storyteller mentioned Queen Tarea he was always careful to add her epithet, "the daughter of Sbona."

The daughter of Sbona, Val thought much later that night, lying by the campfire. He pulled his cloak closer around him, listening to the men shift and settle, hearing a few of them snore.

He knew the story, of course. Sbona had come to earth to find her children, Scathiel and Callabrion. After a month where she had searched and found nothing she saw a wooden hut standing alone in the middle of a plain. She made her way toward it and asked the man within for food.

The man invited her inside. She saw that he had little to eat, but he served her the best that he had, and when night fell he offered her his rough pallet and said that he would sleep on the floor.

"I am the goddess Sbona," she said, thinking to reward him for his kindness to her. "Creator of the earth; kindler of the sun, moon and stars; mother of all. I will grant you anything you wish in exchange for your hospitality here. What is your desire?"

The man said nothing.

"What is your desire?" she asked a second time, and a second time the man said nothing.

The goddess Sbona became angry. She grew in stature and reached up to the rafters, intending to bring the house down around them. "What is your desire?" she asked him for the last time.

The man sank to his knees. She saw then that his reverence had prevented him from speaking his mind to her. She found his thoughts, and knew that his sole desire was to kiss her hand.

She drew him up. Then she kissed him and led him to the

pallet, seeing on his face his astonishment, and terror, and great delight.

Nine months later she returned to the cottage, bringing with her the child they had conceived together. "From her line will come the rulers of Etrara," she said, and she left the daughter with him.

After she found her sons Sbona never came to earth again. Callabrion and Scathiel visited the earth separately, each one sowing his seed in every country he came to, but only the rulers of Etrara could claim descent from the goddess directly.

A son of Sbona, Val thought, a child of the great goddess. The story showed him what his kingship meant. Sbona had cared for her children; a king must think not of himself but of his people.

He had not had any idea of the responsibility he had taken on when he had claimed his birthright. They would follow him heedlessly into any battle, just as they had followed Callia into the war against the Shai. Even he had gone to war; he had enlisted as an officer without thinking of the justice of the cause. They had invaded a country not theirs, had sought to take it from the people who lived there. . . . Surely Callia could have made peace with the Shai. Surely peace was better than war.

And yet he had asked these people to fight again. He could only hope his cause was more honorable than Callia's. He shivered and moved closer to the fire, trying to get warm.

The battle continued the next day. The men clashed together in the strange dusklike light; Val stood at his place by the fountain and tried to make some sense of the dim confused forms. Taja and Kotheg shouted over the sounds of battle, but neither could gain the advantage.

When the bells of the clock tower pealed at noon he saw that the battle had turned again. The Shai had slept in comfort in the palace; they seemed rested, eager to make up for their losses and the humiliation of the day before. His own men had spent the night on hard ground, exposed to the chill of winter.

A trumpet sounded. Val turned. Once again he saw men come marching up the Street of Stones, but this time he understood that Narrion had been right, that Scathiel's pessimism had triumphed. Row after row of Shai soldiers headed toward them, their golden armor shining despite the dim light like a field of wheat struck by sunlight.

It was over, then. Val had seen the men of Etrara put up a brave fight; no king could have done more. Would the Shai let him surrender? Would they take prisoners, with no one left to ransom any of them?

Val looked around him. Taja was speaking, her words inaudible in the din coming from the courtyard. She raised her voice; Val heard a ritual opening verse and an invocation to the gods.

The Shai soldiers came closer. Val clenched his fists impatiently. Poetry and fine phrases were all very well, he thought, but they could be dead if the Shai met them before her spell ended.

"This is how it has to be done," Narrion said. "Slowly, with each verse building on the one before it. I learned that if nothing else when I summoned Callabrion."

Taja spoke her first verse, using the word "street" as a keystone. As Val watched, a thin mist began to curl up from the cobblestones in the street. The strands of mist grew stronger, tighter, webbing themselves together. In the thick fog first one soldier and then another stumbled forward, each unable to see more than a handsbreadth in front of him.

Taja began a second verse, and then a third. Her keystones shuttled through her poetry, acquiring new meanings, meeting each other in seemingly endless variations. The fog in the street thickened to a cloud so dense Val could no longer see the men within it.

The men did not emerge from the cloud. Perhaps Taja had turned them all to stone; Val did not think that lay outside her power. She finished the spell and turned toward the fighting in the courtyard, ready to begin another ritual verse.

All around them the light began to fail; the untimely evening was descending. Taja spoke a verse and Kotheg answered; Val saw with fascination that they both worked together to call up an unearthly light that welled from the ground. Taja recited another verse, weaving Kotheg's keystones into her spell. The light around them strengthened, grew brighter.

Kotheg answered her again, using the meter she had chosen for her verses. The courtyard became bright as day: brighter, for the sun had not shone with so strong a light for many months. Gold flared from the domes and turrets of the palace.

Kotheg continued to speak. A sending formed above the courtyard, a vague mist that the poet-mage began to fashion into a solid apparition. Now Val saw that Kotheg had continued to use Taja's meter, turning it against her; he had worked together with her only for as long as it had taken to learn some of her strengths. Kotheg, like Taja, knew tricks to make the other wizard's magic his own.

He had been watching the battle of magic as a spectator might watch a wrestling match, Val thought. Now he saw that the Shai poet-mage had been cunning indeed, had pretended to weakness in order to trap Taja. The man was even more dangerous than he had realized.

A roiling fire formed above them; its red glare lit the courtyard. Val looked quickly at Taja. She seemed lost; she had been able to counter Kotheg's spells but could not fight an apparition made from her own strengths. She started a verse, using the word "doorway" as her keystone. But she did not repeat the keystone in the second verse, or in the third, and by the fourth she had changed meter for no reason Val could see. Kotheg had unnerved her, Val thought.

Taja looked at Kotheg. He had tricked her, she saw; she had thought him weak, elderly, almost a dotard. Now he had revealed his true power. His verses were strong and supple and oddly beautiful; he seemed to know an infinite number of keystones, learned over a lifetime of study.

The fire grew larger, a vast lowering cloud of heat. Discordant noises sounded above them. She closed her eyes, feeling despair. What did she know, after all? How could she be expected to save Etrara, she who had grown up among simple fisher-folk? She had never truly studied wizardry, knew only the little things Mathary had managed to teach her and what small store of knowledge she had gleaned from the library.

The library. She had been wrong about her knowledge; she had learned a wizardry of sorts in the dusty corridors of the library. She called up a book in her mind, a list of keystones. She spoke the keystone "leap," feeling the power contained within the word as she said it. She saw how it would fit into the verse she had constructed so far, how it would rhyme at the end. A cloud formed to meet the fire.

The two apparitions joined in the sky. Kotheg spoke over her spell; the fire blazed upward. She had used the keystone "leaping" a second time when she spoke of water, and now Kotheg seized on that word to describe a strong red fire leaping against the sky.

She forced herself to become calm, to concentrate on the solid edifice of verses she was building in her mind. Sparks shot from the fire as it met the cloud. The red air above them hissed and turned black. Kotheg spoke louder. She had made him angry, she saw, and the thought delighted her.

She finished her spell. The fire faded and died. She took a deep breath before beginning another spell. Someone shouted in the courtyard.

She looked away from Kotheg and saw that soldiers from both sides had massed again. Andosto stood at the head of a group of men, shouting something she couldn't hear.

Kotheg spoke. An army of great silver cats appeared above them. The cats joined ranks and seemed to walk down from the sky, moving smoothly toward the soldiers. Muscles bunched and relaxed as they came; their fur shone nearly white in the strange light.

The men ran from the apparition. But Andosto spoke something, encouraging them by his words to rally and stand their ground. Someone cheered. Others called out "Andosto!" and "King Valemar!"

She turned quickly and saw that a crowd had formed outside the courtyard. To her surprise she saw Tamra, standing near an old man. Was that Callabrion?

The crowd cheered again. The sight heartened her and she turned to face Kotheg.

But she had missed his last keystone. The cats neared the courtyard. One of them struck out playfully at a soldier, as though it had seen a mouse; the man screamed and fell writhing to the ground.

The bells pealed out again. Andosto was shouting now, screaming into the din. For a moment it seemed as if he would prevail against the panic cast by Kotheg's spell, but then the soldiers broke ranks and ran like madmen in every direction. A cat came to rest in the courtyard and made for Andosto, its tail high.

Andosto raised his sword; Taja had never seen such a gesture of foolish bravery. The cat struck. Andosto fell.

Kotheg was still reciting his verses. His power seemed to emanate from him like a black tide. She had missed more than one keystone, Taja saw; she did not understand the structure of his spell at all. It seemed huge, dizzyingly complex.

Once again she felt despair, knew that she did not have the experience to counter such expert wizardry. And she felt terror as well. What would happen to them if they failed?

She reached out, found his thoughts. They were grim, unyielding, so filled with hatred she nearly recoiled from them. She saw the plan of his entire spell, rhyme upon rhyme creating a strange intricate structure so vast she could barely grasp it all. Finally she made out his last verse and said something to counter it.

Kotheg paused. She saw that he was unaware of what she

had done, knew only that she had anticipated him somehow. For a moment his whole edifice seemed about to come crashing down. He began a verse to steady it.

She countered him before all the words had left his mouth. The cats wavered for a moment. A sudden loud wind struck the courtyard; the cats dispersed like mist.

Taja felt Kotheg's fury grow until it overwhelmed him. She struggled to pull away from his mind, realized that she was caught within the coils of his power and anger. She listened helplessly as he began another spell.

At first she did not understand what he was doing. Then she saw that he had used three keystones in his first verse, and the audacity of it astonished and terrified her. She could not imagine using more than one keystone at first; his wizardry must be strong indeed.

He used four more words of power in his second verse. How in Sbona's name could he possibly tie them all together?

He didn't intend to, she saw. She tried to cry out but his power still held her fast. One of the palace's towers cracked and began to topple dangerously over the courtyard below.

The tower fell. The crash echoed through the courtyard. Soldiers screamed, or shouted curses to the gods. Horses reared and stamped, trying to get free of their riders.

Kotheg's anger overwhelmed her, became her entire world. He hated her for besting him, if only for a moment, hated the strange barbaric land of Etrara, hated even his masters among the Shai for forcing him to fight a battle he could not win. But he would win this battle, she saw, if he had to crack the foundations of the earth to do it.

Another tower fell. Some of the soldiers ran to safety but most stood unable to move; Kotheg had included a spell of binding in his last verse. Lightning shot from the sky and hit Sbona's fountain. Taja saw herself from Kotheg's perspective as she stood near the fountain, unmoving, unable to free herself from the vast machinations of Kotheg's brain.

A jagged rent appeared in the palace wall, running from one of the balconies to the porter's door. Kotheg spoke quickly, sweat pouring down his face. The breach in the palace grew wider; the walls shook.

People ran from the palace. Someone shouted to Kotheg, ordering him to stop. The poet-mage paid no attention.

One of the many ladders leaning against the palace clattered to the ground. Taja heard it but could not see it, her vision limited to what Kotheg looked at. Another ladder fell, and then a third.

Shouts came from the courtyard. "Look!" a voice said.

Kotheg turned toward the palace wall. Someone was descending one of the remaining ladders, a woman, strong and regal. The air around her seemed to burn with her beauty. She stopped halfway down the ladder and gazed out over the courtyard.

"Sbona," someone whispered. "Mother of all." Kotheg looked out across the courtyard; Taja saw Val and Narrion fall to their knees, saw herself standing straight, unyielding, still bound to Kotheg.

Kotheg's anger melted away, turned to fear. Sbona had not come to earth for thousands of years, not since her children were lost. His grip on Taja slackened. She slipped the bonds that held her, slipped them as easily as if they had never existed, and found her body again.

She raised her hand and spoke a short verse. Kotheg stilled, turned to stone. Then she knelt to the goddess.

"I thank you, my lady," she said slowly. "We are unworthy of your help."

"I did not come to aid you," Sbona said to Taja. "I came to find my child, lost on earth a second time." She motioned to the old man Taja had seen in the crowd; Callabrion went toward the ladder unquestioningly.

"I fashioned you for finding," Sbona said. "When my children are lost I need you to discover them for me. And so you have."

She looked out one last time at the ruins in the courtyard, at the people she had created. Then she turned and began to climb the ladder. Callabrion followed her.

"Look where he comes, the Ascending God!" someone said next to Taja. She turned. To her surprise she saw Narrion, still on his knees, watching the god he had rejected climb to the heavens. There was an expression she could not read on his face.

Taja rose; Val and Narrion did the same. All over the courtyard soldiers began to move, freed now from their spell of binding. The men of Shai looked in horror at Kotheg, standing frozen at the turret window. They dropped their weapons and began to run.

The soldiers from Etrara pursued them. Two or three of the Shai went down before their weapons. Someone beside Taja shouted, "Hold!"

She turned. Val had climbed to the small rise near the fountain to stand beside her. "Don't kill them," he said. "Capture them for ransom or let them go."

"Let them go, my lord?" Oldo said scornfully. "After what they've done to us? After Andosto?"

"Will you argue with your king?" Val asked.

Oldo turned away, saying nothing. A moment later Taja saw him forcing men inside the palace. Val left them and moved among the men in the courtyard, stopping to speak to one or two of them.

"Search the palace before you go in," Val said. "And capture only those of the upper rungs. We'll need to ransom them."

The strange light in the courtyard started to dim. She began to speak the spell to restore it, realizing only then how tired she was. "Leave it," Val said. "You can't do any more work here tonight—you're dropping as you stand." He raised his voice. "We'll meet in the council chamber early tomorrow morning."

Fifteen

· · · · · · · ·

BUT TAJA WATCHED, AMAZED, AS VAL WORKED tirelessly through the night. He spoke to the wounded and saw that the fallen were prepared for burial. When he came to the body of Andosto he bowed his head for a moment; as he looked up Taja saw tears in his eyes. "He feasts in Sbona's court tonight," he said.

Finally he motioned to Taja and they went into the palace. He stopped in the banqueting hall, where his men had taken the Shai prisoners, and talked to Oldo; when he left he gave orders that the prisoners were to be fed from the stores in the palace buttery. One of the guards seemed about to protest, but Val stopped him, saying, "When I was a prisoner in Shai they were generous with their food and drink. I would not have them say their hospitality surpasses ours."

He turned and went up the vast stairway. Mariel stood at the doorway of her rooms in the royal apartments. "Is it true?" she asked. "Are the Shai gone?" She looked haggard, even older than she had appeared when she had watched the play in Tobol An.

Val nodded.

"I heard them call you king," she said to Val. "Callia told me the story of your birth."

"And do you contest my right?" Val asked softly.

Half-brother and half-sister stood for a moment, each studying the other. The last of Tariel's children, Taja thought. What will he do if she claims the throne? Will she try to take it from him? She thought that Mariel's rule could prove as disastrous for Etrara as Callia's and Gobro's had.

Mariel looked away first. "No," she said. "No. Gobro has given me no peace since Callia ascended."

"Gobro?" Val said.

"Aye. He haunts me day and night."

"Because—because you killed him?" Val asked softly.

Mariel laughed harshly. "I wish that were so. If he accused me, if he said something about the manner of his death, his haunting might help me atone for the crime of killing him. No—all his talk is of Riel. He asks me daily where she is. He is useless, Gobro is, as useless in death as in life."

Mariel turned back to her room. Val climbed another stairway. Taja followed him. She saw that they were headed toward the turret holding the stone figure of Kotheg, and she began to grow uneasy. "My lord," she said.

Val did not stop. They came to the turret and ascended a small spiral stairway. Kotheg stood with his back to them, unmoving.

"Can you undo your wizardry?" Val asked.

"I— No. No, I don't think so. I was in his mind, trapped there, when Sbona came. I took the knowledge of binding from him. If there is a spell of unbinding it is lost with him."

They walked to the front of the statue. Kotheg's face had frozen in a rictus of fear and anger. "What will you do with him, my lord?" Taja asked. "Bury him? Return him to the Shai?"

"I think I'll keep him where he is. We need something to remind us of the dangers of wizardry." He looked out over the courtyard, seeing his men sleeping by the campfires, and then turned to Taja.

"I first sought to become king to protect myself from Narrion," he said thoughtfully. "I never thought—" He gestured to the men below. "No sane person would seek the office. Gobro, and Callia, and Talenor—they were all mad. And no wonder. I understood yesterday that I am responsible for the deaths I caused."

"But you are responsible for life as well, my lord."

"Aye. For the lives of all these people, each and every one of them."

"And Narrion?" Taja asked. "What will you do with him?"

He seemed not to hear her. "I will need a poet-mage when I am king," he said.

The change of subject nearly caught her off balance, but she took his meaning quickly enough. "I am honored, my lord," she said. "But I'm afraid I must refuse."

"Why?"

"I was— I told you I was bound to Kotheg, trapped in his mind. He was unaware of me, and at first I was able to trick him, to counter his verses before he spoke them. But his anger was so great it overwhelmed me, and I was unable to free myself."

"I don't see—"

Taja stopped him. "My lord," she said. "I understood his anger. Don't you see? I am more like him than I am like anyone in the world. I knew what it felt like to want to crack the foundations of the world, to destroy all of Sbona's creation. And a part of me could not help but delight in that destruction, to rejoice that I had the power to do it."

She hesitated a little and then went on. "I know so little about wizardry, after all. Kotheg's power, and my power—it frightens me. I would like to go back to Tobol An, to spend my days studying the books of magic, to learn whatever Mathary has to teach me."

"Well, then," Val said. He took a long breath. "I will also need a queen."

"No, my lord. I am—I am far beneath you on the ladder. The people will never accept me as queen."

"When I saw you speak your verses against Kotheg I thought the same of you. It seemed to me that you were so far above me on the ladder as to be unreachable. I thought that even a king could never aspire to wed a poet-mage."

"I'm sorry. It is as I said—I would like to return to Tobol An."

"Very well. But even a king—even a king might have reason to consult the library."

She smiled. "That's true."

"Then you will let me visit you?" He looked young, hopeful; for a brief moment she saw the innocent courtier who had once come to Tobol An seeking lodging.

"Of course," she said.

"And perhaps I can persuade you to change your mind."

She said nothing, unable to deny him again. He seemed to take her silence for assent. "I might send you sonnets," he said. "I hope this day has not made you sick to death of poetry."

She laughed, and they went down together into the courtyard.

Narrion sat at the table in the council chamber. To his right sat Oldo, to his left Tamra. Taja and Noddo were across the table. No one had seen Val for hours.

He remembered one of the last times he had sat in this room. Callia had declared war on the Shai, and, by issuing her edicts against the Maegrim, on her own people as well. A great deal had happened since then—the war, the fall of Etrara, the summoning of Callabrion. And the most surprising thing of all—Val's ascension to the throne.

He almost wished they could return to those days. He had understood Callia's ambition, her desire to rule, but he did not know the man Val had become at all. What would Val do with his newfound power? Would he seek revenge for the way Narrion had used him? What judgment would Val pass on him?

Everyone turned toward the door. Val entered, looking drawn; although he had told everyone to go to sleep, he must have worked through the night.

He should have had a herald announce him, Narrion thought. There's so much he doesn't know. I could help him—he could make me the King's Pen, or the King's Axe. He needs me—my position here is not as hopeless as it looks.

Val looked around the table. "I want to thank all of you for your help yesterday," he said. "And for your help in the weeks and months before that. I know what you went through to overthrow the Shai.

"I don't want to spend time on state business now, not while we still have to negotiate with the Shai. But I want to make some appointments before I do anything else. Oldo will be the new King's Axe, and a man named Anthiel my poet-mage. He returned to his village after the war with the Shai—I will send for him later."

A few people looked surprised. But Narrion, who had spoken to Taja that morning, knew why Taja had not accepted the office. Someone started to speak; Val cut him off. "And Narrion—" he began.

Val looked down the table to the man he had once thought of as his cousin. Everyone was silent, looking back at him. Now it comes, Narrion thought, and knew that the others around the table were thinking the same thing. Now we find out what our new king is made of. His heart was beating quickly.

"Narrion, my old friend," Val said. "Twice a year, on the Feasts of the Ascending and Descending God, we are told that Callabrion needs Scathiel, and Scathiel needs Callabrion. The gods are two sides of the same coin, the priests say. But I never understood that, not until this year. You helped me see that. Death exists within life, and life within death."

He's toying with me, Narrion thought. He didn't make speeches when he announced the other appointments.

"In the middle of the battle you called me a fool, and I told you that at the end of it I expected to be made a member of the Society." Val grinned at Noddo, who had started to frown. No king had ever been a Fool; no one could be king and Shadow King at the same time. "Don't worry—I won't hold you to that. I have decided, though, in view of everything you have done for me, to make you my Shadow King. I would have no one else dance and sing for me at the Feast of the Descending God, would trust no one else to issue the proclamations of the Shadow King for that day. That is, of course, if you accept."

Everyone looked at Narrion. He said nothing, his breath nearly taken away by Val's cleverness. Val could have done no different, he thought. The king could not have risked sending him away; he still had friends and influence among the nobility of Etrara. But Val could not have trusted him enough to give him a position of authority either; his desire to rise on the ladder was too well known. "In view of everything you have done for me," the king had said; Narrion had heard the underlying meaning, even if no one else had.

What could he say? The position of Shadow King was many rungs down the ladder from his place as Callia's advisor. Tamra would not like it, Tamra who lived for her position at the king's court. Still, he could not expect Val to offer him anything else.

"Very well, my lord," he said. "I would be honored to become your Shadow King."

After Callabrion ascended to the heavens the days began to move toward spring again. The sun rose earlier and set later, and the crops flourished. After a hard year of winter, a year under cold Scathiel's rule, the citizens of Etrara were only too happy to take Callabrion's advice and enjoy the bounty of the earth.

Even in the first year of his reign people began to call their king Valemar the Good. The Shai had paid a great deal of money to ransom their prisoners and Val used it wisely, helping city folks burned out of their homes by the Shai and farmers who had lost crops to the ravages of winter. He built a triumphal arch to Andosto, and another, because he had promised, to Duke Arion.

But not all his decisions had been popular. The Shai

demanded that he apologize for invading their country and he did so, only to be accused by his own people of love for the king-killers. But he felt strongly that Callia's war against Shai had been wrong.

Six months after Callabrion ascended, on the Feast of the Descending God, he wandered through the streets of Etrara. While the Shadow King ruled he was a private man again, and he enjoyed talking to his people without the strains of ceremony and protocol.

Laughter came from the street ahead. Val made his way toward a crowd of people and saw a Fool struggling with a huge wheeled telescope. The Fool turned; the telescope tipped to point at the ground. Several children screamed with laughter. The Fool stood on tiptoe to look in the eyepiece, and then made a comment on the heavens in the sonorous tones of the astronomer-priests.

Val grinned and moved on. Three Fools stood near the university. Two hit their drums in a simple rhythm; the third joined in several times, always missing the beat. Finally, after much cursing, the three managed to play together, and they began to sing. Men and women around them joined in, singing the traditional words, and after a while Val sang as well.

"There is a skull that bides beneath each skin,
There is a time when high and low must fail.
The prince, the priest, the poet all must die,
When death receives them even kings are pale.

So fill the cup and raise your glasses high
And lift your voices loud to sing the tale.
Today we drink, tomorrow we may die
And lie in earth, our bones as brown as ale."

People smiled to see their king, and waved, and when the song was over they came up shyly to talk to him about one thing or another. A child gave him a mock chain of office made of flowers; he draped it around his shoulders. They could never be totally at their ease with him, knowing that he would assume the land-ring of Etrara the next day, but that day he learned a number of things about his country that his courtiers had not told him.

When the clock at the university struck two he headed back to Palace Hill. Narrion had told him there would be entertainment that afternoon, and he was curious to see what edicts his Shadow King had issued in his absence.

The palace's fallen towers had been replaced, the vast breach in the walls repaired. He looked with satisfaction at the white and gold building, and then glanced up at the stone figure of Kotheg in his turret. Death in life, and life in death, just as he had said to Narrion a half year ago.

He knocked at the palace door. "Who's there?" the porter asked.

"Valemar, a private citizen," he said without hesitation.

The porter opened the door. "Our gracious King Narrion has reserved a few seats for beggars," he said. "Enter." In a lower voice he added, "That's a beautiful chain of office, my lord."

Val looked down and saw that he was still wearing the flowers the child had given him. Well, why not, after all? He grinned at the porter and went inside.

He went to the banqueting hall and took one of the outer seats. Murmurs rose around him: "The king." "Look—King Valemar."

King Valemar the Good looked with pleasure around the hall. At one table sat Lord Oldo, the King's Axe, and near him sat Lord Carrow, who had taken back his office of King's Coin. Lord Varra was at another table near them; Val had ransomed him from the Shai and had confirmed him in the office of King's Pen. And there was Anthiel, the poet-mage.

Many faces were absent, of course; many people had died in the battle against the Shai. And Mariel was not at the banquet; she haunted the royal apartments upstairs like a ghost.

Narrion climbed to the dais. He wore the skeleton and

mask of the Fools, and the land-ring of Etrara, but his tall lean figure was unmistakable. "My people!" he said. He seemed to be enjoying himself hugely. "By edict of your king, Narrion the Good—" Laughter came from the audience. "By edict of Narrion the Good, I say, there will be special entertainment on this day. First we will have a play, *The Comedy of the Two Courtiers.*"

Val tried not to smile. No one knew it, least of all Narrion, but he had written that play, and had given it to an actor to pass off as her own. Dozens of people were writing plays now; hardly a day passed without some young author following the example of their king and traveling to the library at Tobol An for inspiration. No one could remember a time when the invention of poets had flowed so freely.

They thought he went to the library to read the old stories and poems, the ancient histories, and so he did. But he also went to see Taja; her calm strength and her wisdom refreshed him in a way that his courtiers could not. On some days he thought that she might change her mind and become his queen, on others that she would stay at her library, living there like a priest in an observatory. But she had never returned any of the poems he had sent her.

The Shadow King clapped his hands, and the actors climbed to the stage. There were men players as well as women now; one of the first thing Val had done had been to rescind King Tariel's decree forbidding men to appear on stage. He had spent a year acting in one part or another, and it had done no harm to his dignity that he could see.

The men on stage seemed uncertain, unused to performing, but the women faced the audience like the seasoned actors they were. Out of long habit Val looked for Tamra, but did not see her anywhere. One of the men, the Prologue, moved to the front of the stage and began to speak.

A few people in the audience stirred uneasily. They still remembered the play interrupted by the Maegrim a year ago. But no one came into the hall, and the play continued.

The Maegrim's prophecy had come true that year, Val

thought. Nearly everyone in the room that night had fallen from the ladder. But the grim year was over; Callabrion had ascended, thank the gods.

He forced himself to pay attention to the play. The inept courtier was about to say something funny; he hoped that people would laugh. They did. He sat back in his chair, gratified.

The play ended to strong applause. Narrion climbed to the stage again and announced that the banquet would be served.

To Val's surprise Narrion did not return to the dais. Val watched as the Shadow King moved to the back of the hall and sat at an empty chair next to him. "My lord," Val said, "I am a humble beggar, not at all worthy—"

Narrion took off his skeleton mask and brushed back his long black hair. The land-ring of Etrara glittered on his finger; Val wondered briefly, as he would no doubt wonder for years to come, if Narrion would return the ring at the day's end. "I read your book," Narrion said.

At first Val thought he meant the play, and he wondered how on earth Narrion could have known. Then he realized Narrion meant his book about the perfect courtier, the only thing he had published under his own name.

"What did you think?" he asked.

"I can't say I know much about the subject. To be honest, I may be the worst courtier on Sbona's earth."

Surely Narrion hadn't broken with tradition to talk about books. Val waited, knowing that the other man had something on his mind.

"Do you remember when I summoned up Callabrion?" Narrion asked. Val nodded. "He said he had fallen in love with the beauty of the earth. And I asked him why he had never noticed that beauty before—do you remember that?"

Val nodded again.

"The gods fall in love with earthly women, not with abstractions like beauty. I wondered then whether he might have been hiding something, but I said nothing. But as it turned out, I was right. He was in love."

Val remembered Callabrion's impassioned speeches in favor of love at Duchess Sbarra's gatherings. "Riel?" he asked.

"Tamra," Narrion said. "She's pregnant. She says the old stories are true—when a woman carries a god's child she knows it."

Val could not think what to say.

"She thinks she might leave me," Narrion said. "She says I'm too concerned with court politics, with the Society." He looked at Val, his expression unreadable. "They don't care about us, the gods," he said. "I don't say they're evil. But I doubt they're good, either. Don't you see? We mean nothing to them. Sbona didn't care if we destroyed ourselves fighting a wizards' war. All she wanted was her son."

"Do you truly think so? At the end of the battle for Etrara, when Callabrion ascended, I looked at you and I thought—"

"What am I to think, my lord? You made me your fool. It's not that I don't deserve the office—I probably deserve it twenty times over. But what do I say to Tamra? She married a courtier high in Gobro's favor, and now that courtier is nothing but the king's fool, a man who takes office one day a year." He paused. "Sbona fashioned us for finding—the goddess said that the night we overthrew the Shai, the night Callabrion ascended. But did you ever think what the old proverb really means? We were created to search for Sbona's lost children, nothing more. When she found them we had outlived our usefulness. What happens to us then is not their concern."

"I don't think that's true," Val said slowly. "Sbona fashioned us for finding—I think that means she gave us the greatest gift she could. We can understand things, see to the heart of them. The poet-mages are the best at this, of course, but all of us can do it to some extent. I know that to be true from my own experience. At the end of long searching I was able to understand who I am."

"Of course," Narrion said bitterly. "You're the king. But

what about those whose search leads them down less fortunate paths?"

The pages came out of the kitchen and began to serve the
meal. Val studied the man he had thought was his cousin.
They were more than kin, he thought; Narrion was his double,
his dark twin. Summer and winter, they were bound together
for as long as they lived.

He had planned to tell Narrion about the gift of land he
would give him, but now he decided to say nothing. It would
not do for Narrion to think he could sway him in this fashion;
he would find out about the gift soon enough.

"How can you ask me that, my old friend?" Val said.
"You taught me that everything changes, that nothing stands
still. I am sure you will not be a fool forever."

Slowly Narrion's expression eased, lost some of its harshness. Perhaps he had heard rumors of the gift of land, and
Val's hint had confirmed them. Or had Val finally made him
understand something of the god of summer, of the balance
the gods make together?

"The Maegrim are always right," Val said. "Someone's
fortune is always about to change."